EVERYMAN, I will go with thee,
and be thy guide,
In thy most need to go by thy side

SAKI (H.H. MUNRO)

Born at Akyab, Burma, 18 December 1870. From 1902 to 1908 was foreign correspondent of the *Morning Post*. Served as a private in the Royal Fusiliers during World War I, and died at Beaumont-Hamel, 14 November 1916.

SAKI

Short Stories 2

Chosen by Peter Haining

Dent: London and Melbourne
EVERYMAN'S LIBRARY

Phototypeset in 10 on 11½pt VIP Sabon by
Inforum Ltd, Portsmouth,
Made and printed in Great Britain by
Guernsey Press Co. Ltd, Guernsey, C.I. for
J.M. Dent & Sons Ltd
Aldine House, 33 Welbeck Street, London W1M 8LX
First published in Everyman Paperback 1983

British Library Cataloguing in Publication Data

Saki
Short stories.—(Everyman paperback)
2
Rn: Hector Hugh Munro I. Title
II. Haining, Peter
823′ .912[F] PR6025.U675

ISBN 0-460-01354-8

Contents

Preface vii

Dogged 1
Alice in Pall Mall 7
Alice at St Stephen's 9
The Blood-Feud of Toad-Water 11
Reginald on Christmas Presents 14
Reginald's Choir Treat 16
Reginald in Russia 18
The Purple of the Balkan Kings 22
The Soul of Laploshka 25
Judkin of the Parcels 29
The Bag 31
The Lost Sanjak 36
The Saint and the Goblin 42
The Mouse 45
The Recessional 49
The Stampeding of Lady Bastable 53
The Jesting of Arlington Stringham 56
The Talking-Out of Tarrington 60
A Matter of Sentiment 63
Esmé 67
Shock Tactics 72
Clovis on the Alleged Romance of Business 77
The Almanack 78
Tobermory (*original version*) 83
The Music on the Hill 90
Filboid Studge, the Story of a Mouse That Helped 96
The Peace of Mowsle Barton 99
Hermann the Irascible – A Story of the Great Weep 106
The Parting (from *The Unbearable Bassington*) 109
The She-Wolf 114
The Boar-Pig 121
The Cobweb 127
The Elk 131

The Stake 136
The Name-Day 140
'Down Pens' 146
On Approval 150
The Wolves of Cernogratz 155
The Guests 160
The Penance 164
Mark 169
Canossa 174
The Infernal Parliament 178
The Comments of Moung Ka 182
The Gala Programme: An Unrecorded Episode in Roman History 185
Eve and the Forbidden Fruit: A Fragment of Incomplete History 188
How William Came (from *When William Came*) 190
The Toys of Peace 200
An Old Love 206
The C.O.C. 208
The Square Egg: A Badger's-Eye View of the War 210
For the Duration of the War 216

Preface

To be invited to make a selection of stories by a favourite author is certainly a joy to be savoured. The editor approaches his task rather as a gourmet would a *Cordon Bleu* meal. Yet what if the editor finds that someone has gone before; that what may seem like the best stories have already been taken, the choicest dishes already sampled and delightedly consumed?

Yet this should not be allowed to become a deterrent to the task – for surely the most exacting test remains. To discover on a return to the well-spring if there is enough for a second course, another feast which can be prepared and, if possible, spiced with some unexpected relishes?

Such was the position which faced me when contemplating assembling this anthology for Everyman's Library. For Emlyn Williams had already gone before me in 1978 to prepare a selection of his own favourite short stories. There, among his collection of fifty-five tales, were such gems as the chilling *Sredni Vashtar* and the sinister *The Easter Egg*, the high comedy of *The Schartz-Metterklume Method* and the sardonic wit of *The Sex That Doesn't Shop*. At first glance, it was hard to tell what if anything he had left out. But pausing for just a moment to reflect that Saki's output of stories and novels had exceeded 140, I felt sure that there must be more than enough left over. Enough, indeed, for a thoroughly satisfying second course – as I think the reader will find this selection of a further fifty-two quite different stories to be. It is a repast which, I am pleased to be able to say, contains no fewer than four previously uncollected items from Saki's pen. But more of this in a moment.

Saki – or Hector Hugh Munro (1870–1916) to give him his real name – has stood the test of time better than many of his literary contemporaries, and indeed his blend of wit, social commentary and savage observation of human nature, has earned him a distinguished list of champions over the years. Noël Coward, for instance, admitted that Saki was one of the two most significant influences on his career as a writer (the other was E. Nesbit), and believed that the only reason why he was not more popular during his lifetime was 'for the usual reason that he was ahead of his time'. A.A. Milne, on the other hand, felt his comparative obscurity may have had to do with that particular attitude of mind of certain readers to keep 'good things' to themselves. Milne wrote in 1937:

'There are good things which we want to share with the world, and good things which we want to keep to ourselves. The secret of our favourite restaurant, to take a case, is guarded jealously from all but a few intimates; the secret, to take a contrary case, of our infallible remedy for sea-sickness is thrust upon every traveller we meet, even if he be no more than a casual acquaintance about to cross the Serpentine. So with books. There are dearly loved books of which we babble to a neighbour at dinner, insisting that she shall share our delight in them; and there are books, equally dear to us, of which we say nothing, fearing lest the praise of others should cheapen the glory of our discovery. The books of Saki were, for me at least, in the second class.'

Another champion, J.W. Lambert, believes there is no mystery whatsoever as to why Saki remains popular to this day. 'His stories make us laugh,' Lambert explains, 'they up-end respectability, they provide, in broad terms, unflagging entertainment. The deftness of their wit, the ingenuity of their anecdotes, are as effective as ever. The satire is still relevant, although its context was the luxurious, not to say bloated, world of upper-middle-class Edwardian England.'

Concerning the man Hector Hugh Munro who gave us this body of much-admired work, we know really very little beyond the broad outline of his life: his rather claustrophobic childhood in the care of an aunt, his years as a journalist and then successful writer, and, finally, his sad death at the hands of a German sniper while serving with the British Army in France in 1916. This lack of knowledge of the man stems directly from the activities of his intensely possessive sister, Ethel, who immediately upon his death destroyed or suppressed anything she considered might harm his reputation. This, naturally, has fanned the flames of speculation, yet there would certainly be no point – neither is there the space –

to discuss such matters as these here. They are for a biographer with almost endless patience and a relentlessly inquisitive mind. Instead, though, we have Munro's work, in which like the creations of any talented writer, there are clues to his mind and motivations to be found, and in my selection of stories there are several which throw some light on the man and his career, and which I believe require a little exposition here.

My first selection, *Dogged*, was, as far as we know, Munro's very first published item, and appeared in an obscure London journal, *St Paul's*, in February 1899. (It was published, incidentally, under his initials 'H.H.M.', rather than his pen-name, Saki, which he did not use until the following year.) Although at this time, Munro was making his first efforts to become a writer, and had been busy sending submissions to various London newspapers and magazines (all unsuccessfully), why he should have chosen *St Paul's* which was mostly given over to features on live entertainment in the capital, or more particularly why the periodical should have accepted it, remains a mystery. We can speculate that Munro asked no payment for his contribution – anxious as he no doubt was then to secure publication – or that the weekly magazine, one of a multitude that flourished in London at that time, was desperate for copy, and not too particular how far it strayed in search of it. We just don't know. But the mystery should not detract from the importance of the story, for although it is a little laboured and facetious, there are several elements in it which were later to become Saki's favourite themes. The hero, Artemus Gibbon, is a timid and dull young man who is bullied by an implacable matron into taking possession of a yelping terrier dog named Beelzebub. The animal effectively turns his blameless life into one of idleness and dissipation, and the exponent of all this is exposed as a hypocrite into the bargain. The return of *Dogged* to print after almost a century will, I think, be welcomed by all Saki's admirers with more than a little interest.

Whatever the merits of this story, it was not to be long before the young journalist Munro made his mark – and at a stroke revealed himself a master of parody. It was in the late spring of 1900 that Hector was introduced to John Alfred Spender, editor of the influential *Westminster Gazette*, and the two men dreamed up the idea of rewriting the adventures of *Alice in Wonderland* as a satire on the Government, then deeply enmired in the Boer War. The first of Munro's parodies appeared on 25 July, bearing the signature 'Saki' ('Chosen, I think, because the wistful philosophy of Fitzgerald appealed to him and he took the name from that fine poet's verses,' said his friend Rothay Reynolds years later) and they were an immediate success. A decade or so later, Spender himself was to write of this remarkable debut: 'Of the many political squibs I can remember, none had so immediate and complete a success as this. It was quoted everywhere, and the whole town joined in the laugh.'

What Spender also found admirable years on was the sheer timelessness of the Munro contributions. 'Political parodies are generally dead within a few months of their first appearance,' he said, 'but *The Westminster Alice* [as the series became known and was later titled in book form] are still alive and sparkling.' The first of two items he cited as being the best in the series was *Alice in Pall Mall*.

'The White Knight in *Alice in Pall Mall*,' Spender wrote, 'remains the symbol of all the War Ministers who never expected wars, and it is a mere accident that he wears the face of the honoured veteran who happened to be in the saddle in 1899 when the unexpected came.'

Alice at St Stephen's was the editor's other favourite. 'It is in the same way perennial,' he wrote. 'It is addressed to Mr Gully and meant as a delicate rebuke of certain prime lawyer-like habits which had got on the nerves of a private member, but it will do for any Speaker from any member, and is a model of the subtle tactics which must be employed by critics of that illustrious functionary, if they do not wish to be haled to the bar of the House of Commons.'

It is these two items that I have chosen for my selections from *The Westminster Alice*.

While Hector was enjoying the success of *Alice*, he did not abandon the style which he had begun to develop in *Dogged*, and in the spring of 1901 another story with the curious title *The Blood-Feud of Toad-Water* appeared in *The Westminster Gazette*. Like the earlier tale, it was also signed 'H.H.M.' and it appeared as if Munro was still unsure whether or not to immerse himself in his newly conceived pen-name. The story, which is included here, is particularly interesting because Ethel Munro, Hector's protective and not-often-forthcoming sister, has told us that it was inspired by events in her brother's youth. 'The incidents in it really happened,' she wrote in 1924, 'our Rector knew the people. There was also a witch in our neighbourhood who had uncanny powers, but we never met her.'

That same spring of 1901 also saw Hector give literary birth to Reginald, the first of two young men whose exploits in society he was to chronicle through a variety of subsequent delightful and often malicious stories. (The other character was Clovis, to whom we shall come later.) Reginald is a stylish young man-about-town, dedicated to living off other people's finances and scandalizing relatives, friends and acquaintances alike. Of Reginald, Ethel Munro says, 'The characters in the various stories are all imaginary. Reginald is a type composed of several young men, studied during his years of town life. Hector told me that more than one of his acquaintances considered himself the original.'

Like the *Alice* parodies, the stories of Reginald were first published in *The Westminster Gazette*, and like them were bylined 'Saki'. His inspiration for the dandy was evidently Oscar Wilde, and as Grahame Greene has so eloquently pointed out, the influence of Wilde is to be found in both Reginald and, later, Clovis. I quote from Green's essay written about Saki in 1930:

'Reginald and Clovis are the children of Wilde; the epigrams, the absurdities fly unremittingly back and forth, they dazzle and delight, but we are aware of a harsher, less kindly mind behind them than Wilde's. Clovis and Reginald are not creatures of fairy-tale, they belong nearer to the visible world than Ernest Maltravers. While Ernest floats airily like a Rubens' cupid among the over-blue clouds, Clovis and Reginald belong to the Park, the tea-parties of Kensington and evenings at Covent Garden – they even sometimes date, like the suffragettes . . . How often these stories are stories of practical jokes. The victims with their weird names are sufficiently foolish to awaken no sympathy – they are middle-aged, the people with power; it is right that they should suffer a temporary humiliation because the world is always on their side in the long run. Munro, like a chivalrous highwayman, only robs the rich: behind all these stories is an exacting sense of justice.'

Munro may well have believed that Reginald was destined to prove ephemeral – just as ephemeral as he thought the exploits of Alice would be. But once again he was wrong – and in 1904 the stories, which had already attracted something of a following, were collected together in volume form as *Reginald*. I have selected three examples for my collection: *Reginald on Christmas Presents*, which seems to contain the very essence of the character; *Reginald's Choir Treat* which critic Arthur Langguth considers one of Munro's most important convention-breaking stories because of its suggestion of homosexuality, 'for the love that could not speak its name, Saki had spoken, and the name was Reginald'; and, finally, *Reginald in Russia* which gave its name to Munro's next published book (1910) although it was the only story in the collection to feature Reginald and is therefore sometimes missed by admirers of the young dandy.

However, it has to be admitted that it was the success of *The Westminster Alice* (published in book form in 1902) that transformed Hector Munro's fortunes, and shortly afterwards he was recruited by the leading daily newspaper, the *Morning Post*, and forthwith dispatched to one of the European trouble spots, the Balkans, to report on events there. The *Post*'s editor was well pleased with his correspondent's reports, and from there he was reassigned to St Petersburg where he was an eye-witness to the bloody uprising in 1905.

Munro did more than just observe the unrest in Russia, he also found the raw material for more stories, and from this period came *The Purple of the Balkan Kings* which I have included as being typical of his style at the time. Undoubtedly, though, his experiences as a journalist were profoundly changing his character – changes that H.W. Nevinson, a fellow journalist and later close friend, who was also in St Petersburg at this time, noticed:

'One saw the twist of cynicism clearly marked on his face,' Nevinson wrote. 'His aspect of the world was cynical. But the cynicism was humorous and charming, partly assumed as a protective covering to conceal and shelter feeling. This is our English way, and in the suppression of emotion, or of its outward signs, Saki was entirely English.'

On his return to London in the autumn of 1908 after various assignments in Europe, Munro was able to distil his attitude towards life, and society in particular, into the literary style he felt would be most effective – the short story. His first success was *The Soul of Laploshka* which *The Westminster Gazette* featured prominently in the spring of 1909. Once again, Ethel Munro tells us that her brother based the story on a character he had met while in France. 'The place, Porville, was thick with types,' she says, 'one of them was the original of *The Soul of Laploshka*. We found he had a reputation for meanness, and in the fullness of time, Hector played a hoax on him; if there were a crime on which he had no pity, it was meanness, and this man had apparently plenty of money, so there was no shadow of excuse for him.'

Munro wrote prodigiously during 1909, and by the end of the year he was assembling the collection which would be published the following spring as *Reginald in Russia*. As I mentioned earlier, only the title story features Reginald, but from its pages I have also picked *Judkin of the Parcels* (like *The Blood-Feud of Toad-Water* based on real characters Munro had known), the similarly rural, *The Bag*, the grim story of *The Lost Sanjak*, the bizarre account of *The Saint and the Goblin*, and, finally, *The Mouse*, a splendid piece of humorous invention with a twist ending, all about a young man with a mouse caught up in his trousers.

A year later came the book which finally demonstrated that he had reached his literary maturity, *Chronicles of Clovis*. Again these were stories of an effete young man of society, their inspiration partly Hector's own circle and partly Oscar Wilde. Six of my selections are taken from this volume: *The Recessional*, *The Stampeding of Lady Bastable*, *The Jesting of Arlington Stringham*, *The Talking-Out of Tarrington*, *A Matter of Sentiment* and *Esmé*, while to these I have added three scattered pieces, *Shock Tactics* and *Clovis on the Alleged Romance of Business*, from the posthumously published collections, *Toys of Peace* (1919) and *The Square Egg* (1924) respectively, and the Clovis story, *The Almanack*, which had lain forgotten in the files of the *Morning*

Post of 17 July 1913, until its recent discovery.

One of the other stories included in *Chronicles of Clovis*, called *Tobermory*, had a curious history. Written in November 1909 for *The Westminster Gazette*, this tale of a remarkable cat had been just too late to be included in *Reginald in Russia*, so instead Munro decided it should have a place in the new collection – but first, of course, it had to be rewritten to incorporate Clovis. The tale as it appeared in the book has been rightly hailed as one of Saki's masterpieces, but I have long thought it a pity that the original version should be so neglected, and hence it finds a place here, returned to print for the first time in all those years.

Another Saki classic follows *Tobermory*, the much-anthologized supernatural tale, *The Music on the Hill*, which I count among my own very favourite stories. And with it are three other stories which I never hesitate to recommend to new readers, not only because of their quality but because they bear such typical Saki titles, *Filboid Studge, the Story of a Mouse That Helped*, *The Peace of Mowsle Barton* and *Hermann the Irascible – A Story of the Great Weep*.

Highly praised for his short stories as he was, Munro nursed the desire to try his hand at a full-length novel, and a year later published *The Unbearable Bassington* (1912). This story of a possessive mother and her wayward, self-indulgent son, Comus Bassington, who bring inevitable tragedy upon themselves, created enormous interest, as Maurice Baring wrote in a later edition of the book:

'*The Unbearable Bassington* seems to me the key to his work,' Baring said. ' "Bassington", an acute critic once wrote to me, "is what Saki might have become and mysteriously didn't." It is, for this reason, I think, the most interesting, because the most serious and deeply felt, just as from a literary point of view, it is likewise the most "important", because the most artistically executed of his books . . . it is a masterpiece. When published in 1913 it was hailed by critics as "one of the wittiest books, not only of the year, but of the decade".'

What has always intrigued me about this work is the seemingly extraneous episode of the parting of a young man named Courtenay Youghal from his mistress, Molly McQuade. The episode has no bearing on the rest of the novel and might even be a short story inserted by an impatient author to bolster the length of his manuscript. Whatever the case, it is fascinating because of the statement which it makes about love and sex – perhaps the nearest Munro came to revealing his own feelings on these matters in all his works. I have, therefore, extracted this section, titled it *The Parting*, and inserted it here both on account of its own intrinsic merits and because of the further light it throws on its author.

One of the abiding interests of Munro's life was wild animals, and he mirrored this fascination in the collection which followed two years later, *Beasts and Super Beasts* (1914). From the cruel savagery of wolves to the seemingly less dangerous, but equally unpredictable, activities of certain farmyard creatures, he drew fascinating parallels with the 'beastliness' of mankind, and to illustrate this area of his talent I have selected from the pages of that book: *The She-Wolf*, *The Boar Pig*, *The Cobweb*, *The Elk*, *The Stake*, as well as the brooding mystery of *The Name-Day* and the caustic wit of *'Down Pens'* and *On Approval*.

Saki's friend, H.W. Nevinson, was quick to point out about this collection (and by inference all the others) that the reader 'should be warned against swallowing the whole succession one after another as that dulls the appetite for the wit and malice'. He recommends that Saki should be taken 'as an occasional spice, an exquisite *aperitif* – he is best as a defence against the commonplace and sentimentality'. This is a view with which I would concur, and to this end I have selected fifty-two stories for this book – allowing one per week for the abstemious reader.

Beasts and Super Beasts does not, however, represent the sum total of Munro's output during this period of his life, although it was to prove the last collection issued in his lifetime. Those uncollected items from this time were to await exhumation by his sister Ethel in the two posthumous volumes, *Toys of Peace* and *The Square Egg*. From the first I have picked *The Wolves of Cernogratz* (which would seem to have been inspired by his early travels in Europe), *The Guests*, *The Penance*, *Mark* and the exquisite *Canossa*. From the sparse pages of the second collection come *The Infernal Parliament*, *The Comments of Moung Ka* and *The Gala Programme*. To follow this last item, which is subtitled

'An Unrecorded Episode in Roman History', I thought it the ideal place to insert an uncollected story by Saki discovered among his papers, and which is not too disimilar in theme, called *Eve and the Forbidden Fruit* – 'A Fragment of Incomplete History'. It is a teasing little item in which Saki in typical fashion leaves us to make up our own minds as to just how Eve came to do what we all know she did!

As a man who had been eye-witness to political unrest, and seen it become armed conflict in the Balkans and Russia, Munro was among the first to sense the coming upheaval which would change both his own world and that of Britain and Europe beyond recognition. He felt compelled to express this agitation in the best way he knew how – in the form of another novel, the directly titled, *When William Came* (1914), in which, as his friend Rothay Reynolds has said, 'he used his supreme gift of irony to rouse his fellow-countrymen from their torpor and to stir themselves to take measures for the defence of the country'. Also writing of this book – from which I have extracted a crucial episode quite self-contained – Lord Charnwood commented a quarter of a century later with all the assurance of hindsight:

'*When William Came* stands almost alone among works of fiction for the directness and timeliness of its prophetic purpose. The Great War was in a sense a great surprise; for it came upon us, as tremendous things often do, at the moment when many people least expected it; and of course it is not possible or desirable for most of us to be looking forward perpetually to what may happen – and may not. Yet those who forewarned the British people did not labour in vain.'

No one who knew Munro was at all surprised that he took his own message to heart and, despite his age, volunteered for military service when, just as he had predicted, war came. Refusing all offers of a commission, he chose to serve in the ranks, and by all accounts was a popular and dedicated foot soldier serving among men who came from backgrounds vastly different from his own. Even as he served in France, though, the urge to write still possessed him, and my final five selections all date from the period 1914 to 1916. *Toys of Peace*, published in 1914, was to give its title to one of his sister's posthumous collections, while *An*

Old Love, with his thoughts about war, is another previously uncollected Saki item from the *Morning Post* of 23 April 1915. *The C.O.C.*, describing the author's life as a Corporal, has also not been republished since its appearance in *The Bystander* of June 1915. *The Square Egg* is a vivid impression of Munro's life in the trenches (also giving its name to the other posthumous collection), while *For the Duration of the War* was the very last item to come from his pen and demonstrates that even under the shadow of death his spirits remained high.

Mourning his loss years later, Grahame Greene expressed what were undoubtedly the feelings of Munro's many admirers when they heard he had fallen in action. 'It is sad to think', Greene wrote, 'that his sunniness and prattle could not go on for ever, but the worst and cruellest joke was left to the end. Munro's witty, cynical hero, Comus Bassington, died incongruously of fever in a West African village, and in the early morning of 13 November 1916, in a shallow crater near Beaumont-Hamel, Munro was heard to shout, "Put out that bloody cigarette." They were the last, unpredictable words of Clovis and Reginald.'

So passed that 'strange, exotic creature', as A.A. Milne called our author – struck down by the bullet of a sharp-eared German sniper. Behind him he left a memorial in the shape of the stories and novels which can still be read and enjoyed today. Munro, though, might have found the idea that his work would live on beyond his time amusing, a joke to be wryly laughed away.

I like to imagine that wherever he is now, he has lost something of that studied 'twist of cynicism' on his face, of which Rothay Reynolds spoke – for if not, the joke is on him. For wasn't it this most pessimistic of men who remarked through his character Reginald, 'I hate posterity – it's so fond of having the last word'?

In his case, posterity has bestowed immortality.

Suffolk, Christmas 1982 Peter Haining

Dogged

Artemus Gibbon was, by nature and inclination, blameless and respectable, and under happier circumstances the record of his life might have preserved the albino tint of its early promise; but he was of timid and yielding disposition, and had been carefully brought up, so that his case was clearly hopeless from the first. It only remained for the strong and unscrupulous character to come alongside, and the result was a foregone conclusion. And one afternoon it came. It is a well-tried axiom that, in human affairs, as in steeplechasing, the ugliest croppers occur at the 'safest' and most carefully pruned places, and of all conceivable occasions for a young man to go irretrievably wrong, a Church bazaar would seem to offer the least appropriate opportunity. Yet it was at such a function, opened by a bishop's lady, and patronized by the most hopelessly correct people in the neighbourhood, that Artemus Gibbon went unsuspectingly to his undoing.

In the first place it must be admitted that his natural timidity was played upon by the embarrassing absence of anything at the bazaar which a bachelor of prosaic tastes might reasonably be expected to purchase with any approach to hearty conviction that his money was profitably laid out. Baby linen, which seemed to be the staple article on most of the stalls, was not to be thought of for a moment and the innate modesty of his taste in dress caused him to recoil from the 'Jubilee Memento Scarves', handworked with the Royal arms in a delirium of crimson and gold. Hence, when he had purchased a harmless and unnecessary pincushion and two views of Durham Cathedral, he felt that he might, without odium, effect a dexterous retreat. Here it was that the Foreseen and Inevitable stepped in and changed the placid current of his life. He was pounced upon by a severe-looking dame, with an air of one being in authority, who gave him to understand that it was required of him that he should buy a dog.

'Only two guineas; my niece has charge of him over there.

Clara!' Gibbon found himself a moment later confronted by a vivacious damsel – and the dog. The possibility of admitting a canine companion within the narrow compass of his establishment had not been altogether foreign to his speculations on life; a quiet, meek-eyed spaniel for instance, which would occupy an unobtrusive position by his domestic hearth, or participate in his constitutional walks, or, in later days, perhaps, a dignified deerhound with a tendency to statuesque repose – such were the shapes which his occasional ruminations on the subject had taken. But the dog now before him was by no means built according to these patterns. A rakish-looking fox-terrier, stamped with the hall-mark of naked and unashamed depravity, and wearing the yawningly alert air of one who has found the world is vain and likes it all the better for it, such was the specimen of dog-flesh at which Mr Artemus Gibbon found himself gazing in blank dismay.

Before he had quite realized the full force of the cataclysm in which he was involved, he had parted with the demanded forty-two shillings, and learned from the vivacious damsel the appalling fact that his new purchase was named Beelzebub. Something instinctively told him that he had parted too with his peace of mind, and as he was towed out of the bazaar premises in the wake of a yelping and plunging terrier, with an accompaniment of noise and publicity uncongenial to his natural modesty, he was dimly aware that he had started on a downgrade path that led to no good and peaceful end. To the ordinary intellect his position might not have appeared irretrievable; the dog which he had been rushed into buying, and whose personality inspired him with the strongest repugnance, was not necessarily a fixture. An immediate purchaser might be discovered, or the undesired acquisition might be given away, lost, or otherwise disposed of.

But here again the working of inexorable laws sterilized the chances of Gibbon's emancipation. In a conflict between their respective will-powers, the man inevitably succumbed to the fox-terrier, and, when the dinner-hour exposed the bachelor's sitting-room to the observation of a tray-bearing handmaiden, its occupant was discovered in a condition of deprecatory embarrassment; whilst the dog, snugly ensconced in the only arm-chair, was the embodiment of self-composure and critical appraisement. As a general rule, Gibbon was not demonstratively communicative with maidservants, and his intercourse in this direction was usually limited to a perfunctory (vocal) salutation, or a mild request for a forgotten napkin, or such-like trifle. But the advent of Beelzebub had already dislocated the wonted disposition of affairs, and the girl became aware that an appeal of some nature was being addressed to her.

'Er, Mary, this little dog, er, I think you – might say nothing about it to Mrs Mulberry, er, just yet, that is, I will break it to her – I mean – will tell her myself – tomorrow morning.' While Gibbon was delivering himself of this charge he was shoving a warm, moist shilling Mary-wards along the table with a succession of short pats, as if he thought the coin should have some impetus of its own, and start forward in the desired direction. The hush-money staved off the crisis which must assuredly arise when the landlady became aware of the canine presence in her apartments, and Gibbon, having successfully smuggled the contraband article into his bedroom, congratulated himself on having so far made the best of the situation. But, as the dog slipped out next morning on the incoming of the hot water, and chivvied the landlady's cat into the landlady's bedroom, and followed it on to her bed and under the blankets, where a muffled but vigorous battle-royal ensued, it became doubtful whether the shilling had been, after all, a judicious outlay.

Gibbon found that his selection of new rooms was considerably narrowed by the prejudice aroused in the breasts of prospective landladies on the sight of his canine satellite, who accompanied him as a matter of course on all his quests; and finally, having strayed into a suite of chambers furnished in a style of Bohemian extravagance which was wholly out of keeping with his accustomed ways of life, the terrier clinched matters for him by settling down therein and refusing to leave. Gibbon hunted him ineffectually round the place, upset and disarranged the furniture, all to no purpose; and at length, on the suggestion of the proprietor – 'you'd better take the rooms, sir, seems as if it was meant like' – he took alarm at the idea of resisting the possible workings of a Higher Power, and yielded. It was the weak character pitted against the strong once more, and the result was as it ever must be.

To the deteriorating effects of baneful companionship were now added the subtle workings of the laws of environment. Gibbon was too bashfully diffident to remove even the most glaringly uncongenial adornments of his new quarters, and it was a sign of his drifting progress that the views of Durham Cathedral did not find hanging room on the well-covered walls. Instead of these solidly respectable works of art, his eyes were daily confronted with presentiments of ladies who had apparently conquered the love of dress which is attributed to their sex, interspersed with portraits of race-horses noted for their fastness, or of society beauties with a similar reputation. But the chief agent in the moral slump which was becoming more and more pronounced in the person of Artemus Gibbon was undoubtedly Beelzebub. The very name was a stumbling-block to the leading of a respectable life, and a young man who called an already sufficiently unprepossessing animal by such an unseemly appellation was doomed to be dropped by self-respecting acquaintances.

Then with change of friends came also change of habits. Sober constitutionals became a thing of the past since Beelzebub, speedily bored by such tame affairs, contracted a habit of jumping into the nearest empty hansom; the cabman naturally pulled up, and as the dog would not get out, Gibbon had to get in. Having no address that he could give at the moment – it usually happened a few yards from his own door – a restaurant became the necessary destination, and Beelzebub never left much before closing time. The eye of the waiter, scornfully regarding his slowly emptied glass of lager, invariably impelled the naturally temperate Gibbon to order another drink, and the homeward cab was sometimes a matter of convenience as well as dictation.

As fast as the fate-driven dissipator alienated old acquaintances, Beelzebub supplied him with new ones of a stamp more congruous with his altered circumstances; smart sporting youths, lurid in waistcoats and conversation, foregathered with the guileless owner of the indiscriminately social terrier, and one by one the landmarks of the placid past were swept away. Awaking in the harsh crude light of mature morning from late and unrefreshing sleep, Artemus would cast his eyes wearily round his disordered rooms, and everywhere the trail of the dog met his gaze, in powdery cigarette ashes, empty liqueur glasses, vivid-hued sporting periodicals, and tumbled packs of cards.

But the finishing touch was yet to come. Sitting one night in a café where he and his dog were now recognized habitués, slowly imbibing the Scotch and soda which had supplanted the lager of his earlier dissipations, Gibbon had momentarily lost himself in that superstructure of woe which consists of 'remembering happier things'; in particular he was thinking of a certain prodigally inclined young friend of his pre-canine days, by name Hilary Helforlether, whom he had tried to keep, by the force of example and precept, in the straight and narrow way that leads to a respected old age. From the uncomfortable reflections to which this reverie gave rise, he was suddenly aroused by a screamlet of vexed consternation, and turning sharply beheld at an adjoining table a lady, whose entrance had languidly attracted his attention some quarter of an hour ago. She was young and pretty and birdlike – especially with regard to her hair, which was of the tint a Norwich canary aspires to but seldom attains – and there was just a delicate flavour of a possible foreign extraction about her; her attire was a rhapsody (with lucid intervals) of purple and gold, and a magnificent boa of ostrich feather had supplied the finishing touch to an impressive costume. The soft shimmering lengths of this elegant accessory had attracted the attention of the ever-alert Beelzebub, who had quietly abstracted it as it hung negligently from its owner's chair, and by a process of 'little and often' had conscientiously given to each individual feather a separate and independent existence.

Gibbon's horrified gaze, attracted by the lady's excusable agitation, rested on his graceless quadruped snoozing amid the ruin of fluffiness like an eider-duckling in its nest. 'No marvel that the lady wept', or would have if consideration for her complexion had not prevailed, and Beelzebub's owner hastened to gasp out a little hurricane of apologies and inquiries as to the estimated cost of the damage.

The lady really behaved very sweetly considering her provocation, and if in her agitation she placed the price of her ravaged boa somewhat above its Bond Street level, it was only in accordance with the impulse which teaches us to value things the more when we have lost them. Gibbon had not the amount on him, would the lady give him her address, or, well, yes, perhaps that would be better, he would give her his card, tomorrow afternoon, unfailingly, etc., etc., and before he knew what he was doing he had made an assignation with the boa-bereaved damsel.

Gibbon had never before given tea to a lady in his apartments, and was necessarily rather inept in his administration of this unwonted hospitality, but his fair guest supplied the deficiencies of his experience, and knew exactly when the milder beverage should be followed up by liqueurs and cigarettes. That she was not dissatisfied with her entertainment her host gathered from the fact that she graciously forestalled his invitation to come again and continue his education in the art of tea-giving. In short, she was altogether in affable mood, and if she forgot to give the overwhelmed Gibbon any change for his tenner, she at least atoned for the omission by favouring him with a wholly spontaneous kiss.

This unsolicited kindness was conferred on him while opening his outer door for his visitor's departure, which was the appropriate psychological moment for its delivery; it was unfortunate, nevertheless, that Hilary Helforlether should have chosen the same moment for appearing hull-down on the staircase horizon. Artemus, having sped the parting guest, greeted his new visitor with a hastily mobilized smile, which suffered by comparison with the grin on his sometime disciple's face.

'Oh, you pipeclayed sepulchre! Thought you were the blamed whiting of a lifeless flower, and all that sort of thing. *Rats!* Hullo, what a jolly terrier. Does he belong to you?'

'No; I belong to him. Body and soul,' muttered Gibbon, drearily.

Alice in Pall Mall

'The great art in falling off a horse', said the White Knight, 'is to have another handy to fall on to.'

'But wouldn't that be rather difficult to arrange?' asked Alice.

'Difficult, of course,' replied the Knight, 'but in my Department one has to be provided for emergencies. Now, for instance, have you ever conducted a war in South Africa?'

Alice shook her head.

'I have,' said the Knight, with a gentle complacency in his voice.

'And did you bring it to a successful conclusion?' asked Alice.

'Not exactly to a *conclusion* – not a *definite* conclusion, you know – nor entirely successful either. In fact, I believe it's going on still. . . . But you can't think how much forethought it took to get it properly started. I dare say, now, you are wondering at my equipment?'

Alice certainly was; the Knight was riding rather uncomfortably on a sober-paced horse that was prevented from moving any faster by an elaborate housing of red-tape trappings. 'Of course, I see the reason for that,' thought Alice; 'if it were to move any quicker the Knight would come off.' But there were a number of obsolete weapons and appliances hanging about the saddle that didn't seem of the least practical use.

'You see, I had read a book', the Knight went on in a dreamy far-away tone, 'written by someone to prove that warfare under modern conditions was impossible. You may imagine how disturbing that was to a man of my profession. Many men would have thrown up the whole thing and gone home. But I grappled with the situation. You will never guess what I did.'

Alice pondered. 'You went to war, of course –'

'Yes; *but not under modern conditions*.'

The Knight stopped his horse so that he might enjoy the full effect of this announcement.

'Now, for instance,' he continued kindly, seeing that Alice had not recovered her breath, 'you observe this little short-range gun that I have hanging to my saddle? Why do you suppose I sent out guns of that particular kind? Because if they happened to fall into the hands of the enemy they'd be very little use to him. That was my own invention.'

'I see,' said Alice gravely; 'but supposing you wanted to use them against the enemy?'

The Knight looked worried. 'I know there is that to be thought of, but I didn't choose to be putting dangerous weapons into the enemy's hands. And then, again, supposing the Basutos had risen, those would have been just the sort of guns to drive them off with. Of course they *didn't* rise; but they might have done so, you know.'

At this moment the horse suddenly went on again, and the Knight clutched convulsively at its mane to prevent himself from coming off.

'That's the worst of horses,' he remarked apologetically; 'they are so Unforeseen in their movements. Now, if I had had my way I would have done without them as far as possible – in fact, I began that way only it didn't answer. And yet', he went on in an aggrieved tone, 'at Cressy it was the footmen who did the most damage.'

'But', objected Alice, 'if your men hadn't got horses how could they get about from place to place?'

'They couldn't. That would be the beauty of it,' said the White Knight eagerly; 'the fewer places your army moves to, the fewer maps you have to prepare. And we hadn't prepared very many. I'm not very strong at geography, but', he added, brightening, 'you should hear me talk French.'

'But', persisted Alice, 'supposing the enemy went and attacked you at some other place –'

'They did,' interrupted the Knight gloomily; 'they appeared in strength at places that weren't even marked on the ordinary maps. But how do you think they got there?'

He paused and fixed his gentle eyes upon Alice as she walked beside him, and then continued in a hollow voice,

'They rode. Rode and carried rifles. They were no mortal foes – they were Mounted Infantry.'

The Knight swayed about so with the violence of his emotion

that it was inevitable that he should lose his seat, and Alice was relieved to notice that there was another horse with an empty saddle ready for him to scramble on to. There was a frightful dust, of course, but Alice saw him gathering the reins of his new mount into a bunch, and smiling down upon her with increased amiability.

'It's not an easy animal to manage,' he called out to her, 'but if I pat it and speak to it in French it will probably understand where I want it to go. And', he added hopefully, 'it may go there. A knowledge of French and an amiable disposition will see one out of most things.'

'Well,' thought Alice as she watched him settling down uneasily into the saddle, 'it ought not to take long to see him out of that.'

Alice at St Stephen's

'It's very provoking,' said Alice to herself; she had been trying for the previous quarter of an hour to attract the attention of a large and very solemn caterpillar that was perched on the top of a big mushroom with a Gothic fringe. 'I've heard that the only chance of speaking to it is to catch its eye,' she continued, but she found out that however perseveringly she thrust herself into the Caterpillar's range of vision its eye persistently looked beyond her, or beneath her, or around her – never at her. Alice had read somewhere that little girls should be seen and not heard; 'but', she thought, 'I'm not even seen here, and if I'm not to be heard, what am I here at all for?' In any case she determined to make an attempt at conversation.

'If you please –' she began.

'I don't,' said the Caterpillar shortly, without seeming to take any further notice of her.

After an uncomfortable pause she commenced again.

'I should like –'

'You shouldn't,' said the Caterpillar with decision.

Alice felt discouraged, but it was no use to be shut up in this way, so she started again as amiably as she could.

'You can't think, Mr Caterpillar –'

'I can, and I often do,' he remarked stiffly; adding, 'You mustn't make such wild statements. They're not relevant to the discussion.'

'But I only said that in order –'

'You didn't, said the Caterpillar angrily. 'I tell you it was not in order.'

'You are so dreadfully short,' exclaimed Alice; the Caterpillar drew itself up.

'In manner, I mean; no – in memory,' she added hastily, for it was thoroughly angry by this time.

'I'm sure I didn't mean anything,' she continued humbly, for she felt that it was absurd to quarrel with a caterpillar.

The Caterpillar snorted.

'What's the good of talking if you don't mean anything? If you've talked all this time without meaning anything you're not worth listening to.'

'But you put a wrong construction –' Alice began.

'You can't discuss Construction now, you know; that comes on the Estimates. Shrivel!'

'I don't understand,' said Alice.

'Shrivel. Dry up,' explained the Caterpillar, and proceeded to look in another direction, as if it had forgotten her existence.

'Good-bye,' said Alice, after waiting a moment; she half hoped that the Caterpillar might say 'See you later', but it took not the slightest notice of her remark, so she got up reluctantly and walked away.

'Well, of all the gubernatorial –' said Alice to herself when she got outside. She did not quite know that it meant, but it was an immense relief to be able to come out with a word of six syllables.

The Blood-Feud of Toad-Water

A West-Country Epic

The Cricks lived at Toad-Water; and in the same lonely upland spot Fate had pitched the home of the Saunderses, and for miles around these two dwellings there was never a neighbour or a chimney or even a burying-ground to bring a sense of cheerful communion or social intercourse. Nothing but fields and spinneys and barns, lanes and waste-lands. Such was Toad-Water; and, even so, Toad-Water had its history.

Thrust away in the benighted hinterland of a scattered market district, it might have been supposed that these two detached items of the Great Human Family would have leaned towards one another in a fellowship begotten of kindred circumstances and a common isolation from the outer world. And perhaps it had been so once, but the way of things had brought it otherwise. Indeed, otherwise. Fate, which had linked the two families in such unavoidable association of habitat, had ordained that the Crick household should nourish and maintain among its earthly possessions sundry head of domestic fowls, while to the Saunderses was given a disposition towards the cultivation of garden crops. Herein lay the material, ready to hand, for the coming of feud and ill-blood. For the grudge between the man of herbs and the man of live stock is no new thing; you will find traces of it in the fourth chapter of Genesis. And one Sunday afternoon in late spring-time the feud came – came, as such things mostly do come, with seeming aimlessness and triviality. One of the Crick hens, in obedience to the nomadic instincts of her kind, wearied of her legitimate scratching grounds, and flew over the low wall that divided the holdings of the neighbours. And there, on the yonder side, with a hurried consciousness that her time and opportunities might be limited, the misguided bird scratched and scraped and beaked and delved in the soft yielding bed that had been prepared for the solace and well-being of a colony of seeding onions. Little showers of earth-mould and root-fibres went spraying before the hen and behind her, and every minute the area of her operations widened. The onions suffered considerably. Mrs Saunders, sauntering at this luckless moment down the garden path, in order to fill her soul with reproaches at the iniquity of the weeds, which grew faster than she or her good man cared to remove them, stopped in mute discomfiture before the presence of a more magnificent grievance. And then, in the hour of her calamity, she turned instinctively to the Great Mother, and gathered in her capacious hands large clods of the hard brown soil that lay at her feet. With a terrible sincerity of purpose, though with a contemptible inadequacy of aim, she rained her earth bolts at the marauder, and the bursting pellets called forth a flood of cackling protest and panic from the hastily departing fowl. Calmness under misfortune is not an attribute of either hen-folk or womenkind, and while Mrs Saunders declaimed over her onion bed such portions of the slang dictionary as are permitted by the Nonconformist conscience to be said or sung, the Vasco da Gama fowl was waking the echoes of Toad-Water with crescendo bursts of throat music which compelled attention to her griefs. Mrs Crick had a long family, and was therefore licensed, in the eyes of her world, to have a short temper, and when some of her ubiquitous offspring had informed her, with the authority of eye-witnesses, that her neighbour had so far forgotten herself as to heave stones at her hen – her best hen, the best layer in the countryside – her thoughts clothed themselves in language 'unbecoming to a Christian woman' – so at least said Mrs Saunders, to whom most of the language was applied. Nor was she, on her part, surprised at Mrs Crick's conduct in letting her hens stray into other body's gardens, and then abusing of them, seeing as how she remembered things against Mrs Crick – and the latter simultaneously had recollections of lurking episodes in the past of Susan Saunders that were nothing to her credit. 'Fond memory, when all things fade we fly to thee,' and in the paling light of an April afternoon the two women confronted each other from their respective sides of the party wall, recalling with shuddering breath the blots and blemishes of their neighbour's family record. There was that aunt of Mrs Crick's who had died a pauper in Exeter workhouse – everyone knew that Mrs Saunders' uncle on her mother's side drank himself to death – then there was that Bristol cousin of

Mrs Crick's! From the shrill triumph with which his name was dragged in, his crime must have been pilfering from a cathedral at least, but as both remembrancers were speaking at once it was difficult to distinguish his infamy from the scandal which beclouded the memory of Mrs Saunders' brother's wife's mother – who may have been a regicide, and was certainly not a nice person as Mrs Crick painted her. And then, with an air of accumulating and irresistible conviction, each belligerent informed the other that she was no lady – after which they withdrew in a great silence, feeling that nothing further remained to be said. The chaffinches clinked in the apple trees and the bees droned round the berberis bushes, and the waning sunlight slanted pleasantly across the garden plots, but between the neighbour households had sprung up a barrier of hate, permeating and permanent.

The male heads of the families were necessarily drawn into the quarrel, and the children on either side were forbidden to have anything to do with the unhallowed offspring of the other party. As they had to travel a good three miles along the same road to school every day, this was awkward, but such things have to be. Thus all communication between the households was sundered. Except the cats. Much as Mrs Saunders might deplore it, rumour persistently pointed to the Crick he-cat as the presumable father of sundry kittens of which the Saunders she-cat was indisputably the mother. Mrs Saunders drowned the kittens, but the disgrace remained.

Summer succeeded spring, and winter summer, but the feud outlasted the waning seasons. Once, indeed, it seemed as though the healing influences of religion might restore to Toad-Water its erstwhile peace; the hostile families found themselves side by side in the soul-kindling atmosphere of a Revival Tea, where hymns were blended with a beverage that came of tea-leaves and hot water and took after the latter parent, and where ghostly counsel was tempered by garnishings of solidly fashioned buns – and here, wrought up by the environment of festive piety, Mrs Saunders so far unbent as to remark guardedly to Mrs Crick that the evening had been a fine one. Mrs Crick, under the influence of her ninth cup of tea and her fourth hymn, ventured on the hope that it might continue fine, but a maladroit allusion on the part of the Saunders good man to the backwardness of garden crops brought the Feud stalking forth from its corner with all its old bitterness. Mrs Saunders joined heartily in the singing of the final hymn, which told of peace and joy and archangels and golden glories; but her thoughts were dwelling on the pauper aunt of Exeter.

Years have rolled away, and some of the actors in this wayside drama have passed into the Unknown; other onions have arisen, have flourished, have gone their way, and the offending hen has long since expiated her misdeeds and lain with trussed feet and look of ineffable peace under the arched roof of Barnstaple market.

But the Blood-feud of Toad-Water survives to this day.

Reginald on Christmas Presents

I wish it to be distinctly understood (said Reginald) that I don't want a 'George, Prince of Wales' Prayer-book as a Christmas present. The fact cannot be too widely known.

There ought (he continued) to be technical education classes on the science of present-giving. No one seems to have the faintest notion of what anyone else wants, and the prevalent ideas on the subject are not creditable to a civilized community.

There is, for instance, the female relative in the country who 'knows a tie is always useful', and sends you some spotted horror that you could only wear in secret or in Tottenham Court Road. It *might* have been useful had she kept it to tie up currant bushes with, when it would have served the double purpose of supporting the branches and frightening away the birds – for it is an admitted fact that the ordinary tomtit of commerce has a sounder aesthetic taste than the average female relative in the country.

Then there are aunts. They are always a difficult class to deal with in the matter of presents. The trouble is that one never catches them really young enough. By the time one has educated them to an appreciation of the fact that one does not wear red woollen mittens in the West End, they die, or quarrel with the family, or do something equally inconsiderate. That is why the supply of trained aunts is always so precarious.

There is my Aunt Agatha, *par exemple*, who sent me a pair of gloves last Christmas, and even got so far as to choose a kind that was being worn and had the correct number of buttons. But – *they were nines!* I sent them to a boy whom I hated intimately: he didn't wear them, of course, but he could have – that was where the bitterness of death came in. It was nearly as consoling as sending white flowers to his funeral. Of course I wrote and told my aunt that they were the one thing that had been wanting to make existence blossom like a rose; I am afraid she thought me frivolous – she comes from the North, where they live in the fear of Heaven and the Earl of Durham. (Reginald affects an exhaustive knowledge of things political, which furnishes an excellent excuse for not discussing them.) Aunts with a dash of foreign extraction in them are the most satisfactory in the way of understanding these things; but if you can't choose your aunt, it is wisest in the long run to choose the present and send her the bill.

Even friends of one's own set, who might be expected to know better, have curious delusions on the subject. I am *not* collecting copies of the cheaper editions of Omar Khayyám. I gave the last four that I received to the lift-boy, and I like to think of him reading them, with FitzGerald's notes, to his aged mother. Lift-boys always have aged mothers; shows such nice feeling on their part, I think.

Personally, I can't see where the difficulty in choosing suitable presents lies. No boy who had brought himself up properly could fail to appreciate one of those decorative bottles of liqueurs that are so reverently staged in Morel's window – and it wouldn't in the least matter if one did get duplicates. And there would always be the supreme moment of dreadful uncertainty whether it was *crême de menthe* or Chartreuse – like the expectant thrill of seeing your partner's hand turned up at bridge. People may say what they like about the decay of Christianity; the religious system that produced green Chartreuse can never really die.

And then, of course, there are liqueur glasses, and crystallized fruits, and tapestry curtains, and heaps of other necessaries of life that make really sensible presents – not to speak of luxuries, such as having one's bills paid, or getting something quite sweet in the way of jewellery. Unlike the alleged Good Woman of the Bible, I'm not above rubies. When found, by the way, she must have been rather a problem at Christmas-time; nothing short of a blank cheque would have fitted the situation. Perhaps it's as well that she's died out.

The great charm about me (concluded Reginald) is that I am so easily pleased. But I draw the line at a 'Prince of Wales' Prayer-book.

Reginald's Choir Treat

'Never', wrote Reginald to his most darling friend, 'be a pioneer. It's the Early Christian that gets the fattest lion.'

Reginald, in his way, was a pioneer.

None of the rest of his family had anything approaching Titian hair or a sense of humour, and they used primroses as a table decoration.

It follows that they never understood Reginald, who came down late to breakfast, and nibbled toast, and said disrespectful things about the universe. The family ate porridge, and believed in everything, even the weather forecast.

Therefore the family was relieved when the vicar's daughter undertook the reformation of Reginald. Her name was Amabel; it was the vicar's one extravagance. Amabel was accounted a beauty and intellectually gifted; she never played tennis, and was reputed to have read Maeterlinck's *Life of the Bee*. If you abstain from tennis *and* read Maeterlinck in a small country village, you are of necessity intellectual. Also she had been twice to Fécamp to pick up a good French accent from the Americans staying there; consequently she had a knowledge of the world which might be considered useful in dealings with a worldling.

Hence the congratulations in the family when Amabel undertook the reformation of its wayward member.

Amabel commenced operations by asking her unsuspecting pupil to tea in the vicarage garden; she believed in the healthy influence of natural surroundings, never having been in Sicily, where things are different.

And like every woman who has ever preached repentance to unregenerate youth, she dwelt on the sin of an empty life, which always seems so much more scandalous in the country, where people rise early to see if a new strawberry has happened during the night.

Reginald recalled the lilies of the field, 'which simply sat and looked beautiful, and defied competition'.

'But that is not an example for us to follow,' gasped Amabel.

'Unfortunately, we can't afford to. You don't know what a world of trouble I take in trying to rival the lilies in their artistic simplicity.'

'You are really indecently vain of your appearance. A good life is infinitely preferable to good looks.'

'You agree with me that the two are incompatible. I always say beauty is only sin deep.'

Amabel began to realize that the battle is not always to the strong-minded. With the immemorial resource of her sex, she abandoned the frontal attack and laid stress on her unassisted labours in parish work, her mental loneliness, her discouragements – and at the right moment she produced strawberries and cream. Reginald was obviously affected by the latter, and when his preceptress suggested that he might begin the strenuous life by helping her to supervise the annual outing of the bucolic infants who composed the local choir, his eyes shone with the dangerous enthusiasm of a convert.

Reginald entered on the strenuous life alone, as far as Amabel was concerned. The most virtuous women are not proof against damp grass, and Amabel kept her bed with a cold. Reginald called it a dispensation; it had been the dream of his life to stage-manage a choir outing. With strategic insight, he led his shy, bullet-headed charges to the nearest woodland stream and allowed them to bathe; then he seated himself on their discarded garments and discoursed on their immediate future, which, he decreed, was to embrace a Bacchanalian procession through the village. Forethought had provided the occasion with a supply of tin whistles, but the introduction of a he-goat from a neighbouring orchard was a brilliant afterthought. Properly, Reginald explained, there should have been an outfit of panther skins; as it was, those who had spotted handkerchiefs were allowed to wear them, which they did with thankfulness. Reginald recognized the impossibility, in the time at his disposal, of teaching his shivering neophytes a chant in honour of Bacchus, so he started them off with a more familiar, if less appropriate, temperance hymn. After all, he said, it is the spirit of the thing that counts. Following the etiquette of dramatic authors on first nights, he remained discreetly in the background while the procession, with extreme diffidence and the goat, wound its way lugubriously towards the village. The singing had died down long before the main street was reached, but the miserable wailing of pipes brought the inhabitants to their doors. Reginald said he had seen something like it in pictures; the villagers had seen nothing like it in their lives, and remarked as much freely.

Reginald's family never forgave him. They had no sense of humour.

Reginald in Russia

Reginald sat in a corner of the Princess's salon and tried to forgive the furniture, which started out with an obvious intention of being Louise Quinze, but relapsed at frequent intervals into Wilhelm II.

He classified the Princess with that distinct type of woman that looks as if it habitually went out to feed hens in the rain.

Her name was Olga; she kept what she hoped and believed to be a fox-terrier, and professed what she thought were Socialist opinions. It is not necessary to be called Olga if you are a Russian Princess; in fact, Reginald knew quite a number who were called Vera; but the fox-terrier and the Socialism are essential.

'The Countess Lomshen keeps a bull-dog,' said the Princess suddenly. 'In England is it more chic to have a bull-dog than a fox-terrier?'

Reginald threw his mind back over the canine fashions of the last ten years and gave an evasive answer.

'Do you think her handsome, the Countess Lomshen?' asked the Princess.

Reginald thought the Countess's complexion suggested an exclusive diet of macaroons and pale sherry. He said so.

'But that cannot be possible,' said the Princess triumphantly; 'I've seen her eating fish-soup at Donon's.'

The Princess always defended a friend's complexion if it was really bad. With her, as with a great many of her sex, charity began at homeliness and did not generally progress much farther.

Reginald withdrew his macaroon and sherry theory, and became interested in a case of miniatures.

'That?' said the Princess; 'that is the old Princess Lorikoff. She lived in Millionaya Street, near the Winter Palace, and was one of the Court ladies of the Old Russian school. Her knowledge of people and events was extremely limited; but she used to patronize everyone who came in contact with her. There was a story that when she died and left the Millionaya for Heaven she addressed St Peter in her formal staccato French: "Je suis la Princesse Lor-i-koff. Il me donne grand plaisir à faire votre connaissance. Je vous en prie me présenter au Bon Dieu." St Peter made the desired introduction, and the Princess addressed le Bon Dieu: "Je suis la Princesse Lor-i-koff. Il me donne grand plaisir à faire votre connaissance. On a souvent parlé de vous à l'église de la rue Million." '

'Only the old and the clergy of Established churches know how to be flippant gracefully,' commented Reginald; 'which reminds me that in the Anglican Church in a certain foreign capital, which shall be nameless, I was present the other day when one of the junior chaplains was preaching in aid of distressed somethings or other, and he brought a really eloquent passage to a close with the remark, "The tears of the afflicted, to what shall I liken them – to diamonds?" The other junior chaplain, who had been dozing out of professional jealousy, awoke with a start and asked hurriedly, "Shall I play to diamonds, partner?" It didn't improve matters when the senior chaplain remarked dreamily, but with painful distinctness, "Double Diamonds". Everyone looked at the preacher, half expecting him to redouble, but he contented himself with scoring what points he could under the circumstances.'

'You English are always so frivolous,' said the Princess. 'In Russia we have too many troubles to permit of our being light-hearted.'

Reginald gave a delicate shiver, such as an Italian greyhound might give in contemplating the approach of an ice age of which he personally disapproved, and resigned himself to the inevitable political discussion.

'Nothing that you hear about us in England is true,' was the Princess's hopeful beginning.

'I always refused to learn Russian geography at school,' observed Reginald; 'I was certain some of the names must be wrong.'

'Everything is wrong with our system of government,' continued the Princess placidly. 'The Bureaucrats think only of their pockets, and the people are exploited and plundered in every direction, and everything is mismanaged.'

'With us,' said Reginald, 'a Cabinet usually gets the credit of being depraved and worthless beyond the bounds of human conception by the time it has been in office about four years.'

'But if it is a bad Government you can turn it out at the election,' argued the Princess.

'As far as I remember, we generally do,' said Reginald.

'But here it is dreadful, everyone goes to such extremes. In England you never go to extremes.'

'We go to the Albert Hall,' explained Reginald.

'There is always a see-saw with us between repression and violence,' continued the Princess; 'and the pity of it is the people are really not in the least inclined to be anything but peaceable. Nowhere will you find people more good-natured, or family circles where there is more affection.'

'There I agree with you,' said Reginald. 'I know a boy who lives somewhere on the French Quay who is a case in point. His hair curls naturally, especially on Sundays, and he plays bridge well, even for a Russian, which is saying much. I don't think he has any other accomplishments, but his family affection is really of a very high order. When his maternal grandmother died he didn't go as far as to give up bridge altogether but he declared on nothing but black suits for the next three months. That, I think, was really beautiful.'

The Princess was not impressed.

'I think you must be very self-indulgent and live only for amusement,' she said. 'A life of pleasure-seeking and card-playing and dissipation brings only dissatisfaction. You will find that out some day.'

'Oh, I know it turns out that way sometimes,' assented Reginald. 'Forbidden fizz is often the sweetest.'

But the remark was wasted on the Princess, who preferred champagne that had at least a suggestion of dissolved barley-sugar.

'I hope you will come and see me again,' she said in a tone that prevented the hope from becoming too infectious; adding as a happy after-thought, 'you must come to stay with us in the country'.

Her particular part of the country was a few hundred versts the other side of Tamboff, with some fifteen miles of agrarian disturbance between her and the nearest neighbour. Reginald felt that there is some privacy which should be sacred from intrusion.

The Purple of the Balkan Kings

Luitpold Wolkenstein, financier and diplomat on a small, obtrusive, self-important scale, sat in his favoured café in the worldwise Habsburg capital, confronted with the *Neue Freie Presse* and the cup of cream-topped coffee and attendant glass of water that a sleek-headed piccolo had just brought him. For years longer than a dog's lifetime sleek-headed piccolos had placed the *Neue Freie Presse* and a cup of cream-topped coffee on his table; for years he had sat at the same spot, under the dust-coated, stuffed eagle, that had once been a living, soaring bird on the Styrian mountains, and was now made monstrous and symbolical with a second head grafted on to its neck and a gilt crown planted on either dusty skull. Today Luitpold Wolkenstein read no more than the first article in his paper, but he read it again and again.

'The Turkish fortress of Kirk Kilisseh has fallen. . . . The Serbs, it is officially announced, have taken Kumanovo. . . . The fortress of Kirk Kilisseh lost, Kumanovo taken by the Serbs, these are tidings for Constantinople resembling something out of Shakespeare's tragedies of the kings. . . . The neighbourhood of Adrianople and the Eastern region, where the great battle is now in progress, will not reveal merely the future of Turkey, but also what position and what influence the Balkan States are to have in the world.'

For years longer than a dog's lifetime Luitpold Wolkenstein had disposed of the pretensions and strivings of the Balkan States over the cup of cream-topped coffee that sleek-headed piccolos had brought him. Never travelling further eastward than the horse-fair at Temesvar, never inviting personal risk in an encounter with anything more potentially desperate than a hare or partridge, he had constituted himself the critical appraiser and arbiter of the military and national prowess of the small countries that fringed the Dual Monarchy on its Danube border. And his judgment had been one of unsparing contempt for small-scale efforts, of unquestioning respect for the big battalions and full purses. Over the whole scene of the Balkan territories and their troubled histories had loomed the commanding magic of the words 'the Great Powers' – even more imposing in their Teutonic rendering, 'Die Grossmächte'.

Worshipping power and force and money-mastery as an elderly nerve-ridden woman might worship youthful physical energy, the comfortable, plump-bodied café-oracle had jested and gibed at the ambitions of the Balkan kinglets and their peoples, had unloosed against them that battery of strange lip-sounds that a Viennese employs almost as an auxiliary language to express the thoughts when his thoughts are not complimentary. British travellers had visited the Balkan lands and reported high things of the Bulgarians and their future, Russian officers had taken peeps at their army and confessed 'this is a thing to be reckoned with, and it is not we who have created it, they have done it by themselves'. But over his cups of coffee and his hour-long games of dominoes the oracle had laughed and wagged his head and distilled the worldly wisdom of his caste. The Grossmächte had not succeeded in stifling the roll of the war-drum, that was true; the big battalions of the Ottoman Empire would have to do some talking, and then the big purses and big threatenings of the Powers would speak and the last word would be with them. In imagination Luitpold heard the onward tramp of the red-fezzed bayonet bearers echoing through the Balkan passes, saw the little sheepskin-clad mannikins driven back to their villages, saw the augustly chiding spokesmen of the Powers dictating, adjusting, restoring, settling things once again in their allotted places, sweeping up the dust of conflict, and now his ears had to listen to the war-drum rolling in quite another direction, had to listen to the tramp of battalions that were bigger and bolder and better skilled in war-craft than he had deemed possible in that quarter; his eyes had to read in the columns of his accustomed newspaper a warning to the Grossmächte that they had something new to learn, something new to reckon with, much that was time-honoured to relinquish. 'The Great Powers will have no little difficulty in persuading the Balkan States of the inviolability of the principle that Europe cannot permit any fresh partition of territory in the East without her approval. Even now, while the campaign is still undecided, there are rumours of a project of fiscal unity, extending over the entire Balkan lands, and further of a constitutional union in imitation of the German Empire. That is perhaps only a political straw blown by the storm, but it is not possible to dismiss the reflection that the Balkan States leagued together command a military strength with which the Great Powers will have to reckon. . . . The people who have poured out their blood on the battlefields and sacrificed the available armed men of an entire generation in order to encompass a union with their kinsfolk will not remain any longer in an attitude of dependence on the Great Powers or on Russia, but will go their own ways. . . . The blood that has been poured forth today gives for the first time a genuine tone to the purple of the Balkan Kings. The Great Powers cannot overlook the fact that a people that has tasted victory will not let itself be driven back again within its former limits. Turkey has lost today not only Kirk Kilisseh and Kumanovo, but Macedonia also.'

Luitpold Wolkenstein drank his coffee, but the flavour had somehow gone out of it. His world, his pompous, imposing, dictating world, had suddenly rolled up into narrower dimensions. The big purses and the big threats had been pushed unceremoniously on one side; a force that he could not fathom, could not comprehend, had made itself rudely felt. The august Cæsars of Mammon and armament had looked down frowningly on the combat, and those about to die had *not* saluted, had no intention of saluting. A lesson was being imposed on unwilling learners, a lesson of respect for certain fundamental principles, and it was not the small struggling States who were being taught the lesson.

Luitpold Wolkenstein did not wait for the quorum of domino players to arrive. They would all have read the article in the *Freie Presse*. And there are moments when an oracle finds its greatest salvation in withdrawing itself from the area of human questioning.

The Soul of Laploshka

Laploshka was one of the meanest men I have ever met, and quite one of the most entertaining. He said horrid things about other people in such a charming way that one forgave him for the equally horrid things he said about oneself behind one's back. Hating anything in the way of ill-natured gossip ourselves, we are always grateful to those who do it for us and do it well. And Laploshka did it really well.

Naturally Laploshka had a large circle of acquaintances, and as he exercised some care in their selection it followed that an appreciable proportion were men whose bank balances enabled them to acquiesce indulgently in his rather one-sided views on hospitality. Thus, although possessed of only moderate means, he was able to live comfortably within his income, and still more comfortably within those of various tolerantly disposed associates.

But towards the poor or to those of the same limited resources as himself his attitude was one of watchful anxiety; he seemed to be haunted by a besetting fear lest some fraction of a shilling or franc, or whatever the prevailing coinage might be, should be diverted from his pocket or service into that of a hard-up companion. A two-franc cigar would be cheerfully offered to a wealthy patron, on the principle of doing evil that good may come, but I have known him indulge in agonies of perjury rather than admit the incriminating possession of a copper coin when change was needed to tip a waiter. The coin would have been duly returned at the earliest opportunity – he would have taken means to ensure against forgetfulness on the part of the borrower – but accidents might happen, and even the temporary estrangement from his penny or sou was a calamity to be avoided.

The knowledge of this amiable weakness offered a perpetual temptation to play upon Laploshka's fears of involuntary generosity. To offer him a lift in a cab and pretend not to have enough money to pay the fare, to fluster him with a request for a sixpence when his hand was full of silver just received in change, these were a few of the petty torments that ingenuity prompted as occasion afforded. To do justice to Laploshka's resourcefulness it must be admitted that he always emerged somehow or other from the most embarrassing dilemma without in any way compromising his reputation for saying 'No'. But the gods send opportunities at some time to most men, and mine came one evening when Laploshka and I were supping together in a cheap boulevard restaurant. (Except when he was the bidden guest of someone with an irreproachable income, Laploshka was wont to curb his appetite for high living; on such fortunate occasions he let it go on an easy snaffle.) At the conclusion of the meal a somewhat urgent message called me away, and without heeding my companion's agitated protest, I called back cruelly, 'Pay my share; I'll settle with you tomorrow.' Early on the morrow Laploshka hunted me down by instinct as I walked along a side street that I hardly ever frequented. He had the air of a man who had not slept.

'You owe me two francs from last night,' was his breathless greeting.

I spoke evasively of the situation in Portugal, where more trouble seemed brewing. But Laploshka listened with the abstraction of the deaf adder, and quickly returned to the subject of the two francs.

'I'm afraid I must owe it to you,' I said lightly and brutally. 'I haven't a sou in the world,' and I added mendaciously, 'I'm going away for six months or perhaps longer.'

Laploshka said nothing, but his eyes bulged a little and his cheeks took on the mottled hues of an ethnographical map of the Balkan Peninsula. That same day, at sundown, he died. 'Failure of the heart's action' was the doctor's verdict; but I, who knew better, knew that he had died of grief.

There arose the problem of what to do with his two francs. To have killed Laploshka was one thing; to have kept his beloved money would have argued a callousness of feeling of which I am not capable. The ordinary solution, of giving it to the poor, would by no means fit the present situation, for nothing would have distressed the dead man more than such a misuse of his property. On the other hand, the bestowal of two francs on the rich was an operation which called for some tact. An easy way out of the difficulty seemed, however, to present itself the following Sunday, as I was wedged into the cosmopolitan crowd which filled the side-aisle of one of the most popular Paris churches. A collecting-bag, for 'the poor of Monsieur le Curé', was buffeting its tortuous way across the seemingly impenetrable human sea, and a German in front of me, who evidently did not wish his appreciation of the magnificent music to be marred by a suggestion of payment, made audible criticisms to his companion on the claims of the said charity.

'They do not want money,' he said; 'they have too much money. They have no poor. They are all pampered.'

If that were really the case my way seemed clear. I dropped Laploshka's two francs into the bag with a murmured blessing on the rich of Monsieur le Curé.

Some three weeks later chance had taken me to Vienna, and I sat one evening regaling myself in a humble but excellent little Gasthaus up in the Währinger quarter. The appointments were primitive, but the Schnitzel, the beer, and the cheese could not have been improved on. Good cheer brought good custom, and with the exception of one small table near the door every place was occupied. Half-way through my meal I happened to glance in the direction of that empty seat, and saw that it was no longer empty. Poring over the bill of fare with the absorbed scrutiny of one who seeks the cheapest among the cheap was Laploshka. Once he looked across at me, with a comprehensive glance at my repast, as though to say, 'It is my two francs you are eating', and then looked swiftly away. Evidently the poor of Monsieur le Curé had been genuine poor. The Schnitzel turned to leather in my mouth, the beer seemed tepid; I left the Emmenthaler untasted. My one idea was to get away from the room, away from the table where *that* was seated; and as I fled I felt Laploshka's reproachful eyes watching the amount that I gave to the piccolo – out of his two francs. I lunched next day at an expensive restaurant which I felt sure that the living Laploshka would never have entered on his own account, and I hoped that the dead Laploshka would observe the same barriers. I was not mistaken, but as I came out I found him miserably studying the bill of fare stuck up on the portals.

Then he slowly made his way over to a milk-hall. For the first time in my experience I missed the charm and gaiety of Vienna life.

After that, in Paris or London or wherever I happened to be, I continued to see a good deal of Laploshka. If I had a seat in a box at a theatre I was always conscious of his eyes furtively watching me from the dim recesses of the gallery. As I turned into my club on a rainy afternoon I would see him taking inadequate shelter in a doorway opposite. Even if I indulged in the modest luxury of a penny chair in the Park he generally confronted me from one of the free benches, never staring at me, but always elaborately conscious of my presence. My friends began to comment on my changed looks, and advised me to leave off heaps of things. I should have liked to have left off Laploshka.

On a certain Sunday – it was probably Easter, for the crush was worse than ever – I was again wedged into the crowd listening to the music in the fashionable Paris church, and again the collection-bag was buffeting its way across the human sea. An English lady behind me was making ineffectual efforts to convey a coin into the still distant bag, so I took the money at her request and helped it forward to its destination. It was a two-franc piece. A swift inspiration came to me, and I merely dropped my own sou into the bag and slid the silver coin into my pocket. I had withdrawn Laploshka's two francs from the poor, who should never have had that legacy. As I backed away from the crowd I heard a woman's voice say, 'I don't believe he put my money in the bag. There are swarms of people in Paris like that!' But my mind was lighter than it had been for a long time.

The delicate mission of bestowing the retrieved sum on the deserving rich still confronted me. Again I trusted to the inspiration of accident, and again fortune favoured me. A shower drove me, two days later, into one of the historic churches on the left bank of the Seine, and there I found, peering at the old woodcarvings, the Baron R., one of the wealthiest and most shabbily dressed men in Paris. It was now or never. Putting a strong American inflection into the French which I usually talked with an unmistakable British accent, I catechized the Baron as to the date of the church's building, its dimensions, and other details which an American tourist would be certain to want to know. Having acquired such information as the Baron was able to impart on short notice, I solemnly placed the two-franc piece in his hand, with the hearty assurance that it was 'pour vous', and turned to go. The Baron was slightly taken aback, but accepted the situation with a good grace. Walking over to a small box fixed in the wall, he dropped Laploshka's two francs into the slot. Over the box was the inscription, 'Pour les pauvres de M. le Curé'.

That evening, at the crowded corner by the Café de la Paix, I caught a fleeting glimpse of Laploshka. He smiled, slightly raised his hat, and vanished. I never saw him again. After all, the money had been *given* to the deserving rich, and the soul of Laploshka was at peace.

Judkin of the Parcels

A figure in an indefinite tweed suit, carrying brown-paper parcels. That is what we met suddenly, at the bend of a muddy Dorsetshire lane, and the roan mare stared and obviously thought of a curtsey. The mare is road-shy, with intervals of stolidity, and there is no telling what she will pass and what she won't. We call her Redford. That was my first meeting with Judkin, and the next time the circumstances were the same; the same muddy lane, the same rather apologetic figure in the tweed suit, the same – or very similar – parcels. Only this time the roan looked straight in front of her.

Whether I asked the groom or whether he advanced the information, I forget, but someway I gradually reconstructed the life-history of this trudger of the lanes. It was much the same, no doubt, as that of many others who are from time to time pointed out to one as having been aforetime in crack cavalry regiments and noted performers in the saddle; men who have breathed into their lungs the wonder of the East, have romped through life as through a cotillon, have had a thrust perhaps at the Viceroy's Cup, and done fantastic horse-fleshy things around the Gulf of Aden. And then a golden stream has dried up, the sunlight has faded suddenly out of things, and the gods have nodded, 'Go'. And they have not gone. They have turned instead to the muddy lanes and cheap villas and the marked-down ills of life, to watch pear trees growing and to encourage hens for their eggs. And Judkin was even as these others; the wine had been suddenly spilt from his cup of life, and he had stayed to suck at the dregs which the wise throw away. In the days of his scorn for most things he would have stared the roan mare and her turnout out of all pretension to smartness, as he would have frozen a cheap claret behind its cork, or a plain woman behind her veil; and now he was walking stoically through the mud, in a tweed suit that would eventually go on to the gardener's boy, and would perhaps fit him. The dear gods, who know the end before the beginning, were perhaps growing a gardener's boy somewhere to fit the garments, and Judkin was only a caretaker, inhabiting a portion of them. That is what I like to think, and I am probably wrong. And Judkin, whose clothes had been to him once more than a religion, scarcely less sacred than a family quarrel, would carry those parcels back to his villa and to the wife who awaited him and them – a wife who may, for all we know to the contrary, have had a figure once, and perhaps has yet a heart of gold – of nine-caret gold, let us say at the least – but assuredly a soul of tape. And he that has fetched and carried will explain how it had fared with him in his dealings, and if he has brought the wrong sort of sugar or thread he will wheedle away the displeasure from that leaden face as a pastry-cook girl will drive bluebottles off a stale bun. And that man has known what it was to coax the fret of a thoroughbred, to soothe its toss and sweat as it danced beneath him in the glee and chafe of its pulses and the glory of its thews. He has been in the raw places of the earth, where the desert beasts have whimpered their unthinkable psalmody, and their eyes have shone back the reflex of the midnight stars – and he can immerse himself in the tending of an incubator. It is horrible and wrong, and yet when I have met him in the lanes his face has worn a look of tedious cheerfulness that might pass for happiness. Has Judkin of the Parcels found something in the lees of life that I have missed in going to and fro over many waters? Is there more wisdom in her perverseness than in the madness of the wise? The dear gods know.

I don't think I saw Judkin more than three times all told, and always the lane was our point of contact; but as the roan mare was taking me to the station one heavy, cloud-smeared day, I passed a dull-looking villa that the groom, or instinct, told me was Judkin's home. From beyond a hedge of ragged elder-bushes could be heard the thud, thud of a spade, with an occasional clink and pause, as if someone had picked out a stone and thrown it to a distance, and I knew that *he* was doing nameless things to the roots of a pear tree. Near by him, I felt sure, would be lying a large and late vegetable marrow, and its largeness and lateness would be a theme of conversation at luncheon. It would be suggested that it should grace the harvest thanksgiving service; the harvest having been so generally unsatisfactory, it would be unfair to let the farmers supply all the material for rejoicing.

And while I was speeding townwards along the rails Judkin would be plodding his way to the vicarage bearing a vegetable marrow and a basketful of dahlias. The basket to be returned.

The Bag

'The Mayor is coming in to tea,' said Mrs Hoopington to her niece. 'He's just gone round to the stables with his horse. Be as bright and lively as you can; the poor man's got a fit of the glooms.'

Major Pallaby was a victim of circumstances, over which he had no control, and of his temper, over which he had very little. He had taken on the Mastership of the Pexdale Hounds in succession to a highly popular man who had fallen foul of his committee, and the Major found himself confronted with the overt hostility of at least half the hunt, while his lack of tact and amiability had done much to alienate the remainder. Hence subscriptions were beginning to fall off, foxes grew provokingly scarcer, and wire obtruded itself with increasing frequency. The Major could plead reasonable excuse for his fit of the glooms.

In ranging herself as a partisan on the side of Major Pallaby Mrs Hoopington had been largely influenced by the fact that she had made up her mind to marry him at an early date. Against his notorious bad temper she set his three thousand a year, and his prospective succession to a baronetcy gave a casting vote in his favour. The Major's plans on the subject of matrimony were not at present in such an advanced stage as Mrs Hoopington's, but he was begining to find his way over to Hoopington Hall with a frequency that was already being commented on.

'He had a wretchedly thin field out again yesterday,' said Mrs Hoopington. 'Why you didn't bring one or two hunting men down with you, instead of that stupid Russian boy, I can't think.'

'Vladimir isn't stupid,' protested her niece; 'he's one of the most amusing boys I ever met. Just compare him for a moment with some of your heavy hunting men –'

'Anyhow, my dear Norah, he can't ride.'

'Russians never can; but he shoots.'

'Yes; and what does he shoot? Yesterday he brought home a woodpecker in his game-bag.'

'But he'd shot three pheasants and some rabbits as well.'

'That's no excuse for including a woodpecker in his game-bag.'

'Foreigners go in for mixed bags more than we do. A Grand Duke pots a vulture just as seriously as we should stalk a bustard. Anyhow, I've explained to Vladimir that certain birds are beneath his dignity as a sportsman. And as he's only nineteen, of course, his dignity is a sure thing to appeal to.'

Mrs Hoopington sniffed. Most people with whom Vladimir came in contact found his high spirits infectious, but his present hostess was guaranteed immune against infection of that sort.

'I hear him coming in now,' she observed. 'I shall go and get ready for tea. We're going to have it here in the hall. Entertain the Major if he comes in before I'm down, and, above all, be bright.'

Norah was dependent on her aunt's good graces for many little things that made life worth living, and she was conscious of a feeling of discomfiture because the Russian youth whom she had brought down as a welcome element of change in the country-house routine was not making a good impression. That young gentleman, however, was supremely unconscious of any short-comings, and burst into the hall, tired, and less sprucely groomed than usual, but distinctly radiant. His game-bag looked comfortably full.

'Guess what I have shot,' he demanded.

'Pheasants, wood-pigeons, rabbits,' hazarded Norah.

'No; a large beast; I don't know what you call it in English. Brown, with a darkish tail.' Norah changed colour.

'Does it live in a tree and eat nuts?' she asked, hoping that the use of the adjective 'large' might be an exaggeration.

Vladimir laughed.

'Oh, no; not a *biyelka*.'

'Does it swim and eat fish?' asked Norah, with a fervent prayer in her heart that it might turn out to be an otter.

'No,' said Vladimir, busy with the straps of his game-bag; 'it lives in the woods, and eats rabbits and chickens.'

Norah sat down suddenly, and hid her face in her hands.

'Merciful Heaven!' she wailed; 'he's shot a fox!'

Vladimir looked up at her in consternation. In a torrent of agitated words she tried to explain the horror of the situation. The boy understood nothing, but was thoroughly alarmed.

'Hide it, hide it!' said Norah frantically, pointing to the still unopened bag. 'My aunt and the Major will be here in a moment. Throw it on the top of that chest; they won't see it there.'

Vladimir swung the bag with fair aim; but the strap caught in its flight on the outstanding point of an antler fixed in the wall, and the bag, with its terrible burden, remained suspended just above the alcove where tea would presently be laid. At that moment Mrs Hoopington and the Major entered the hall.

'The Major is going to draw our covers tomorrow,' announced the lady, with a certain heavy satisfaction. 'Smithers is confident that we'll be able to show him some sport; he swears he's seen a fox in the nut copse three times this week.'

'I'm sure I hope so; I hope so,' said the Major moodily. 'I must break this sequence of blank days. One hears so often that a fox has settled down as a tenant for life in certain covers, and then when you go to turn him out there isn't a trace of him. I'm certain a fox was shot or trapped in Lady Widden's woods the very day before we drew them.'

'Major, if anyone tried that game on in my woods they'd get short shrift,' said Mrs Hoopington.

Norah found her way mechanically to the tea-table and made her fingers frantically busy in rearranging the parsley round the sandwich dish. On one side of her loomed the morose countenance of the Major, on the other she was conscious of the scared, miserable eyes of Vladimir. And above it all hung *that*. She dared not raise her eyes above the level of the tea-table, and she almost expected to see a spot of accusing vulpine blood drip down and stain the whiteness of the cloth. Her aunt's manner signalled to her the repeated message to 'be bright'; for the present she was fully occupied in keeping her teeth from chattering.

'What did you shoot today?' asked Mrs Hoopington suddenly of the unusually silent Vladimir.

'Nothing – nothing worth speaking of,' said the boy.

Norah's heart, which had stood still for a space, made up for lost time with a most disturbing bound.

'I wish you'd find something that was worth speaking about,' said the hostess; 'everyone seems to have lost their tongues.'

'When did Smithers last see that fox?' said the Major.

'Yesterday morning; a fine dog-fox, with a dark brush,' confided Mrs Hoopington.

'Aha, we'll have a good gallop after that brush tomorrow,' said the Major, with a transient gleam of good humour. And then gloomy silence settled again round the tea-table, a silence broken only by despondent munchings and the occasional feverish rattle of a teaspoon in its saucer. A diversion was at last afforded by Mrs Hoopington's fox-terrier, which had jumped on to a vacant chair, the better to survey the delicacies of the table, and was now sniffing in an upward direction at something apparently more interesting than cold tea-cake.

'What is exciting him?' asked his mistress, as the dog suddenly broke into short, angry barks, with a running accompaniment of tremulous whines.

'Why,' she continued, 'it's your game-bag, Vladimir! What *have* you got in it?'

'By Gad,' said the Major, who was now standing up; 'there's a pretty warm scent!'

And then a simultaneous idea flashed on himself and Mrs Hoopington. Their faces flushed to distinct but harmonious tones of purple, and with one accusing voice they screamed, 'You've shot the fox!'

Norah tried hastily to palliate Vladimir's misdeed in their eyes, but it is doubtful whether they heard her. The Major's fury clothed and reclothed itself in words as frantically as a woman up in town for one day's shopping tries on a succession of garments. He reviled and railed at fate and the general scheme of things, he pitied himself with a strong, deep pity too poignant for tears, he condemned everyone with whom he had ever come in contact to endless and abnormal punishments. In fact, he conveyed the impression that if a destroying angel had been lent to him for a week it would have had very little time for private study. In the lulls of his outcry could be heard the querulous monotone of Mrs Hoopington and the sharp staccato barking of the fox-terrier. Vladimir, who did not understand a tithe of what was being said, sat fondling a cigarette and repeating under his breath from time to time a vigorous English adjective which he had long ago taken affectionately into his vocabulary. His mind strayed back to the youth in the old Russian folk-tale who shot an enchanted bird with dramatic results. Meanwhile, the Major, roaming round the hall like an imprisoned cyclone, had caught sight of and joyfully pounced on the telephone apparatus, and lost no time in ringing up the hunt secretary and announcing his resignation of the Mastership. A servant had by this time brought his horse round to the door, and in a few seconds Mrs Hoopington's shrill monotone had the field to itself. But after the Major's display her best efforts at vocal violence missed their full effect; it was as though one had come straight out from a Wagner opera into a rather tame thunderstorm. Realizing, perhaps, that her tirades were something of an anticlimax, Mrs Hoopington broke suddenly into some rather necessary tears and marched out of the room, leaving behind her a silence almost as terrible as the turmoil which had preceded it.

'What shall I do with – *that*?' asked Vladimir at last.

'Bury it,' said Norah.

'Just plain burial?' said Vladimir, rather relieved. He had almost expected that some of the local clergy would have insisted on being present, or that a salute might have to be fired over the grave.

And thus it came to pass that in the dusk of a November evening the Russian boy, murmuring a few of the prayers of his Church for luck, gave hasty but decent burial to a large polecat under the lilac trees at Hoopington.

The Lost Sanjak

The prison Chaplain entered the condemned's cell for the last time, to give such consolation as he might.

'The only consolation I crave for', said the condemned, 'is to tell my story in its entirety to someone who will at least give it a respectful hearing.'

'We must not be too long over it,' said the Chaplain, looking at his watch.

The condemned repressed a shiver and commenced.

'Most people will be of opinion that I am paying the penalty of my own violent deeds. In reality I am a victim to a lack of specialization in my education and character.'

'Lack of specialization!' said the Chaplain.

'Yes. If I had been known as one of the few men in England familiar with the fauna of the Outer Hebrides, or able to repeat stanzas of Camoëns' poetry in the original, I should have had no difficulty in proving my identity in the crisis when my identity became a matter of life and death for me. But my education was merely a moderately good one, and my temperament was of the general order that avoids specialization. I know a little in a general way about gardening and history and old masters, but I could never tell you off-hand whether "Stella van der Loopen" was a chrysanthemum or a heroine of the American War of Independence, or something by Romney in the Louvre.'

The Chaplain shifted uneasily in his seat. Now that the alternatives had been suggested they all seemed dreadfully possible.

'I fell in love, or thought I did, with the local doctor's wife,' continued the condemned. 'Why I should have done so, I cannot say, for I do not remember that she possessed any particular attractions of mind or body. On looking back at past events it seems to me that she must have been distinctly ordinary, but I suppose the doctor had fallen in love with her once, and what man has done man can do. She appeared to be pleased with the attentions which I paid her, and to that extent I suppose I might say she encouraged me, but I think she was honestly unaware that I meant anything more than a little neighbourly interest. When one is face to face with Death one wishes to be just.'

The Chaplain murmured approval. 'At any rate, she was genuinely horrified when I took advantage of the doctor's absence one evening to declare what I believed to be my passion. She begged me to pass out of her life and I could scarcely do otherwise than agree, though I hadn't the dimmest idea of how it was to be done. In novels and plays I knew it was a regular occurrence, and if you mistook a lady's sentiments or intentions you went off to India and did things on the frontier as a matter of course. As I stumbled along the doctor's carriage-drive I had no very clear idea as to what my line of action was to be, but I had a vague feeling that I must look at the *Times* Atlas before going to bed. Then, on the dark and lonely highway, I came suddenly on a dead body.'

The Chaplain's interest in the story visibly quickened.

'Judging by the clothes it wore the corpse was that of a Salvation Army captain. Some shocking accident seemed to have struck him down, and the head was crushed and battered out of all human semblance. Probably, I thought, a motor-car fatality; and then, with a sudden overmastering insistence, came another thought, that here was a remarkable opportunity for losing my identity and passing out of the life of the doctor's wife for ever. No tiresome and risky voyage to distant lands, but a mere exchange of clothes and identity with the unknown victim of an unwitnessed accident. With considerable difficulty I undressed the corpse, and clothed it anew in my own garments. Anyone who has valeted a dead Salvation Army captain in an uncertain light will appreciate the difficulty. With the idea, presumably, of inducing the doctor's wife to leave her husband's roof-tree for some habitation which would be run at my expense, I had crammed my pockets with a store of banknotes, which represented a good deal of my immediate worldly wealth. When, therefore, I stole away into the world in the guise of a nameless Salvationist, I was not without resources which would easily support so humble a role for a considerable period. I tramped to a neighbouring market-town, and, late as the hour was, the production of a few shillings procured me supper and a night's lodging in a cheap coffee-house. The next day I started forth on an aimless course of wandering from one small town to another. I was already somewhat disgusted with the upshot of my sudden break; in a few hours' time I was considerably more so. In the contents-bill of a local news sheet I read the announcement of my own murder at the hands of some person unknown; on buying a copy of the paper for a detailed account of the tragedy, which at first had aroused in me a certain grim amusement, I found that the deed was ascribed to a wandering Salvationist of doubtful antecedents, who had been seen lurking in the roadway near the scene of the crime. I was no longer amused. The matter promised to be embarrassing. What I had mistaken for a motor accident was evidently a case of savage assault and murder, and, until the real culprit was found, I should have much difficulty in explaining my intrusion into the affair. Of course I could establish my own identity; but how, without disagreeably involving the doctor's wife, could I give any adequate reason for changing clothes with the murdered man? While my brain worked feverishly at this problem, I subconsciously obeyed a secondary instinct – to get as far away as possible from the scene of the crime, and to get rid at all costs of my incriminating uniform. There I found a difficulty. I tried two or three obscure clothes shops, but my entrance invariably aroused an attitude of hostile suspicion in the proprietors, and on one excuse or another they avoided serving me with the now ardently desired change of clothing. The uniform that I had so thoughtlessly donned seemed as difficult to get out of as the fatal shirt of – You know, I forget the creature's name.'

'Yes, yes,' said the Chaplain hurriedly. 'Go on with your story.'

'Somehow, until I could get out of those compromising garments, I felt it would not be safe to surrender myself to the police. The thing that puzzled me was why no attempt was made to arrest me, since there was no question as to the suspicion which followed me, like an inseparable shadow, wherever I went. Stares, nudgings, whisperings, and even loud-spoken remarks of "that's 'im" greeted my every appearance, and the meanest and most deserted eating-house that I patronized soon became filled with a crowd of furtively watching customers. I began to sympathize with the feelings of Royal personages trying to do a little private shopping under the unsparing scrutiny of an irrepressible public. And still, with all this inarticulate shadowing, which weighed on my nerves almost worse than open hostility would have done, no attempt was made to interfere with my liberty. Later on I discovered the reason. At the time of the murder on the lonely highway a series of important bloodhound trials had been taking place in the near neighbourhood, and some dozen and a half couples of trained animals had been put on the track of the supposed murderer – on my track. One of our most public-spirited London dailies had offered a princely prize to the owner of the pair that should first track me down, and betting on the chances of the respective competitors became rife throughout the land. The dogs ranged far and wide over about thirteen counties, and though my own movements had become by this time perfectly well known to police and public alike, the sporting instincts of the nation stepped in to prevent my premature arrest. "Give the dogs a chance", was the prevailing sentiment, whenever some ambitious local constable wished to put an end to my drawn-out evasion of justice. My final capture by the winning pair was not a very dramatic episode, in fact, I'm not sure that they would have taken any notice of me if I hadn't spoken to them and patted them, but the event gave rise to an extraordinary amount of partisan excitement. The owner of the pair who were next nearest up at the finish was an American, and he lodged a protest on the ground that an otterhound had married into the family of the winning pair six generations ago, and that the prize had been offered to the first pair of bloodhounds to capture the murderer, and that a dog that had one sixty-fourth part of otterhound blood in it couldn't technically be considered a bloodhound. I forget how the matter was ultimately settled, but it aroused a tremendous amount of acrimonious discussion on both sides of the Atlantic. My own contribution to the controversy consisted in pointing out that the whole dispute was beside the mark, as the actual murderer had not yet been captured; but I soon discovered that on this point there was not the least divergence of public or expert opinion. I had looked forward apprehensively to the proving of my identity and the establishment of my motives as a disagreeable necessity; I speedily found out that the most disagreeable part of the business was that it couldn't be done. When I saw in the glass the haggard and hunted expression which the experiences of the past few weeks had stamped on my erstwhile placid countenance, I could scarcely feel surprised that the few friends and relations I possessed refused to recognize me in my altered guise, and persisted in their obstinate but widely shared belief that it was I who had been done to death on the highway. To make matters worse, infinitely worse, an aunt of the really murdered man, an appalling female of an obviously low order of intelligence, identified me as her nephew, and gave the authorities a lurid account of my depraved youth and of her laudable but unavailing efforts to spank me into a better way. I believe it was even proposed to search me for finger-prints.'

'But', said the Chaplain, 'surely your educational attainments –'

'That was just the crucial point,' said the condemned; 'that was where my lack of specialization told so fatally against me. The dead Salvationist, whose identity I had so lightly and so disastrously adopted, had possessed a veneer of cheap modern education. It should have been easy to demonstrate that my learning was on altogether another plane to his, but in my nervousness I bungled miserably over test after test that was put to me. The little French I had ever known deserted me; I could not render a simple phrase about the gooseberry of the gardener into that language, because I had forgotten the French for gooseberry.'

The Chaplain again wriggled uneasily in his seat. 'And then', resumed the condemned, 'came the final discomfiture. In our village we had a modest little debating club, and I remembered having promised, chiefly, I suppose, to please and impress the doctor's wife, to give a sketchy kind of lecture on the Balkan Crisis. I had relied on being able to get up my facts from one or two standard works, and the back-numbers of certain periodicals. The prosecution had made a careful note of the circumstance that the man whom I claimed to be – and actually was – had posed locally as some sort of second-hand authority on Balkan affairs, and, in the midst of a string of questions on indifferent topics, the examining counsel asked me with a diabolical suddenness if I could tell the Court the whereabouts of Novibazar. I felt the question to be a crucial one; something told me that the answer was St Petersburg or Baker Street. I hesitated, looked helplessly round at the sea of tensely expectant faces, pulled myself together, and chose Baker Street. And then I knew that everything was lost. The prosecution had no difficulty in demonstrating that an individual, even moderately versed in the affairs of the Near East, could never have so unceremoniously dislocated Novibazar from its accustomed corner of the map. It was an answer which the Salvation Army captain might conceivably have made – and I had made it. The circumstantial evidence connecting the Salvationist with the crime was overwhelmingly convincing, and I had inextricably identified myself with the Salvationist. And thus it comes to pass that in ten minutes' time I shall be hanged by the neck until I am dead in expiation of the murder of myself, which murder never took place, and of which, in any case, I am necessarily innocent.'

When the Chaplain returned to his quarters, some fifteen minutes later, the black flag was floating over the prison tower. Breakfast was waiting for him in the dining-room, but he first passed into his library, and taking up the *Times* Atlas, consulted a map of the Balkan Peninsula. 'A thing like that', he observed, closing the volume with a snap, 'might happen to anyone.'

The Saint and the Goblin

The little stone Saint occupied a retired niche in a side aisle of the old cathedral. No one quite remembered who he had been, but that in a way was a guarantee of respectability. At least so the Goblin said. The goblin was a very fine specimen of quaint stone carving, and lived up in the corbel on the wall opposite the niche of the little Saint. He was connected with some of the best cathedral folk, such as the queer carvings in the choir stalls and chancel screen, and even the gargoyles high up on the roof. All the fantastic beasts and manikins that sprawled and twisted in wood or stone or lead overhead in the arches or away down in the crypt were in some way akin to him; consequently he was a person of recognized importance in the cathedral world.

The little stone Saint and the Goblin got on very well together, though they looked at most things from different points of view. The Saint was a philanthropist in an old-fashioned way; he thought the world, as he saw it, was good, but might be improved. In particular he pitied the church mice, who were miserably poor. The Goblin, on the other hand, was of opinion that the world, as he knew it, was bad, but had better be let alone. It was the function of the church mice to be poor.

'All the same,' said the Saint, 'I feel very sorry for them.'

'Of course you do,' said the Goblin; 'it's *your* function to feel sorry for them. If they were to leave off being poor you couldn't fulfil your functions. You'd be a sinecure.'

He rather hoped that the Saint would ask him what a sinecure meant, but the latter took refuge in a stony silence. The Goblin might be right, but still, he thought, he would like to do something for the church mice before winter came on; they were so very poor.

Whilst he was thinking the matter over he was startled by something falling between his feet with a hard metallic clatter. It was a bright new thaler; one of the cathedral jackdaws, who collected such things, had flown in with it to a stone cornice just above his niche, and the banging of the sacristy door had startled him into dropping it. Since the invention of gunpowder the family nerves were not what they had been.

'What have you got there?' asked the Goblin.

'A silver thaler,' said the Saint. 'Really,' he continued, 'it is most fortunate; now I can do something for the church mice.'

'How will you manage it?' asked the Goblin.

The Saint considered.

'I will appear in a vision to the vergeress who sweeps the floors. I will tell her that she will find a silver thaler between my feet, and that she must take it and buy a measure of corn and put it on my shrine. When she finds the money she will know that it was a true dream, and she will take care to follow my directions. Then the mice will have food all winter.'

'Of course *you* can do that,' observed the Goblin. 'Now, *I* can only appear to people after they have had a heavy supper of indigestible things. My opportunities with the vergeress would be limited. There is some advantage in being a saint after all.'

All this while the coin was lying at the Saint's feet. It was clean and glittering and had the Elector's arms beautifully stamped upon it. The Saint began to reflect that such an opportunity was too rare to be hastily disposed of. Perhaps indiscriminate charity might be harmful to the church mice. After all, it was their function to be poor; the Goblin had said so, and the Goblin was generally right.

'I've been thinking', he said to that personage, 'that perhaps it would be really better if I ordered a thaler's worth of candles to be placed on my shrine instead of the corn.'

He often wished, for the look of the thing, that people would sometimes burn candles at his shrine; but as they had forgotten who he was it was not considered a profitable speculation to pay him that attention.

'Candles would be more orthodox,' said the Goblin.

'More orthodox, certainly,' agreed the Saint, 'and the mice could have the ends to eat; candle-ends are most fattening.'

The Goblin was too well bred to wink; besides, being a stone goblin, it was out of the question.

'Well, if it ain't there, sure enough!' said the vergeress next morning. She took the shining coin down from the gusty niche and turned it over and over in her grimy hands. Then she put it to her mouth and bit it.

'She can't be going to eat it,' thought the Saint, and fixed her with his stoniest stare.

'Well,' said the woman, in a somewhat shriller key, 'who'd have thought it! A saint, too!'

Then she did an unaccountable thing. She hunted an old piece of tape out of her pocket, and tied it crosswise, with a big loop, round the thaler, and hung it round the neck of the little Saint.

Then she went away.

'The only possible explanation', said the Goblin, 'is that it's a bad one.'

'What is that decoration your neighbour is wearing?' asked a wyvern that was wrought into the capital of an adjacent pillar.

The Saint was ready to cry with mortification, only, being of stone, he couldn't.

'It's a coin of – ahem! – fabulous value,' replied the Goblin tactfully.

And the news went round the Cathedral that the shrine of the little stone Saint had been enriched by a priceless offering.

'After all, it's something to have the conscience of a goblin,' said the Saint to himself.

The church mice were as poor as ever, but that was their function.

The Mouse

Theodoric Voler had been brought up, from infancy to the confines of middle age, by a fond mother whose chief solicitude had been to keep him screened from what she called the coarser realities of life. When she died she left Theodoric alone in a world that was as real as ever, and a good deal coarser than he considered it had any need to be. To a man of his temperament and upbringing even a simple railway journey was crammed with petty annoyances and minor discords, and as he settled himself down in a second-class compartment one September morning he was conscious of ruffled feelings and general mental discomposure. He had been staying at a country vicarage, the inmates of which had been certainly neither brutal nor bacchanalian, but their supervision of the domestic establishment had been of that lax order which invites disaster. The pony carriage that was to take him to the station had never been properly ordered, and when the moment for his departure drew near the handy-man who should have produced the required article was nowhere to be found. In this emergency Theodoric, to his mute but very intense disgust, found himself obliged to collaborate with the vicar's daughter in the task of harnessing the pony, which necessitated groping about in an ill-lighted outhouse called a stable, and smelling very like one – except in patches where it smelt of mice. Without being actually afraid of mice, Theodoric classed them among the coarser incidents of life, and considered that Providence, with a little exercise of moral courage, might long ago have recognized that they were not indispensable, and have withdrawn them from circulation. As the train glided out of the station Theodoric's nervous imagination accused himself of exhaling a weak odour of stableyard, and possibly of displaying a mouldy straw or two on his usually well-brushed garments. Fortunately the only other occupant of the compartment, a lady of about the same age as himself, seemed inclined for slumber rather than scrutiny; the train was not due to stop till the terminus was reached, in about an hour's time, and the carriage was of the old-fashioned sort, that held no communication with a corridor, therefore no further travelling companions were likely to intrude on Theodoric's semi-privacy. And yet the train had scarcely attained its normal speed before he became reluctantly but vividly aware that he was not alone with the slumbering lady; he was not even alone in his own clothes. A warm, creeping movement over his flesh betrayed the unwelcome and highly resented presence, unseen but poignant, of a strayed mouse, that had evidently dashed into its present retreat during the episode of the pony harnessing. Furtive stamps and shakes and wildly directed pinches failed to dislodge the intruder, whose motto, indeed, seemed to be Excelsior; and the lawful occupant of the clothes lay back against the cushions and endeavoured rapidly to evolve some means of putting an end to the dual ownership. It was unthinkable that he should continue for the space of a whole hour in the horrible position of a Rowton House for vagrant mice (already his imagination had at least doubled the numbers of the alien invasion). On the other hand, nothing less drastic than partial disrobing would ease him of his tormentor, and to undress in the presence of a lady, even for so laudable a purpose, was an idea that made his eartips tingle in a blush of abject shame. He had never been able to bring himself even to the mild exposure of open-work socks in the presence of the fair sex. And yet – the lady in this case was to all appearances soundly and securely asleep; the mouse, on the other hand, seemed to be trying to crowd a Wanderjahr into a few strenuous minutes. If there is any truth in the theory of transmigration, this particular mouse must certainly have been in a former state a member of the Alpine Club. Sometimes in its eagerness it lost its footing and slipped for half an inch or so; and then, in fright, or more probably temper, it bit. Theodoric was goaded into the most audacious undertaking of his life. Crimsoning to the hue of a beetroot and keeping an agonized watch on his slumbering fellow-traveller, he swiftly and noiselessly secured the ends of his railway-rug to the racks on either side of the carriage, so that a substantial curtain hung athwart the compartment. In the narrow dressing-room that he had thus improvised he proceeded with violent haste to extricate himself partially and the mouse entirely from the surrounding casings of tweed and half-wool. As the unravelled mouse gave a wild leap to the floor, the rug, slipping its fastening at either end, also came down with a heart-curdling flop, and almost simultaneously the awakened sleeper opened her eyes. With a movement almost quicker than the mouse's, Theodoric pounced on the rug, and hauled its ample folds chin-high over his dismantled person as he collapsed into the further corner of the carriage. The blood raced and beat in the veins of his neck and forehead, while he waited dumbly for the communication-cord to be pulled. The lady, however, contented herself with a silent stare at her strangely muffled companion. How much had she seen, Theodoric queried to himself, and in any case what on earth must she think of his present posture?

'I think I have caught a chill,' he ventured desperately.

'Really, I'm sorry,' she replied. 'I was just going to ask you if you would open this window.'

'I fancy it's malaria,' he added, his teeth chattering slightly, as much from fright as from a desire to support his theory.

'I've got some brandy in my hold-all, if you'll kindly reach it down for me,' said his companion.

'Not for worlds – I mean, I never take anything for it,' he assured her earnestly.

'I suppose you caught it in the Tropics?'

Theodoric, whose acquaintance with the Tropics was limited to an annual present of a chest of tea from an uncle in Ceylon, felt that even the malaria was slipping from him. Would it be possible, he wondered, to disclose the real state of affairs to her in small instalments?

'Are you afraid of mice?' he ventured, growing, if possible, more scarlet in the face.

'Not unless they came in quantities, like those that ate up Bishop Hatto. Why do you ask?'

'I had one crawling inside my clothes just now,' said Theodoric in a voice that hardly seemed his own. 'It was a most awkward situation.'

'It must have been, if you wear your clothes at all tight,' she observed; 'but mice have strange ideas of comfort.'

'I had to get rid of it while you were asleep,' he continued; then, with a gulp, he added, 'it was getting rid of it that brought me to – to this.'

'Surely leaving off one small mouse wouldn't bring on a chill,' she exclaimed, with a levity that Theodoric accounted abominable.

Evidently she had detected something of his predicament, and was enjoying his confusion. All the blood in his body seemed to have mobilized in one concentrated blush, and an agony of abasement, worse than a myriad mice, crept up and down over his soul. And then, as reflection began to assert itself, sheer terror took the place of humiliation. With every minute that passed the train was rushing nearer to the crowded and bustling terminus where dozens of prying eyes would be exchanged for the one paralysing pair that watched him from the further corner of the carriage. There was one slender despairing chance, which the next few minutes must decide. His fellow-traveller might relapse into a blessed slumber. But as the minutes throbbed by, that chance ebbed away. The furtive glance which Theodoric stole at her from time to time disclosed only an unwinking wakefulness.

'I think we must be getting near now,' she presently observed.

Theodoric had already noted with growing terror the recurring stacks of small, ugly dwellings that heralded the journey's end. The words acted as a signal. Like a hunted beast breaking cover and dashing madly towards some other haven of momentary safety he threw aside his rug, and struggled frantically into his dishevelled garments. He was conscious of dull suburban stations racing past the window, of a choking, hammering sensation of his throat and heart, and of an icy silence in that corner towards which he dared not look. Then as he sank back in his seat, clothed and almost delirious, the train slowed down to a final crawl, and the woman spoke.

'Would you be so kind', she asked, 'as to get me a porter to put me into a cab? It's a shame to trouble you when you're feeling unwell, but being blind makes one so helpless at a railway station.'

The Recessional

Clovis sat in the hottest zone but two of a Turkish bath, alternately inert in statuesque contemplation and rapidly manœuvering a fountain-pen over the pages of a note-book.

'Don't interrupt me with your childish prattle,' he observed to Bertie van Tahn, who had slung himself languidly into a neighbouring chair and looked conversationally inclined; 'I'm writing deathless verse.'

Bertie looked interested.

'I say, what a boon you would be to portrait painters if you really got to be notorious as a poetry writer. If they couldn't get your likeness hung in the Academy as "Clovis Sangrail, Esq, at work on his latest poem", they could slip you in as a Study of the Nude or Orpheus descending into Jermyn Street. They always complain that modern dress handicaps them, whereas a towel and a fountain-pen –'

'It was Mr Packletide's suggestion that I should write this thing,' said Clovis, ignoring the bypaths to fame that Bertie van Tahn was pointing out to him. 'You see, Loona Bimberton had a Coronation Ode accepted by the *New Infancy*, a paper that has been started with the idea of making the *New Age* seem elderly and hidebound. "So clever of you, dear Loona," the Packletide remarked when she had read it; "of course, anyone could write a Coronation Ode, but no one else would have thought of doing it." Loona protested that these things were extremely difficult to do, and gave us to understand that they were more or less the province of a gifted few. Now the Packletide has been rather decent to me in many ways, a sort of financial ambulance, you know, that carries you off the field when you're hard hit, which is a frequent occurrence with me, and I've no use whatever for Loona Bimberton, so I chipped in and said I could turn out that sort of stuff by the square yard if I gave my mind to it. Loona said I couldn't, and we got bets on, and between you and me I think the money's fairly safe. Of course, one of the conditions of the wager is that the thing has to be published in something or other, local newspapers barred; but Mrs Packletide has endeared herself by many little acts of thoughtfulness to the editor of the *Smoky Chimney*, so if I can hammer out anything at all approaching the level of the usual Ode output we ought to be all right. So far I'm getting along so comfortably that I begin to be afraid that I must be one of the gifted few.'

'It's rather late in the day for a Coronation Ode, isn't it?' said Bertie.

'Of course,' said Clovis; 'this is going to be a Durbar Recessional, the sort of thing that you can keep by you for all time if you want to.'

'Now I understand your choice of a place to write it in,' said Bertie van Tahn, with the air of one who has suddenly unravelled a hitherto obscure problem; 'you want to get the local temperature.'

'I came here to get freedom from the inane interruptions of the mentally deficient,' said Clovis, 'but it seems I asked too much of fate.'

Bertie van Tahn prepared to use his towel as a weapon of precision, but reflecting that he had a good deal of unprotected coast-line himself, and that Clovis was equipped with a fountain-pen as well as a towel, he relapsed pacifically into the depths of his chair.

'May one hear extracts from the immortal work?' he asked. 'I promise that nothing that I hear now shall prejudice me against borrowing a copy of the *Smoky Chimney* at the right moment.'

'It's rather like casting pearls into a trough,' remarked Clovis pleasantly, 'but I don't mind reading you bits of it. It begins with a general dispersal of the Durbar participants:

> "Back to their homes in Himalayan heights
> The stale pale elephants of Cutch Behar
> Roll like great galleons on a tideless sea –" '

'I don't believe Cutch Behar is anywhere near the Himalayan region,' interrupted Bertie. 'You ought to have an atlas on hand when you do this sort of thing; and why stale and pale?'

'After the late hours and the excitement, of course,' said Clovis;

'and I said their *homes* were in the Himalayas. You can have Himalayan elephants in Cutch Behar, I suppose, just as you have Irish-bred horses running at Ascot.'

'You said they were going back to the Himalayas,' objected Bertie.

'Well, they would naturally be sent home to recuperate. It's the usual thing out there to turn elephants loose in the hills, just as we put horses out to grass in this country.'

Clovis could at least flatter himself that he had infused some of the reckless splendour of the East into his mendacity.

'Is it all going to be in blank verse?' asked the critic.

'Of course not; "Durbar" comes at the end of the fourth line.'

'That seems so cowardly; however, it explains why you picked on Cutch Behar.'

'There is more connection between geographical place-names and poetical inspiration than is generally recognized; one of the chief reasons why there are so few really great poems about Russia in our language is that you can't possibly get a rhyme to names like Smolensk and Tobolsk and Minsk.'

Clovis spoke with the authority of one who has tried.

'Of course, you could rhyme Omsk with Tomsk,' he continued; 'in fact, they seem to be there for that purpose, but the public wouldn't stand that sort of thing indefinitely.'

'The public will stand a good deal,' said Bertie malevolently, 'and so small a proportion of it knows Russian that you could always have an explanatory footnote asserting that the last three letters in Smolensk are not pronounced. It's quite as believable as your statement about putting elephants out to grass in the Himalayan range.'

'I've got rather a nice bit,' resumed Clovis with unruffled serenity, 'giving an evening scene on the outskirts of a jungle village:

"Where the coiled cobra in the gloaming gloats,
And prowling panthers stalk the wary goats." '

'There is practically no gloaming in tropical countries,' said Bertie indulgently; 'but I like the masterly reticence with which you treat the cobra's motive for gloating. The unknown is proverbially the uncanny. I can picture nervous readers of the *Smoky Chimney* keeping the light turned on in their bedrooms all night out of sheer sickening uncertainty as to *what* the cobra might have been gloating about.'

'Cobras gloat naturally,' said Clovis, 'just as wolves are always ravening from mere force of habit, even after they've hopelessly overeaten themselves. I've got a fine bit of colour painting later on,' he added, 'where I describe the dawn coming up over the Brahma-putra river:

"The amber dawn-drenched East with sun-shafts kissed,
Stained sanguine apricot and amethyst,
O'er the washed emerald of the mango groves
Hangs in a mist of opalescent mauves,
While painted parrot-flights impinge the haze
With scarlet, chalcedon and chrysoprase." '

'I've never seen the dawn come up over the Brahma-putra river,' said Bertie, 'so I can't say if it's a good description of the event, but it sounds more like an account of an extensive jewel robbery. Anyhow, the parrots give a good useful touch of local colour. I suppose you've introduced some tigers into the scenery? An Indian landscape would have rather a bare, unfinished look without a tiger or two in the middle distance.'

'I've got a hen-tiger somewhere in the poem,' said Clovis, hunting through his notes. 'Here she is:

"The tawny tigress 'mid the tangled teak
Drags to her purring cubs' enraptured ears
The harsh death-rattle in the pea-fowl's beak,
A jungle lullaby of blood and tears." '

Bertie van Tahn rose hurriedly from his recumbent position and made for the glass door leading into the next compartment.

'I think your idea of home life in the jungle is perfectly horrid,' he said. 'The cobra was sinister enough, but the improvised rattle in the tiger-nursery is the limit. If you're going to make me turn hot and cold all over I may as well go into the steam room at once.'

'Just listen to this line,' said Clovis; 'it would make the reputation of any ordinary poet:

"and overhead
The pendulum-patient Punkah, parent of stillborn breeze." '

'Most of your readers will think "punkah" is a kind of iced drink or half-time at polo,' said Bertie, and disappeared into the steam.

The *Smoky Chimney* duly published the 'Recessional', but it proved to be its swan song, for the paper never attained to another issue.

Loona Bimberton gave up her intention of attending the Durbar and went into a nursing-home on the Sussex Downs. Nervous breakdown after a particularly strenuous season was the usually accepted explanation, but there are three or four people who know that she never really recovered from the dawn breaking over the Brahma-putra river.

The Stampeding of Lady Bastable

'It would be rather nice if you would put Clovis up for another six days while I go up north to the MacGregors',' said Mrs Sangrail sleepily across the breakfast-table. It was her invariable plan to speak in a sleepy, comfortable voice whenever she was unusually keen about anything; it put people off their guard, and they frequently fell in with her wishes before they had realized that she was really asking for anything. Lady Bastable, however, was not so easily taken unawares; possibly she knew that voice and what it betokened – at any rate, she knew Clovis.

She frowned at a piece of toast and ate it very slowly, as though she wished to convey the impression that the process hurt her more than it hurt the toast; but no extension of hospitality on Clovis's behalf rose to her lips.

'It would be a great convenience to me,' pursued Mrs Sangrail, abandoning the careless tone. 'I particularly don't want to take him to the MacGregors', and it will only be for six days.'

'It will seem longer,' said Lady Bastable dismally. 'The last time he stayed here for a week –'

'I know,' interrupted the other hastily, 'but that was nearly two years ago. He was younger then.'

'But he hasn't improved,' said her hostess; 'it's no use growing older if you only learn new ways of misbehaving yourself.'

Mrs Sangrail was unable to argue the point; since Clovis had reached the age of seventeen she had never ceased to bewail his irrepressible waywardness to all her circle of acquaintances, and a polite scepticism would have greeted the slightest hint at a prospective reformation. She discarded the fruitless effort at cajolery and resorted to undisguised bribery.

'If you'll have him here for these six days I'll cancel that outstanding bridge account.'

It was only for forty-nine shillings, but Lady Bastable loved shillings with a great, strong love. To lose money at bridge and not to have to pay it was one of those rare experiences which gave the card-table a glamour in her eyes which it could never otherwise have possessed. Mrs Sangrail was almost equally devoted to her card winnings, but the prospect of conveniently warehousing her offspring for six days, and incidentally saving his railway fare to the north, reconciled her to the sacrifice; when Clovis made a belated appearance at the breakfast-table the bargain had been struck.

'Just think,' said Mrs Sangrail sleepily; 'Lady Bastable has very kindly asked you to stay on here while I go to the MacGregors'.'

Clovis said suitable things in a highly unsuitable manner, and proceeded to make punitive expeditions among the breakfast dishes with a scowl on his face that would have driven the purr out of a peace conference. The arrangement that had been concluded behind his back was doubly distasteful to him. In the first place, he particularly wanted to teach the MacGregor boys, who could well afford the knowledge, how to play poker-patience; secondly, the Bastable catering was of the kind that is classified as a rude plenty, which Clovis translated as a plenty that gives rise to rude remarks. Watching him from behind ostentatiously sleepy lids, his mother realized, in the light of long experience, that any rejoicing over the success of her manœuvre would be distinctly premature. It was one thing to fit Clovis into a convenient niche of the domestic jig-saw puzzle; it was quite another matter to get him to stay there.

Lady Bastable was wont to retire in state to the morning-room immediately after breakfast and spend a quiet hour in skimming through the papers; they were there, so she might as well get their money's worth out of them. Politics did not greatly interest her, but she was obsessed with a favourite foreboding that one of these days there would be a great social upheaval, in which everybody would be killed by everybody else. 'It will come sooner than we think,' she would observe darkly; a mathematical expert of exceptionally high powers would have been puzzled to work out the approximate date from the slender and confusing groundwork which this assertion afforded.

On this particular morning the sight of Lady Bastable enthroned among her papers gave Clovis the hint towards which his mind had been groping all breakfast time. His mother had gone upstairs to supervise packing operations, and he was alone on the ground-floor with his hostess – and the servants. The latter were the key to the situation. Bursting wildly into the kitchen quarters, Clovis screamed a frantic though strictly non-committal summons: 'Poor Lady Bastable! In the morning-room! Oh, quick!' The next moment the butler, cook, page-boy, two or three maids, and a gardener who had happened to be in one of the outer kitchens were following a hot scurry after Clovis as he headed back for the morning-room. Lady Bastable was roused from the world of newspaper lore by hearing a Japanese screen in the hall go down with a crash. Then the door leading from the hall flew open and her young guest tore madly through the room, shrieked at her in passing, 'The jacquerie! They're on us!' and dashed like an escaping hawk out through the French window. The scared mob of servants burst in on his heels, the gardener still clutching the sickle with which he had been trimming hedges, and the impetus of their headlong haste carried them, slipping and sliding, over the smooth parquet flooring towards the chair where their mistress sat in panic-stricken amazement. If she had had a moment granted for her reflection she would have behaved, as she afterwards explained, with considerable dignity. It was probably the sickle which decided her, but anyway she followed the lead that Clovis had given her through the French window, and ran well and far across the lawn before the eyes of her astonished retainers.

Lost dignity is not a possession which can be restored at a moment's notice, and both Lady Bastable and the butler found the process of returning to normal conditions almost as painful as a slow recovery from drowning. A jacquerie, even if carried out with the most respectful of intentions, cannot fail to leave some traces of embarrassment behind it. By lunch-time, however, decorum had reasserted itself with enhanced rigour as a natural rebound from its recent overthrow, and the meal was served in a frigid stateliness that might have been framed on a Byzantine model. Half-way through its duration Mrs Sangrail was solemnly presented with an envelope lying on a silver salver. It contained a cheque for forty-nine shillings.

The MacGregor boys learned how to play poker-patience; after all, they could afford to.

The Jesting of Arlington Stringham

Arlington Stringham made a joke in the House of Commons. It was a thin House, and a very thin joke; something about the Anglo-Saxon race having a great many angles. It is possible that it was unintentional, but a fellow-member, who did not wish it to be supposed that he was asleep because his eyes were shut, laughed. One or two of the papers noted 'a laugh' in brackets, and another, which was notorious for the carelessness of its political news, mentioned 'laughter'. Things often begin in that way.

'Arlington made a joke in the House last night,' said Eleanor Stringham to her mother; 'in all the years we've been married neither of us has made jokes, and I don't like it now. I'm afraid it's the beginning of the rift in the lute.'

'What lute?' said her mother.

'It's a quotation,' said Eleanor.

To say that anything was a quotation was an excellent method, in Eleanor's eyes, for withdrawing it from discussion, just as you could always defend indifferent lamb late in the season by saying 'It's mutton.'

And, of course, Arlington Stringham continued to tread the thorny path of conscious humour into which Fate had beckoned him.

'The country's looking very green, but, after all, that's what it's there for,' he remarked to his wife two days later.

'That's very modern, and I dare say very clever, but I'm afraid it's wasted on me,' she observed coldly. If she had known how much effort it had cost him to make the remark she might have greeted it in a kinder spirit. It is the tragedy of human endeavour that it works so often unseen and unguessed.

Arlington said nothing, not from injured pride, but because he was thinking hard for something to say. Eleanor mistook his silence for an assumption of tolerant superiority, and her anger prompted her to a further gibe.

'You had better tell it to Lady Isobel. I've no doubt she would appreciate it.'

Lady Isobel was seen everywhere with a fawn coloured collie at a time when every one else kept nothing but Pekinese, and she had once eaten four green apples at an afternoon tea in the Botanical Gardens, so she was widely credited with a rather unpleasant wit. The censorious said she slept in a hammock and understood Yeats's poems, but her family denied both stories.

'The rift is widening to an abyss,' said Eleanor to her mother that afternoon.

'I shall not tell that to anyone,' remarked her mother, after long reflection.

'Naturally, I should not talk about it very much,' said Eleanor, 'but why shouldn't I mention it to anyone?'

'Because you can't have an abyss in a lute. There isn't room.'

Eleanor's outlook on life did not improve as the afternoon wore on. The page-boy had brought from the library *By Mere and Wold* instead of *By Mere Chance*, the book which everyone denied having read. The unwelcome substitute appeared to be a collection of nature notes contributed by the author to the pages of some Northern weekly, and when one had been prepared to plunge with disapproving mind into a regrettable chronicle of ill-spent lives it was intensely irritating to read 'the dainty yellow-hammers are now with us, and flaunt their jaundiced livery from every bush and hillock'. Besides, the thing was so obviously untrue; either there must be hardly any bushes or hillocks in those parts or the country must be fearfully overstocked with yellow-hammers. The thing scarcely seemed worth telling such a lie about. And the page-boy stood there, with his sleekly brushed and parted hair, and his air of chaste and callous indifference to the desires and passions of the world. Eleanor hated boys, and she would have liked to have whipped this one long and often. It was perhaps the yearning of a woman who had no children of her own.

She turned at random to another paragraph. 'Lie quietly concealed in the fern and bramble in the gap by the old rowan tree, and you may see, almost every evening during early summer, a pair of lesser whitethroats creeping up and down the nettles and hedge-growth that mask their nesting-place.'

The insufferable monotony of the proposed recreation! Eleanor would not have watched the most brilliant performance at His Majesty's Theatre for a single evening under such uncomfortable circumstances, and to be asked to watch lesser whitethroats creeping up and down a nettle 'almost every evening' during the height of the season struck her as an imputation on her intelligence that was positively offensive. Impatiently she transferred her attention to the dinner menu, which the boy had thoughtfully brought in as an alternative to the more solid literary fare. 'Rabbit curry', met her eye, and the lines of disapproval deepened on her already puckered brow. The cook was a great believer in the influence of environment, and nourished an obstinate conviction that if you brought rabbit and curry-powder together in one dish a rabbit curry would be the result. And Clovis and the odious Bertie van Tahn were coming to dinner. Surely, thought Eleanor, if Arlington knew how much she had had that day to try her, he would refrain from joke-making.

At dinner that night it was Eleanor herself who mentioned the name of a certain statesman, who may be decently covered under the disguise of X.

'X', said Arlington Stringham, 'has the soul of a meringue.'

It was a useful remark to have on hand, because it applied equally well to four prominent statesmen of the day, which quadrupled the opportunities for using it.

'Meringues haven't got souls,' said Eleanor's mother.

'It's a mercy that they haven't,' said Clovis; 'they would be always losing them, and people like my aunt would get up missions to meringues, and say it was wonderful how much one could teach them and how much more one could learn from them.'

'What could you learn from a meringue?' asked Eleanor's mother.

'My aunt has been known to learn humility from an ex-Viceroy,' said Clovis.

'I wish cook would learn to make curry, or have the sense to leave it alone,' said Arlington, suddenly and savagely.

Eleanor's face softened. It was like one of his old remarks in the days when there was no abyss between them.

It was during the debate on the Foreign Office vote that Stringham made his great remark that 'the people of Crete unfortunately make more history than they can consume locally'. It was not brilliant, but it came in the middle of a dull speech, and the House was quite pleased with it. Old gentlemen with bad memories said it reminded them of Disraeli.

It was Eleanor's friend, Gertrude Ilpton, who drew her attention to Arlington's newest outbreak. Eleanor in these days avoided the morning papers.

'It's very modern, and I suppose very clever,' she observed.

'Of course it's clever,' said Gertrude; 'all Lady Isobel's sayings are clever, and luckily they bear repeating.'

'Are you sure it's one of her sayings?' asked Eleanor.

'My dear, I've heard her say it dozens of times.'

'So that is where he gets his humour,' said Eleanor slowly, and the hard lines deepened round her mouth.

The death of Eleanor Stringham from an overdose of chloral, occurring at the end of a rather uneventful season, excited a certain amount of unobtrusive speculation. Clovis, who perhaps exaggerated the importance of curry in the home, hinted at domestic sorrow.

And of course Arlington never knew. It was the tragedy of his life that he should miss the fullest effect of his jesting.

The Talking-Out of Tarrington

'Heavens!' exclaimed the aunt of Clovis, 'here's someone I know bearing down on us. I can't remember his name, but he lunched with us once in Town. Tarrington – yes, that's it. He's heard of the picnic I'm giving for the Princess, and he'll cling to me like a lifebelt till I give him an invitation; then he'll ask if he may bring all his wives and mothers and sisters with him. That's the worst of these small watering-places; one can't escape from anybody.'

'I'll fight a rearguard action for you if you like to do a bolt now,' volunteered Clovis; 'you've a clear ten yards start if you don't lose time.'

The aunt of Clovis responded gamely to the suggestion, and churned away like a Nile steamer, with a long brown ripple of Pekingese spaniel trailing in her wake.

'Pretend you don't know him,' was her parting advice, tinged with the reckless courage of the non-combatant.

The next moment the overtures of an affably disposed gentleman were being received by Clovis with a 'silent-upon-a-peak-in-Darien' stare which denoted an absence of all previous acquaintance with the object scrutinized.

'I expect you don't know me with my moustache,' said the new-comer; 'I've only grown it during the last two months.'

'On the contrary,' said Clovis, 'the moustache is the only thing about you that seemed familiar to me. I felt certain that I had met it somewhere before.'

'My name is Tarrington,' resumed the candidate for recognition.

'A very useful kind of name,' said Clovis; 'with a name of that sort no one would blame you if you did nothing in particular heroic or remarkable, would they? And yet if you were to raise a troop of light horse in a moment of national emergency, "Tarrington's Light Horse" would sound quite appropriate and pulse-quickening; whereas if you were called Spoopin, for instance, the thing would be out of the question. No one, even in a moment of national emergency, could possibly belong to Spoopin's Horse.'

The new-comer smiled weakly, as one who is not to be put off by mere flippancy, and began again with patient persistence:

'I think you ought to remember my name –'

'I shall,' said Clovis, with an air of immense sincerity. 'My aunt was asking me only this morning to suggest names for four young owls she's just had sent her as pets. I shall call them all Tarrington; then if one or two of them die or fly away, or leave us in any of the ways that pet owls are prone to, there will be always one or two left to carry on your name. And my aunt won't *let* me forget it; she will always be asking "Have the Tarringtons had their mice?" and questions of that sort. She says if you keep wild creatures in captivity you ought to see after their wants, and of course she's quite right there.'

'I met you at luncheon at your aunt's house once –' broke in Mr Tarrington, pale but still resolute.

'My aunt never lunches,' said Clovis; 'she belongs to the National Anti-Luncheon League, which is doing quite a lot of good work in a quiet, unobtrusive way. A subscription of half a crown per quarter entitles you to go without ninety-two luncheons.'

'This must be something new,' exclaimed Tarrington.

'It's the same aunt that I've always had,' said Clovis coldly.

'I perfectly well remember meeting you at a luncheon-party

given by your aunt,' persisted Tarrington, who was beginning to flush an unhealthy shade of mottled pink.

'What was there for lunch?' asked Clovis.

'Oh, well, I don't remember that –'

'How nice of you to remember my aunt when you can no longer recall the names of the things you ate. Now my memory works quite differently. I can remember a menu long after I've forgotten the hostess that accompanied it. When I was seven years old I recollect being given a peach at a garden-party by some Duchess or other; I can't remember a thing about her, except that I imagine our acquaintance must have been of the slightest, as she called me a 'nice little boy', but I have unfading memories of that peach. It was one of those exuberant peaches that meet you half-way, so to speak, and are all over you in a moment. It was a beautiful unspoiled product of a hothouse, and yet it managed quite successfully to give itself the airs of a compote. You had to bite it and imbibe it at the same time. To me there has always been something charming and mystic in the thought of that delicate velvet globe of fruit, slowly ripening and warming to perfection through the long summer days and perfumed nights, and then coming suddenly athwart my life in the supreme moment of its existence. I can never forget it, even if I wished to. And when I had devoured all that was edible of it, there still remained the stone, which a heedless, thoughtless child would doubtless have thrown away; I put it down the neck of a young friend who was wearing a very *décolleté* sailor suit. I told him it was a scorpion, and from the way he wriggled and screamed he evidently believed it, though where the silly kid imagined I could procure a live scorpion at a garden-party I don't know. Altogether, that peach is for me an unfading and happy memory –'

The defeated Tarrington had by this time retreated out of ear-shot, comforting himself as best he might with the reflection that a picnic which included the presence of Clovis might prove a doubtfully agreeable experience.

'I shall certainly go in for a Parliamentary career,' said Clovis to himself as he turned complacently to rejoin his aunt. 'As a talker-out of inconvenient bills I should be invaluable.'

A Matter of Sentiment

It was the eve of the great race, and scarcely a member of Lady Susan's house-party had as yet a single bet on. It was one of those unsatisfactory years when one horse held a commanding market position, not by reason of any general belief in its crushing superiority, but because it was extremely difficult to pitch on any other candidate to whom to pin one's faith. Peradventure II was the favourite, not in the sense of being a popular fancy, but by virtue of a lack of confidence in any one of his rather undistinguished rivals. The brains of clubland were much exercised in seeking out possible merit where none was very obvious to the naked intelligence, and the house-party at Lady Susan's was possessed by the same uncertainty and irresolution that infected wider circles.

'It is just the time for bringing off a good coup,' said Bertie van Tahn.

'Undoubtedly. But with what?' demanded Clovis for the twentieth time.

The women of the party were just as keenly interested in the matter, and just as helplessly perplexed; even the mother of Clovis, who usually got good racing information from her dressmaker, confessed herself fancy free on this occasion. Colonel Drake, who was professor of military history at a minor cramming establishment, was the only person who had a definite selection for the event, but as his choice varied every three hours he was worse than useless as an inspired guide. The crowning difficulty of the problem was that it could only be fitfully and furtively discussed. Lady Susan disapproved of racing. She disapproved of many things; some people went as far as to say that she disapproved of most things. Disapproval was to her what neuralgia and fancy needlework are to many other women. She disapproved of early morning tea and auction bridge, of ski-ing and the two-step, of the Russian ballet and the Chelsea Arts Club ball, of the French policy in Morocco and the British policy everywhere. It was not that she was particularly strict or narrow in her views of life, but she had been the eldest sister of a large family of self-indulgent children, and her particular form of indulgence had consisted in openly disapproving of the foibles of the others. Unfortunately the hobby had grown up with her. As she was rich, influential, and very, very kind, most people were content to count their early tea as well lost on her behalf. Still, the necessity for hurriedly dropping the discussion of an enthralling topic, and suppressing all mention of it during her presence on the scene, was an affliction at a moment like the present, when time was slipping away and indecision was the prevailing note.

After a lunch-time of rather strangled and uneasy conversation, Clovis managed to get most of the party together at the further end of the kitchen gardens, on the pretext of admiring the Himalayan pheasants. He had made an important discovery. Motkin, the butler, who (as Clovis expressed it) had grown prematurely grey in Lady Susan's service, added to his other excellent qualities an intelligent interest in matters connected with the Turf. On the subject of the forthcoming race he was not illuminating, except in so far that he shared the prevailing unwillingness to see a winner in Peradventure II. But where he outshone all the members of the house-party was in the fact that he had a second cousin who was head stable-lad at a neighbouring racing establishment, and usually gifted with much inside information as to private form and possibilities. Only the fact of her ladyship having taken it into her head to invite a houseparty for the last week of May had prevented Mr Motkin from paying a visit of consultation to his relative with respect to the big race; there was still time to cycle over if he could get leave of absence for the afternoon on some specious excuse.

'Let's jolly well hope he does,' said Bertie van Tahn; 'under the circumstances a second cousin is almost as useful as second sight.'

'That stable ought to know something, if knowledge is to be found anywhere,' said Mrs Packletide hopefully.

'I expect you'll find he'll echo my fancy for Motorboat,' said Colonel Drake.

At this moment the subject had to be hastily dropped. Lady Susan bore down upon them, leaning on the arm of Clovis's mother, to whom she was confiding the fact that she disapproved of the craze for Pekingese spaniels. It was the third thing she had found time to disapprove of since lunch, without counting her silent and permanent disapproval of the way Clovis's mother did her hair.

'We have been admiring the Himalayan pheasants,' said Mrs Packletide suavely.

'They went off to a bird-show at Nottingham early this morning,' said Lady Susan, with the air of one who disapproves of hasty and ill-considered lying.

'Their house, I mean; such perfect roosting arrangements, and all so clean,' resumed Mrs Packletide, with an increased glow of enthusiasm. The odious Bertie van Tahn was murmuring audible prayers for Mrs Packletide's ultimate estrangement from the paths of falsehood.

'I hope you don't mind dinner being a quarter of an hour late tonight,' said Lady Susan; 'Motkin has had an urgent summons to go and see a sick relative this afternoon. He wanted to bicycle there, but I am sending him in the motor.'

'How very kind of you! Of course we don't mind dinner being put off.' The assurances came with unanimous and hearty sincerity.

At the dinner-table that night an undercurrent of furtive curiosity directed itself towards Motkin's impassive countenance. One or two of the guests almost expected to find a slip of paper concealed in their napkins, bearing the name of the second cousin's selection. They had not long to wait. As the butler went round with the murmured question, 'Sherry?' he added in an even lower tone the cryptic words, 'Better not'. Mrs Packletide gave a start of alarm, and refused the sherry; there seemed some sinister suggestion in the butler's warning, as though her hostess had suddenly become addicted to the Borgia habit. A moment later the explanation flashed on her that 'Better Not' was the name of one of the runners in the big race. Clovis was already pencilling it on his cuff, and Colonel Drake, in his turn, was signalling to everyone in hoarse whispers and dumb-show the fact that he had all along fancied 'B.N.'

Early next morning a sheaf of telegrams went Townward,

representing the market commands of the house-party and servants' hall.

It was a wet afternoon, and most of Lady Susan's guests hung about the hall, waiting apparently for the appearance of tea, though it was scarcely yet due. The advent of a telegram quickened everyone into a flutter of expectancy; the page who brought the telegram to Clovis waited with unusual alertness to know if there might be an answer.

Clovis read the message and gave an exclamation of annoyance.

'No bad news, I hope,' said Lady Susan. Everyone else knew that the news was not good.

'It's only the result of the Derby,' he blurted out; 'Sadowa won; an utter outsider.'

'Sadowa!' exclaimed Lady Susan; 'you don't say so. How remarkable! It's the first time I've ever backed a horse; in fact I disapprove of horse-racing, but just for once in a way I put money on this horse, and it's gone and won.'

'May I ask', said Mrs Packletide, amid the general silence, 'why you put your money on this particular horse? None of the sporting prophets mentioned it as having an outside chance.'

'Well,' said Lady Susan, 'you may laugh at me, but it was the name that attracted me. You see, I was always mixed up with the Franco-German war; I was married on the day that the war was declared, and my eldest child was born the day that peace was signed, so anything connected with the war has always interested me. And when I saw there was a horse running in the Derby called after one of the battles in the Franco-German war, I said I *must* put some money on it, for once in a way, though I disapprove of racing. And it's actually won.'

There was a general groan. No one groaned more deeply than the professor of military history.

Esmé

'All hunting stories are the same,' said Clovis; 'just as all Turf stories are the same, and all –'

'My hunting story isn't a bit like any you've ever heard,' said the Baroness. 'It happened quite a while ago, when I was about twenty-three. I wasn't living apart from my husband then; you see, neither of us could afford to make the other a separate allowance. In spite of everything that proverbs may say, poverty keeps together more homes than it breaks up. But we always hunted with different packs. All this has nothing to do with the story.'

'We haven't arrived at the meet yet. I suppose there was a meet,' said Clovis.

'Of course there was a meet,' said the Baroness; 'all the usual crowd were there, especially Constance Broddle. Constance is one of those strapping florid girls that go so well with autumn scenery or Christmas decorations in church. "I feel a presentiment that something dreadful is going to happen," she said to me; "am I looking pale?"

'She was looking about as pale as a beetroot that has suddenly heard bad news.

' "You're looking nicer than usual," I said, "but that's so easy for you." Before she had got the right bearings of this remark we had settled down to business; hounds had found a fox lying out in some gorse-bushes.'

'I knew it,' said Clovis; 'in every fox-hunting story that I've ever heard there's been a fox and some gorse-bushes.'

'Constance and I were well mounted,' continued the Baroness serenely, 'and we had no difficulty in keeping ourselves in the first flight, though it was a fairly stiff run. Towards the finish, however, we must have held rather too independent a line, for we lost the hounds, and found ourselves plodding aimlessly along miles away from anywhere. It was fairly exasperating, and my temper was beginning to let itself go by inches, when on pushing our way through an accommodating hedge we were gladdened by the sight of hounds in full cry in a hollow just beneath us.

' "There they go," cried Constance, and then added in a gasp, "In Heaven's name, what are they hunting?"

'It was certainly no mortal fox. It stood more than twice as high, had a short, ugly head, and an enormous thick neck.

' "It's a hyæna," I cried; "it must have escaped from Lord Pabham's Park."

'At that moment the hunted beast turned and faced its pursuers, and the hounds (there were only about six couple of them) stood round in a half-circle and looked foolish. Evidently they had broken away from the rest of the pack on the trail of this alien scent, and were not quite sure how to treat their quarry now they had got him.

'The hyæna hailed our approach with unmistakable relief and demonstrations of friendliness. It had probably been accustomed to uniform kindness from humans, while its first experience of a pack of hounds had left a bad impression. The hounds looked more than ever embarrassed as their quarry paraded its sudden intimacy with us, and the faint toot of a horn in the distance was seized on as a welcome signal for unobtrusive departure. Constance and I and the hyæna were left alone in the gathering twilight.

' "What are we to do?" asked Constance.

' "What a person you are for questions," I said.

' "Well, we can't stay here all night with a hyæna," she retorted.

' "I don't know what your ideas of comfort are," I said; "but I shouldn't think of staying here all night even without a hyæna. My home may be an unhappy one, but at least it has hot and cold water laid on, and domestic service, and other conveniences which we shouldn't find here. We had better make for that ridge of trees to the right; I imagine the Crowley road is just beyond.'

'We trotted off slowly along a faintly marked cart-track, with the beast following cheerfully at our heels.

' "What on earth are we to do with the hyæna?" came the inevitable question.

' "What does one generally do with hyænas?" I asked crossly.

' "I've never had anything to do with one before," said Constance.

' "Well, neither have I. If we even knew its sex we might give it a name. Perhaps we might call it Esmé. That would do in either case."

'There was still sufficient daylight for us to distinguish wayside objects, and our listless spirits gave an upward perk as we came upon a small half-naked gipsy brat picking blackberries from a low-growing bush. The sudden apparition of two horsewomen and a hyæna set it off crying, and in any case we should scarcely have gleaned any useful geographical information from that source; but there was a probability that we might strike a gipsy encampment somewhere along our route. We rode on hopefully but uneventfully for another mile or so.

' "I wonder what that child was doing there," said Constance presently.

' "Picking blackberries. Obviously."

' "I don't like the way it cried," pursued Constance; "somehow its wail keeps ringing in my ears."

'I did not chide Constance for her morbid fancies; as a matter of fact the same sensation, of being pursued by a persistent fretful wail, had been forcing itself on my rather over-tired nerves. For company's sake I hulloed to Esmé, who had lagged somewhat behind. With a few springy bounds he drew up level, and then shot past us.

'The wailing accompaniment was explained. The gipsy child was firmly, and I expect painfully, held in his jaws.

' "Merciful Heaven!" screamed Constance, "what on earth shall we do? What are we to do?"

'I am perfectly certain that at the Last Judgment Constance will ask more questions than any of the examining Seraphs.

' "Can't we do something?" she persisted tearfully, as Esmé cantered easily along in front of our tired horses.

'Personally I was doing everything that occurred to me at the moment. I stormed and scolded and coaxed in English and French and gamekeeper language; I made absurd, ineffectual cuts in the air with my thongless hunting-crop; I hurled my sandwich case at the brute; in fact, I really don't know what more I could have done. And still we lumbered on through the deepening dusk, with that dark uncouth shape lumbering ahead of us, and a drone of lugubrious music floating in our ears. Suddenly Esmé bounded aside into some thick bushes, where we could not follow; the wail rose to a shriek and then stopped altogether. This part of the story I always hurry over, because it is really rather horrible. When the beast joined us again, after an absence of a few minutes, there was an air of patient understanding about him, as though he knew that he had done something of which we disapproved, but which he felt to be thoroughly justifiable.

' "How can you let that ravening beast trot by your side?" asked Constance. She was looking more than ever like an albino beetroot.

' "In the first place, I can't prevent it," I said; "and in the second place, whatever else he may be, I doubt if he's ravening at the present moment."

'Constance shuddered. "Do you think the poor little thing suffered much?" came another of her futile questions.

' "The indications were all that way," I said; "on the other hand, of course, it may have been crying from sheer temper. Children sometimes do."

'It was nearly pitch-dark when we emerged suddenly into the high road. A flash of lights and the whir of a motor went past us at the same moment at uncomfortably close quarters. A thud and a sharp screeching yell followed a second later. The car drew up, and when I had ridden back to the spot I found a young man bending over a dark motionless mass lying by the roadside.

' "You have killed my Esmé," I exclaimed bitterly.

' "I'm so awfully sorry," said the young man; "I keep dogs myself, so I know what you must feel about it. I'll do anthing I can in reparation."

' "Please bury him at once," I said; "that much I think I may ask of you."

' "Bring the spade, William," he called to the chauffeur. Evidently hasty roadside interments were contingencies that had been provided against.

'The digging of a sufficiently large grave took some little time. "I say, what a magnificent fellow," said the motorist as the corpse was rolled over into the trench. "I'm afraid he must have been rather a valuable animal."

' "He took second in the puppy class at Birmingham last year," I said resolutely.

'Constance snorted loudly.

' "Don't cry, dear," I said brokenly; "it was all over in a moment. He couldn't have suffered much."

' "Look here," said the young fellow desperately, "you simply must let me do something by way of reparation."

'I refused sweetly, but as he persisted I let him have my address.

'Of course, we kept our own counsel as to the earlier episodes of the evening. Lord Pabham never advertised the loss of his hyæna; when a strictly fruit-eating animal strayed from his park a year or two previously he was called upon to give compensation in eleven cases of sheep-worrying and practically to re-stock his neighbours' poultry-yards, and an escaped hyæna would have mounted up to something on the scale of a Government grant. The gipsies were equally unobtrusive over their missing offspring; I don't suppose in large encampments they really know to a child or two how many they've got.'

The Baroness paused reflectively, and then continued:

'There was a sequel to the adventure, though. I got through the post a charming little diamond brooch, with the name Esmé set in a sprig of rosemary. Incidentally, too, I lost the friendship of Constance Broddle. You see, when I sold the brooch I quite properly refused to give her any share of the proceeds. I pointed out that the Esmé part of the affair was my own invention, and the hyæna part of it belonged to Lord Pabham, if it really was his hyæna, of which, of course, I've no proof.

Shock Tactics

On a late spring afternoon Ella McCarthy sat on a green-painted chair in Kensington Gardens, staring listlessly at an uninteresting stretch of park landscape, that blossomed suddenly into tropical radiance as an expected figure appeared in the middle distance.

'Hullo, Bertie!' she exclaimed sedately, when the figure arrived at the painted chair that was the nearest neighbour to her own, and dropped into it eagerly, yet with a certain due regard for the set of its trousers; 'hasn't it been a perfect spring afternoon?'

The statement was a distinct untruth as far as Ella's own feelings were concerned; until the arrival of Bertie the afternoon had been anything but perfect.

Bertie made a suitable reply, in which a questioning note seemed to hover.

'Thank you ever so much for those lovely handkerchiefs,' said Ella, answering the unspoken question; 'they were just what I've been wanting. There's only one thing spoilt my pleasure in your gift,' she added, with a pout.

'What was that?' asked Bertie anxiously, fearful that perhaps he had chosen a size of handkerchief that was not within the correct feminine limit.

'I should have liked to have written and thanked you for them as soon as I got them,' said Ella, and Bertie's sky clouded at once.

'You know what mother is,' he protested; 'she opens all my letters, and if she found I'd been giving presents to anyone there'd have been something to talk about for the next fortnight.'

'Surely, at the age of twenty –' began Ella.

'I'm not twenty till September,' interrupted Bertie.

'At the age of nineteen years and eight months,' persisted Ella, 'you might be allowed to keep your correspondence private to yourself.'

'I ought to be, but things aren't always what they ought to be. Mother opens every letter that comes into the house, whoever it's for. My sisters and I have made rows about it time and again, but she goes on doing it.'

'I'd find some way to stop her if I were in your place,' said Ella valiantly, and Bertie felt that the glamour of his anxiously deliberated present had faded away in the disagreeable restriction that hedged round its acknowledgment.

'Is anything the matter?' asked Bertie's friend Clovis when they met that evening at the swimming-bath.

'Why do you ask?' said Bertie.

'When you wear a look of tragic gloom in a swimming-bath,' said Clovis, 'it's especially noticeable from the fact that you're wearing very little else. Didn't she like the handkerchiefs?'

Bertie explained the situation.

'It is rather galling, you know,' he added, 'when a girl has a lot of things she wants to write to you and can't send a letter except by some roundabout, underhand way.'

'One never realizes one's blessings while one enjoys them,' said Clovis; 'now I have to spend a considerable amount of ingenuity inventing excuses for not having written to people.'

'It's not a joking matter,' said Bertie resentfully: 'you wouldn't find it funny if your mother opened all your letters.'

'The funny thing to me is that you should let her do it.'

'I can't stop it. I've argued about it –'

'You haven't used the right kind of argument, I expect. Now, if every time one of your letters was opened you lay on your back on the dining-table during dinner and had a fit, or roused the entire family in the middle of the night to hear you recite one of Blake's "Poems of Innocence", you would get a far more respectful hearing for future protests. People yield more consideration to a mutilated mealtime or a broken night's rest, than ever they would to a broken heart.'

'Oh, dry up,' said Bertie crossly, inconsistently splashing Clovis from head to foot as he plunged into the water.

It was a day or two after the conversation in the swimming-bath that a letter addressed to Bertie Heasant slid into the letter-box at his home, and thence into the hands of his mother. Mrs Heasant was one of those empty-minded individuals to whom other people's affairs are perpetually interesting. The more private they are intended to be the more acute is the interest they arouse. She would have opened this particular letter in any case; the fact that it was marked 'private', and diffused a delicate but penetrating aroma merely caused her to open it with headlong haste rather than matter-of-course deliberation. The harvest of sensation that rewarded her was beyond all expectations.

> 'Bertie, carissimo,' it began, 'I wonder if you will have the nerve to do it: it will take some nerve, too. Don't forget the jewels. They are a detail, but details interest me.
>
> 'Yours as ever,
> 'CLOTILDE.
>
> 'Your mother must not know of my existence. If questioned swear you never heard of me.'

For years Mrs Heasant had searched Bertie's correspondence diligently for traces of possible dissipation or youthful entanglements, and at last the suspicions that had stimulated her inquisitorial zeal were justified by this one splendid haul. That anyone wearing the exotic name 'Clotilde' should write to Bertie under the incriminating announcement 'as ever' was sufficiently electrifying, without the astounding allusion to the jewels. Mrs Heasant could recall novels and dramas wherein jewels played an exciting and commanding role, and here, under her own roof, before her very eyes as it were, her own son was carrying on an intrigue in which jewels were merely an interesting detail. Bertie was not due home for another hour, but his sisters were available for the immediate unburdening of a scandal-laden mind.

'Bertie is in the toils of an adventuress,' she screamed; 'her name is Clotilde,' she added, as if she thought they had better know the worst at once. There are occasions when more harm than good is done by shielding young girls from a knowledge of the more deplorable realities of life.

By the time Bertie arrived his mother had discussed every possible and improbable conjecture as to his guilty secret; the girls limited themselves to the opinion that their brother had been weak rather than wicked.

'Who is Clotilde?' was the question that confronted Bertie almost before he had got into the hall. His denial of any knowledge of such a person was met with an outburst of bitter laughter.

'How well you have learned your lesson!' exclaimed Mrs Heasant. But satire gave way to furious indignation when she realized that Bertie did not intend to throw any further light on her discovery.

'You shan't have any dinner till you've confessed everything,' she stormed.

Bertie's reply took the form of hastily collecting material for an impromptu banquet from the larder and locking himself into his bedroom. His mother made frequent visits to the locked door and shouted a succession of interrogations with the persistence of one who thinks that if you ask a question often enough an answer will eventually result. Bertie did nothing to encourage the supposition. An hour had passed in fruitless one-sided palaver when another letter addressed to Bertie and marked 'private' made its appearance in the letter-box. Mrs Heasant pounced on it with the enthusiasm of a cat that has missed its mouse and to whom a second has been unexpectedly vouchsafed. If she hoped for further disclosures assuredly she was not disappointed.

> 'So you have really done it!' the letter abruptly commenced; 'Poor Dagmar. Now she is done for I almost pity her. You did it very well, you wicked boy, the servants all think it was suicide, and there will be no fuss. Better not touch the jewels till after the inquest.
>
> 'CLOTILDE.'

Anything that Mrs Heasant had previously done, in the way of outcry was easily surpassed as she raced upstairs and beat frantically at her son's door.

'Miserable boy, what have you done to Dagmar?'

'It's Dagmar now, is it?' he snapped; 'it will be Geraldine next.'

'That it should come to this, after all my efforts to keep you at home of an evening,' sobbed Mrs Heasant; 'it's no use you trying to hide things from me; Clotilde's letter betrays everything.'

'Does it betray who she is?' asked Bertie; 'I've heard so much about her, I should like to know something about her home-life. Seriously, if you go on like this I shall fetch a doctor; I've often enough been preached at about nothing, but I've never had an imaginary harem dragged into the discussion.'

'Are these letters imaginary?' screamed Mrs Heasant; 'what about the jewels, and Dagmar, and the theory of suicide?'

No solution of these problems was forthcoming through the bedroom door, but the last post of the evening produced another letter for Bertie, and its contents brought Mrs Heasant that enlightenment which had already dawned on her son.

> 'Dear Bertie,' it ran; 'I hope I haven't distracted your brain with the spoof letters I've been sending in the name of a fictitious Clotilde. You told me the other day that the servants, or somebody at your home, tampered with your letters, so I thought I would give anyone that opened them something exciting to read. The shock might do them good.
>
> 'Yours,
>
> 'CLOVIS SANGRAIL.'

Mrs Heasant knew Clovis slightly, and was rather afraid of him. It was not difficult to read between the lines of his successful hoax. In a chastened mood she rapped once more at Bertie'd door.

'A letter from Mr Sangrail. It's all been a stupid hoax. He wrote those other letters. Why, where are you going?'

Bertie had opened the door; he had on his hat and overcoat.

'I'm going for a doctor to come and see if anything's the matter with you. Of course it was all a hoax, but no person in his right mind could have believed all that rubbish about murder and suicide and jewels. You've been making enough noise to bring the house down for the last hour or two.'

'But what was I to think of those letters?' whimpered Mrs Heasant.

'I should have known what to think of them,' said Bertie; 'if you choose to excite yourself over other people's correspondence it's your own fault. Anyhow, I'm going for a doctor.'

It was Bertie's great opportunity, and he knew it. His mother was conscious of the fact that she would look rather ridiculous if the story got about. She was willing to pay hush-money.

'I'll never open your letters again,' she promised.

And Clovis has no more devoted slave than Bertie Heasant.

Clovis on the Alleged Romance of Business

'It is the fashion nowadays,' said Clovis, 'to talk about the romance of Business. There isn't such a thing. The romance has all been the other way, with the idle apprentice, the truant, the runaway, the individual who couldn't be bothered with figures and book-keeping and left business to look after itself. I admit that a grocer's shop is one of the most romantic and thrilling things that I have ever happened on, but the romance and thrill are centred in the groceries, not the grocer. The citron and spices and nuts and dates, the barrelled anchovies and Dutch cheeses, the jars of *caviar* and the chests of tea, they carry the mind away to Levantine coast towns and tropic shores, to the Old World wharfs and quays of the Low Countries, to dusty Astrachan and far Cathay; if the grocer's apprentice has any romance in him it is not a business education he gets behind the grocer's counter, it is a standing invitation to dream and to wander, and to remain poor. As a child such places as South America and Asia Minor were brought painstakingly under my notice, the names of their principal rivers and the height of their chief mountain peaks were committed to my memory, and I was earnestly enjoined to consider them as parts of the world that I lived in; it was only when I visited a large well-stocked grocer's shop that I realized that they certainly existed. Such galleries of romance and fascination are not bequeathed to us by the business man; he is only the dull custodian, who talks glibly of Spanish olives and Rangoon rice, a Spain that he has never known or wished to know, a Rangoon that he has never imagined or could imagine. It was the unledgered wanderer, the careless-hearted seafarer, the aimless outcast, who opened up new trade routes, tapped new markets, brought home samples or cargoes of new edibles and unknown condiments. It was they who brought the glamour and romance to the threshold of business life, where it was promptly reduced to pounds, shillings and pence; invoiced, double-entried, quoted, written-off, and so forth; most of those terms are probably wrong, but a little inaccuracy sometimes saves tons of explanation.

On the other side of the account there is the industrious apprentice, who grew up into the business man, married early and worked late, and lived, thousands and thousands of him, in little villas outside big towns. He is buried by the thousand in Kensal Green and other large cemeteries; any romance that was ever in him was buried prematurely in shop and warehouse and office. Whenever I feel in the least tempted to be business-like or methodical of even decently industrious I go to Kensal Green and look at the graves of those who died in business.'

The Almanack

'Has it ever struck you,' said Vera Durmot to Clovis, 'that one might make a comfortable income by compiling a local almanack, on prophetic lines, like those that the general public buy by the half million?'

'An income, perhaps,' said Clovis, 'but not a comfortable one. The prophet has proverbially a thin sort of time in his own country, and you would be too closely mixed up with the people you were prophesying about to be able to get much comfort out of the job. If the man who foretells tragic happenings for the Crowned Heads of Europe had to meet them at luncheon parties and tea-fights every other day of the week he would not find his business a comfortable one, especially towards the last days of the year, when the tragedies were getting overdue.'

'I should sell it just before the New Year,' said Vera, ignoring the suggestion of possible embarrassments, 'at eighteenpence a copy, and get a friend to type it for me, so that every copy I sold would be clear profit. Everyone would buy it out of curiosity, just to see how many of the predictions would be falsified.'

'Wouldn't it be rather a trying time for you later on,' asked

Clovis, 'when the predictions began to "lack confirmation"?'

'The thing would be', said Vera, 'to arrange your forecast so that it couldn't go very far wrong. I should begin with the prediction that the vicar would preach a moving New Year sermon from a text in Colossians; he always has done so since I can remember, and at his time of life men dislike change. Then one could safely foretell for the month of January that "more than one well-known family in this neighbourhood will be faced with a serious financial outlook which, however, will not develop into actual crisis". Every other head of a family down here discovers about that time of year that his household is living far beyond its income, and that severe retrenchment will be necessary. For April or May or thereabouts I should hint that one of the Dibcuster girls would make the happiest choice of her life. There are eight of them, and it's really time that one of the family married or went on the stage or took to writing worldly novels.'

'They never have done anything of the kind within human memory,' objected Clovis.

'One must take some risks,' said Vera. 'I should be on safer ground', she added, 'in predicting serious servant troubles from February to November. "Some of the best mistresses and house managers in this locality will be faced with vexatious servant difficulties, which will be temporarily tided over." '

'Another safe forecast', suggested Clovis, 'could be fitted into the dates when there are medal competitions at the golf club. "One or two of the most brilliant local players will encounter extraordinary and persistent back luck, which will rob them of the deserved guerdon of good play." At least a dozen men will think your prophecies positively inspired.'

Vera made a note of the suggestion.

'I'll let you have an advance copy at half price,' she said; 'on the other hand, I expect you to see that your mother buys one at market rates.'

'She shall buy two,' said Clovis; 'she can give one to Lady Adela, who never buys anything that she can borrow.'

The almanack had a big sale, and most of its predictions came sufficiently near fulfilment to sustain the compiler's claim to prophetic powers of an eighteenpenny standard. One of the

Dibcuster girls made up her mind to be a hospital nurse and another of them gave up piano playing, both of which might be considered happy decisions, while the forecast of servant troubles and unmerited bad luck on the golf links received ample confirmation in the annals of the home and the club.

'I don't see how she was to know that I was going to change my cook twice in seven months,' said Mrs Duff, who easily recognized an allusion to herself as one of the best mistresses of the neighbourhood.

'And it's come quite true about phenomenal vegetable products being recorded from a local garden,' said Mrs Openshaw; 'it said "a garden which has long been the admiration of the neighbourhood for its magnificent flowers will this year produce some marvels in the way of vegetables". Our garden is the admiration of everybody, and yesterday Henry brought in some carrots, well, you wouldn't see anything to equal them at a show.'

'Oh, but I think that refers to *our* garden,' said Mrs Duff; 'it has always been admired for its flowers, and now we've got some Glory of the South parsnips that beat anything I've ever seen. We've taken their measurements, and I got Phyllis to photograph them. I shall certainly buy the almanack if it comes out another year.'

'I've ordered it already,' said Mrs Openshaw; 'after what it foretold about my garden I thought I ought to.'

While the general verdict was in favour of the almanack as an inspired production, or, at any rate, a very fair compilation of successful prediction, there were critics who pointed out that most of the events foretold were of the nature of things that happened in one form or another in any given year.

'I couldn't risk being very definite about any particular event,' said Vera to Clovis towards the end of the twelve-month; 'as it is I have rather tied myself up over Jocelyn Vanner. I hinted that the hunting field was not a safe place for her during November and December. It never is a safe place for her at any time, she is always coming off a jump or getting bolted with or something of that sort. And now she has taken alarm at my prediction, and only comes to the meets on foot. Nothing very serious can happen to her under those circumstances.'

'It must be ruining her hunting season,' said Clovis.

'It's ruining the reputation of my almanack,' said Vera; 'it's the one thing that has definitely miscarried. I felt so sure she would have a spill of some sort that could be magnified into a serious accident.'

'I'm afraid I can't offer to ride over her, or incite hounds to tear her to pieces in mistake for a fox,' said Clovis; 'I should earn your undying devotion, but there would be a wearisome fuss about it, and I should have to hunt with another pack in the future, and that would be dreadfully inconvenient.'

'As your mother says, you are a mass of selfishness,' commented Vera.

An opportunity for being unselfish occurred to Clovis a day or two later, when he found himself at close quarters with Jocelyn near Bludberry Gate, where hounds were drawing a long woody hollow in search of an elusive fox.

'Scent is poor, and there's an interminable amount of cover,' grumbled Clovis from his saddle; 'we shall be here for hours before we get a fox away.'

'All the more time for you to talk to me,' said Jocelyn archly.

'The question is,' said Clovis darkly, 'whether I ought to be seen talking to you. I may be involving you.'

'Heavens! Involving me in what?' gasped Jocelyn.

'Do you know anything about Bukowina?' Clovis asked with seeming inconsequence.

'Bukowina? It's somewhere in Asia Minor, isn't it – or Central Asia – or is it part of the Balkans?' hazarded Jocelyn; 'I really forget for the moment. Where exactly is it?'

'On the brink of a revolution,' said Clovis impressively; 'that's what I want to warn you about. When I was staying with my aunt in Bucharest' (Clovis invented aunts as lavishly as other people invent golfing experiences) 'I got mixed up in the affair without knowing what I was in for. There was a Princess –'

'Ah,' said Jocelyn knowingly, 'there is always a beautiful and alluring Princess in these affairs.'

'As plain and boring a woman as one could find in eastern Europe,' said Clovis; 'one of the sort that call just before lunch and stay till it's time to dress for dinner. Well, it seems that some

Rumanian Jew is willing to finance the revolution if he could be assured of getting certain mineral concessions. The Jew is cruising in a yacht somewhere off the English coast, and the Princess had made up her mind that I was the safest person to convey the concession papers to him. My aunt whispered, "For Heaven's sake agree to what she asks or she'll stay on to dinner." At the moment any sacrifice seemed better than *that*, and so here I am, with my breast pocket bulging with compromising documents, and my life not worth a minute's purchase.'

'But', said Jocelyn, 'you are safe here in England, aren't you?'

'Do you see that man over there, on the roan?' asked Clovis, pointing to a man with a heavy black moustache, who was probably an auctioneer from a neighbouring town, and at any rate was a stranger to the hunt. 'That man was outside my aunt's door when I escorted the Princess to her carriage. He was on the platform of the railway station when I left Bucharest. He was on the landing-stage when I arrived in England. I can go nowhere without finding him at my elbow. I was not surprised to see him at the meet this morning.'

'But what can he do to you?' asked Jocelyn tremulously; 'he can't kill you.'

'Not before witnesses, if he can avoid it. The moment hounds find and the field scatters will be his opportunity. He means to have those papers today.'

'But how can he be sure you've got them on you?'

'He can't; I might have slipped them over to you while we were talking. That is why he is trying to make up his mind which of us to go for at the critical moment.'

'Us?' screamed Jocelyn; 'do you mean to say –?'

'I warned you that it was dangerous to be seen talking to me.'

'But this is awful! What am I to do?'

'Slip away into the undergrowth the moment that hounds get moving, and run like a rabbit. It is your only chance, and remember, if you escape, no talking. Many lives will be involved if you breathe a word of what I've told you. My aunt at Bucharest –'

At that moment there was a whimper from hounds down in the hollow, and a general ripple of movement passed through the scattered groups of waiting horsemen. A louder and more assured burst of noise came up from the valley.

'They've found!' cried Clovis and turned eagerly to join in the stampede. A crashing, scrunching noise as of a body rapidly and resolutely forcing its way through birch thicket and dead bracken was all that remained to him of his late companion.

Jocelyn's most intimate friends never knew the exact nature of the deadly peril she had incurred in the hunting field that day, but enough was made known to ensure the almanack a brisk sale at its new price of three shillings.

Tobermory

(Original version)

It was a chill, rain-washed afternoon of a late August day, that indefinite season when partridges are still in security or cold storage, and there is nothing to hunt – unless one is bounded on the north by the Bristol Channel, in which case one may lawfully gallop after fat red stags. Lady Blemley's house-party was not bounded on the north by the Bristol Channel, hence there was a full gathering of her guests round the tea-table on this particular afternoon. And, in spite of the blankness of the season and the triteness of the occasion, there was no trace in the company of that fatigued restlessness which means a dread of the pianola and a subdued hankering for auction bridge. The undisguised open-mouthed attention of the entire party was fixed on the homely negative personality of Mr Cornelius Appin. Of all her guests, he was the one who had come to Lady Blemley with the vaguest reputation. Someone had said he was 'clever', and he had got his invitation in the moderate expectation, on the part of his hostess, that some portion at least of his cleverness would be contributed to the general entertainment. Until tea-time that day she had been unable to discover in what direction, if any, his cleverness lay. He was neither a wit nor a croquet champion, a hypnotic force nor a begetter of amateur theatricals. Neither did his exterior suggest the sort of man in whom women are willing to pardon a generous measure of mental deficiency. He had subsided into mere Mr Appin, and the Cornelius seemed a piece of transparent baptismal bluff. And now he was claiming to have launched on the world a discovery beside which the invention of gunpowder, of the printing-press, and of steam locomotion were inconsiderable trifles. Science had made bewildering strides in many directions during recent decades, but this thing seemed to belong to the domain of miracle rather than to scientific achievement.

'And do you really ask us to believe', Sir Wilfrid was saying, 'that you have discovered a means for instructing animals in the art of human speech, and that dear old Tobermory has proved your first successful pupil?'

'It is a problem at which I have worked for the last seventeen years,' said Mr Appin, 'but only during the last eight or nine months have I been rewarded with glimmerings of success. Of course I have experimented with thousands of animals, but latterly only with cats, those wonderful creatures which have assimilated themselves so marvellously with our civilization while retaining all their highly developed feral instincts. Here and there among cats one comes across an outstanding superior intellect, just as one does among the ruck of human beings, and when I made the acquaintance of Tobermory a week ago I saw at once that I was in contact with a "Beyond-cat" of extraordinary intelligence. I had gone far along the road to success in recent experiments; with Tobermory, as you call him, I have reached the goal.'

Mr Appin concluded his remarkable statement in a voice which he strove to divest of a triumphant inflection. No one said 'rats', though Bertie van Tahn's lips moved in a monosyllabic contortion which probably invoked those rodents of disbelief.

'And do you mean to say', asked Miss Resker, after a slight pause, 'that you have taught Tobermory to say and understand easy sentences of one syllable?'

'My dear Miss Resker,' said the wonder-worker patiently, 'one teaches little children and savages and backward adults in that piecemeal fashion; when one has once solved the problem of making a beginning with an animal of highly developed intelligence one has no need for those halting methods. Tobermory can speak our language with perfect correctness.'

This time Bertie van Tahn very distinctly said 'Beyond-rats!' Sir Wilfrid was more polite, but equally sceptical.

'Hadn't we better have the cat in and judge for ourselves?' suggested Lady Blemley.

Sir Wilfrid went in search of the animal, and the company settled themselves down to the languid expectation of witnessing some more or less adroit drawing-room ventriloquism.

In a minute Sir Wilfrid was back in the room, his face white beneath its tan and his eyes dilated with excitement.

'By Gad, it's true!'

His agitation was unmistakably genuine, and his hearers started forward in a thrill of awakened interest.

Collapsing into an armchair, he continued breathlessly: 'I found him dozing in the smoking-room, and called out to him to come for his tea. He blinked at me in his usual way, and I said, "Come on, Toby; don't keep us waiting"; and, by Gad! he drawled out in a most horribly natural voice that he'd come when he dashed well pleased! I nearly jumped out of my skin!'

Appin had preached to absolutely incredulous hearers; Sir Wilfrid's statement carried instant conviction. A Babel-like chorus of startled exclamation arose, amid which the scientist sat mutely enjoying the first fruit of his stupendous discovery.

In the midst of the clamour Tobermory entered the room and made his way with velvet tread and studied unconcern across to the group seated round the tea-table.

A sudden hush of awkwardness and constraint fell on the company. Somehow there seemed an element of embarrassment in addressing on equal terms a domestic cat of acknowledged mental ability.

'Will you have some milk, Tobermory?' asked Lady Blemley in a rather strained voice.

'I don't mind if I do,' was the response, couched in a tone of even indifference. A shiver of suppressed excitement went through the listeners, and Lady Blemley might be excused for pouring out the saucerful of milk rather unsteadily.

'I'm afraid I've spilt a good deal of it,' she said apologetically.

'After all, it's not my Axminster,' was Tobermory's rejoinder.

Another silence fell on the group, and then Miss Resker, in her best district-visitor manner, asked if the human language had been difficult to learn. Tobermory looked squarely at her for a moment and then fixed his gaze serenely on the middle distance. It was obvious that boring questions lay outside his scheme of life.

'What do you think of human intelligence?' asked Mavis Pellington lamely.

'Of whose intelligence in particular?' asked Tobermory coldly.

'Oh, well, mine, for instance,' said Mavis with a feeble laugh.

'You put me in an embarrassing position,' said Tobermory, whose tone and attitude certainly did not suggest a shred of embarrassment. 'When your inclusion in this house-party was suggested Sir Wilfrid protested that you were the most brainless woman of his acquaintance, and that there was a wide distinction between hospitality and the care of the feeble-minded. Lady Blemley replied that your lack of brain-power was the precise quality which had earned you your invitation, as you were the only person she could think of who might be idiotic enough to buy their old car. You know, the one they call "The Envy of Sisyphus", because it goes quite nicely up hill if you push it.'

Lady Blemley's protestations would have had greater effect if she had not casually suggested to Mavis only that morning that the car in question would be just the thing for her down at her Devonshire home.

Major Barfield plunged in heavily to effect a diversion.

'How about your carryings-on with the tortoiseshell puss up at the stables, eh?'

The moment he had said it everyone realized the blunder.

'One does not usually discuss these matters in public,' said Tobermory frigidly. 'From a slight observation of your ways since you've been in this house I should imagine you'd find it inconvenient if I were to shift the conversation on to your own little affairs.'

The panic which ensued was not confined to the Major.

'Would you like to go and see if cook has got your dinner ready?' suggested Lady Blemley hurriedly, affecting to ignore the fact that it wanted at least two hours to Tobermory's dinner-time.

'Thanks,' said Tobermory, 'not quite so soon after my tea. I don't want to die of indigestion.'

'Cats have nine lives, you know,' said Sir Wilfrid heartily.

'Possibly,' answered Tobermory; 'but only one liver.'

'Adelaide!' said Mrs Cornett, 'do you mean to encourage that cat to go out and gossip about us in the servants' hall?'

The panic had indeed become general. A narrow ornamental balustrade ran in front of most of the bedroom windows at the Towers, and it was recalled with dismay that this had formed a favourite promenade for Tobermory at all hours, whence he could watch the pigeons – and heaven knew what else besides. If he intended to become reminiscent in his present outspoken strain the effect would be something more than disconcerting. Mrs Cornett, who spent much time at her toilet table, and whose complexion was reputed to be of a nomadic though punctual disposition, looked as ill at ease as the Major. Miss Scrawen, who wrote fiercely sensuous poetry and led a blameless life, merely displayed irritation; if you are methodical and virtuous in private you don't necessarily want everyone to know it. Bertie van Tahn, who was so depraved at seventeen that he had long ago given up trying to be any worse, turned a dull shade of gardenia white, but he did not commit the error of dashing out of the room like Odo Finsberry, a young gentleman who was understood to be reading for the Church and who was possibly disturbed at the thought of scandals he might hear concerning other people.

Even in a delicate situation like the present, Agnes Resker could not endure to remain too long in the background.

'Why did I ever come down here?' she asked dramatically.

Tobermory immediately accepted the opening.

'Judging by what you said to Mrs Cornett on the croquet-lawn yesterday, you were out for food. You described the Blemleys as the dullest people to stay with that you knew, but said they were clever enough to employ a first-rate cook; otherwise they'd find it difficult to get anyone to come down a second time.'

'There's not a word of truth in it! I appeal to Mrs Cornett –' exclaimed the discomfited Agnes.

'Mrs Cornett repeated your remark afterwards to Bertie van Tahn,' continued Tobermory, 'and said "That woman is a regular

Hunger Marcher; she'd go anywhere for four square meals a day," and Bertie van Tahn said –'

At this point the chronicle mercifully ceased. Tobermory had caught a glimpse of the big yellow Tom from the Rectory, working his way through the shrubbery towards the stable wing. In a flash he had vanished through the open French window.

With the disappearance of his too brilliant pupil Cornelius Appin found himself beset by a hurricane of bitter upbraiding, anxious inquiry, and frightened entreaty. The responsibility for the situation lay with him, and he must prevent matters from becoming worse. Could Tobermory impart his dangerous gift to other cats? was the first question he had to answer. It was possible, he replied, that he might have initiated his intimate friend the stable puss into his new accomplishment, but it was unlikely that his teaching could have taken a wider range as yet.

'Then,' said Mrs Cornett, 'Tobermory may be a valuable cat and a great pet; but I'm sure you'll agree, Adelaide, that both he and the stable cat must be done away with without delay.'

'You don't suppose I've enjoyed the last quarter of an hour, do you?' said Lady Blemley bitterly. 'My husband and I are very fond of Tobermory – at least, we were before this horrible accomplishment was infused into him; but now, of course, the only thing is to have him destroyed as soon as possible.'

'We can put some strychnine in the scraps he always gets at dinner-time,' said Sir Wilfrid, 'and I will go and drown the stable cat myself. The coachman will be very sore at losing his pet, but I'll say a very catching form of mange has broken out in both cats and we're afraid of it spreading to the kennels.'

'But my great discovery!' expostulated Mr Appin; 'after all my years of research and experiment –'

'You can go and experiment on the shorthorns at the farm, who are under proper control,' said Mrs Cornett, 'or the elephants at the Zoological Gardens. They're said to be highly intelligent, and they have this recommendation, that they don't come creeping about our bedrooms and under chairs, and so forth.'

An archangel ecstatically proclaiming the Millennium, and then finding that it clashed unpardonably with Henley and would have to be indefinitely postponed, could hardly have felt more crestfallen than Cornelius Appin at the reception of his wonderful achievement. Public opinion, however, was against him – in fact, had the general voice been consulted on the subject it is probable that a strong minority vote would have been in favour of including him in the strychnine diet.

Defective train arrangements and a nervous desire to see matters brought to a finish prevented an immediate dispersal of the party: but dinner that evening was not a social success. Sir Wilfrid had had rather a trying time with the stable cat and subsequently with the coachman. Agnes Resker ostentatiously limited her repast to a morsel of dry toast, which she bit as though it were a personal enemy; while Mavis Pellington maintained a vindictive silence throughout the meal. Lady Blemley kept up a flow of what she hoped was conversation, but her attention was fixed on the doorway. A plateful of carefully dosed fish scraps was in readiness on the sideboard, but sweets and savoury and dessert went their way, and no Tobermory appeared either in the dining-room or kitchen.

The sepulchral dinner was cheerful compared with the subsequent vigil in the smoking-room. Eating and drinking had at least supplied a distraction and cloak to the prevailing embarrassment. Bridge was out of the question in the general tension of nerves and tempers, and after Odo Finsberry had given a lugubrious rendering of 'Melisande in the Wood' to a frigid audience music was tacitly avoided. At eleven the servants went to bed, announcing that the small window in the pantry had been left open as usual for Tobermory's private use. The guests read steadily through the current batch of magazines, and fell back gradually on the 'Badminton Library' and bound volumes of 'Punch'. Lady Blemley made periodic visits to the pantry, returning each time with an expression of listless depression which forestalled questioning.

At two o'clock Bertie van Tahn broke the dominating silence.

'He won't turn up tonight. He's probably in the local newspaper office at the present moment, dictating the first instalment of his reminiscences. What's-her-name's book won't be in it. It will be the event of the day.'

Having made this contribution to the general cheerfulness,

Bertie van Tahn went to bed. At long intervals the various members of the house-party followed his example.

The servants taking round the early tea made a uniform announcement in reply to a uniform question. Tobermory had not returned.

Breakfast was, if anything, a more unpleasant function than dinner had been, but before its conclusion the situation was relieved. Tobermory's corpse was brought in from the shrubbery, where a gardener had just discovered it. From the bites on his throat and the yellow fur which coated his claws it was evident that he had fallen in unequal combat with the big Tom from the Rectory.

By midday most of the guests had quitted the Towers, and after lunch Lady Blemley had sufficiently recovered her spirits to write an extremely nasty letter to the Rectory about the loss of her valuable pet.

Tobermory had been Appin's one successful pupil, and he was destined to have no successor. A few weeks later an elephant in the Dresden Zoological Garden, which had shown no previous signs of irritability, broke loose and killed an Englishman who had apparently been teasing it. The victim's name was variously reported in the papers as Oppin and Eppelin, but his front name was faithfully rendered Cornelius.

'If he was trying German irregular verbs on the poor beast,' said Bertie van Tahn, 'he deserved all he got.'

The Music on the Hill

Sylvia Seltoun ate her breakfast in the morning-room at Yessney with a pleasant sense of ultimate victory, such as a fervent Ironside might have permitted himself on the morrow of Worcester fight. She was scarcely pugnacious by temperament, but belonged to that more successful class of fighters who are pugnacious by circumstance. Fate had willed that her life should be occupied with a series of small struggles, usually with the odds slightly against her, and usually she had just managed to come through winning. And now she felt that she had brought her hardest and certainly her most important struggle to a successful issue. To have married Mortimer Seltoun, 'Dead Mortimer' as his more intimate enemies called him, in the teeth of the cold hostility of his family, and in spite of his unaffected indifference to women, was indeed an achievement that had needed some determination and adroitness to carry through; yesterday she had brought her victory to its concluding stage by wrenching her husband away from Town and its group of satellite watering-places and 'settling him down', in the vocabulary of her kind, in this remote wood-girt manor farm which was his country house.

'You will never get Mortimer to go,' his mother had said carpingly, 'but if he once goes he'll stay; Yessney throws almost as much a spell over him as Town does. One can understand what holds him to Town, but Yessney –' and the dowager had shrugged her shoulders.

There was a sombre almost savage wildness about Yessney that was certainly not likely to appeal to town-bred tastes, and Sylvia, notwithstanding her name, was accustomed to nothing much more sylvan than 'leafy Kensington'. She looked on the country as something excellent and wholesome in its way, which was apt to become troublesome if you encouraged it overmuch. Distrust of town-life had been a new thing with her, born of her marriage with Mortimer, and she had watched with satisfaction the gradual fading of what she called 'the Jermyn-street-look' in his eyes as the woods and heather of Yessney had closed in on them yesternight. Her will-power and strategy had prevailed; Mortimer would stay.

Outside the morning-room windows was a triangular slope of turf, which the indulgent might call a lawn, and beyond its low hedge of neglected fuchsia bushes a steeper slope of heather and bracken dropped down into cavernous combes overgrown with oak and yew. In its wild open savegery there seemed a stealthy linking of the joy of life with the terror of unseen things. Sylvia smiled complacently as she gazed with a School-of-Art appreciation at the landscape, and then of a sudden she almost shuddered.

'It is very wild,' she said to Mortimer, who had joined her; 'one could almost think that in such a place the worship of Pan had never quite died out.'

'The worship of Pan never has died out,' said Mortimer. 'Other newer gods have drawn aside his votaries from time to time, but he is the Nature-God to whom all must come back at last. He has been called the Father of all the Gods, but most of his children have been stillborn.'

Sylvia was religious in an honest vaguely devotional kind of way, and did not like to hear her beliefs spoken of as mere aftergrowths, but it was at least something new and hopeful to hear Dead Mortimer speak with such energy and conviction on any subject.

'You don't really believe in Pan?' she asked incredulously.

'I've been a fool in most things,' said Mortimer quietly, 'but I'm not such a fool as not to believe in Pan when I'm down here. And if you're wise you won't disbelieve in him too boastfully while you're in his country.'

It was not till a week later, when Sylvia had exhausted the attractions of the woodland walks round Yessney, that she ventured on a tour of inspection of the farm buildings. A farmyard suggested in her mind a scene of cheerful bustle, with churns and flails and smiling dairymaids, and teams of horses drinking knee-deep in duck-crowded ponds. As she wandered among the gaunt grey buildings of Yessney manor farm her first impression was one of crushing stillness and desolation, as though she had happened on some lone deserted homestead long given over to owls and cobwebs; then came a sense of furtive watchful hostility, the same shadow of unseen things that seemed to lurk in the wooded combes and coppices. From behind heavy doors and shuttered windows came the restless stamp of hoof or rasp of chain halter, and at times a muffled bellow from some stalled beast. From a distant corner a shaggy dog watched her with intent unfriendly eyes; as she drew near it slipped quietly into its kennel, and slipped out again as noiselessly when she had passed by. A few hens, questing for food under a rick, stole away under a gate at her approach. Sylvia felt that if she had come across any human beings in this wilderness of barn and byre they would have fled wraith-like from her gaze. At last, turning a corner quickly, she came upon a living thing that did not fly from her. Astretch in a pool of mud was an enormous sow, gigantic beyond the town-woman's wildest computation of swine-flesh, and speedily alert to resent and if necessary repel the unwonted intrusion. It was Sylvia's turn to make an unobtrusive retreat. As she threaded her way past rickyards and cowsheds and long blank walls, she started suddenly at a strange sound – the echo of a boy's laughter, golden and equivocal. Jan, the only boy employed on the farm, a tow-headed, wizen-faced yokel, was visibly at work on a potato clearing half-way up the nearest hill-side, and Mortimer, when questioned, knew of no other probable or possible begetter of the hidden mockery that had ambushed Sylvia's retreat. The memory of that untraceable echo was added to her other impressions of a furtive sinister 'something' that hung around Yessney.

Of Mortimer she saw very little; farm and woods and trout-streams seemed to swallow him up from dawn till dusk. Once, following the direction she had seen him take in the morning, she came to an open space in a nut copse, further shut in by huge yew trees, in the centre of which stood a stone pedestal surmounted by a small bronze figure of a youthful Pan. It was a beautiful piece of workmanship, but her attention was chiefly held by the fact that a newly cut bunch of grapes had been placed as an offering at its feet. Grapes were none too plentiful at the manor house, and Sylvia snatched the bunch angrily from the pedestal. Contemptuous annoyance dominated her thoughts as she strolled slowly homeward, and then gave way to a sharp feeling of something that was very near fright; across a thick tangle of undergrowth a boy's face was scowling at her, brown and beautiful, with unutterably evil eyes. It was a lonely pathway, all pathways round Yessney were lonely for the matter of that, and she sped forward without waiting to give a closer scrutiny to this sudden apparition. It was not till she had reached the house that she discovered that she had dropped the bunch of grapes in her flight.

'I saw a youth in the wood today,' she told Mortimer that

evening, 'brown-faced and rather handsome, but a scoundrel to look at. A gipsy lad, I suppose.'

'A reasonable theory,' said Mortimer, 'only there aren't any gipsies in these parts at present.'

'Then who was he?' asked Sylvia, and as Mortimer appeared to have no theory of his own, she passed on to recount her finding of the votive offering.

'I suppose it was your doing,' she observed; 'it's a harmless piece of lunacy, but people would think you dreadfully silly if they knew of it.'

'Did you meddle with it in any way?' asked Mortimer.

'I – I threw the grapes away. It seemed so silly,' said Sylvia, watching Mortimer's impassive face for a sign of annoyance.

'I don't think you were wise to do that,' he said reflectively. 'I've heard it said that the Wood Gods are rather horrible to those who molest them.'

'Horrible perhaps to those that believe in them, but you see I don't,' retorted Sylvia.

'All the same,' said Mortimer in his even, dispassionate tone, 'I should avoid the woods and orchards if I were you, and give a wide berth to the horned beasts on the farm.'

It was all nonsense, of course, but in that lonely wood-girt spot nonsense seemed able to rear a bastard brood of uneasiness.

'Mortimer,' said Sylvia suddenly, 'I think we will go back to Town some time soon.'

Her victory had not been so complete as she had supposed; it had carried her on to ground that she was already anxious to quit.

'I don't think you will ever go back to Town,' said Mortimer. He seemed to be paraphrasing his mother's prediction as to himself.

Sylvia noted with dissatisfaction and some self-contempt that the course of her next afternoon's ramble took her instinctively clear of the network of woods. As to the horned cattle, Mortimer's warning was scarcely needed, for she had always regarded them as of doubtful neutrality at the best: her imagination unsexed the most matronly dairy cows and turned them into bulls liable to 'see red' at any moment. The ram who fed in the narrow paddock below the orchards she had adjudged, after ample and cautious probation, to be of docile temper; today, however, she decided to leave his docility untested, for the usually tranquil beast was roaming with every sign of restlessness from corner to corner of his meadow. A long, fitful piping, as of some reedy flute, was coming from the depth of a neighbouring copse, and there seemed to be some subtle connection between the animal's restless pacing and the wild music from the wood. Sylvia turned her steps in an upward direction and climbed the heather-clad slopes that stretched in rolling shoulders high above Yessney. She had left the piping notes behind her, but across the wooded combes at her feet the wind brought her another kind of music, the straining bay of hounds in full chase. Yessney was just on the outskirts of the Devon-and-Somerset country, and the hunted deer sometimes came that way. Sylvia could presently see a dark body, breasting hill after hill, and sinking again and again out of sight as he crossed the combes, while behind him steadily swelled that relentless chorus, and she grew tense with the excited sympathy that one feels for any hunted thing in whose capture one is not directly interested. And at last he broke through the outermost line of oak scrub and fern and stood panting in the open, a fat September stag carrying a well-furnished head. His obvious course was to drop down to the brown pools of Undercombe, and thence make his way towards the red deer's favoured sanctuary, the sea. To Sylvia's surprise, however, he turned his head to the upland slope and came lumbering resolutely onward over the heather. 'It will be dreadful,' she thought, 'the hounds will pull him down under my very eyes.' But the music of the pack seemed to have died away for a moment, and in its place she heard again that wild piping, which rose now on this side, now on that, as though urging the failing stag to a final effort. Sylvia stood well aside from his path, half hidden in a thick growth of whortle bushes, and watched him swing stiffly upward, his flanks dark with sweat, the coarse hair on his neck showing light by contrast. The pipe music shrilled suddenly around her, seeming to come from the bushes at her very feet, and at the same moment the great beast slewed round and bore directly down upon her. In an instant her pity for the hunted animal was changed to wild terror at her own danger; the thick heather roots mocked her scrambling efforts at flight, and she looked frantically downward for a glimpse of oncoming hounds. The huge antler spikes were within a few yards of her, and in a flash of numbing fear she remembered Mortimer's warning, to beware of horned beasts on the farm. And then with a quick throb of joy she saw that she was not alone; a human figure stood a few paces aside, knee-deep in the whortle bushes.

'Drive it off!' she shrieked. But the figure made no answering movement.

The antlers drove straight at her breast, the acrid smell of the hunted animal was in her nostrils, but her eyes were filled with the horror of something she saw other than her oncoming death. And in her ears rang the echo of a boy's laughter, golden and equivocal.

Filboid Studge, the Story of a Mouse That Helped

'I want to marry your daughter,' said Mark Spayley with faltering eagerness. 'I am only an artist with an income of two hundred a year, and she is the daughter of an enormously wealthy man, so I suppose you will think my offer a piece of presumption.'

Duncan Dullamy, the great company inflator, showed no outward sign of displeasure. As a matter of fact, he was secretly relieved at the prospect of finding even a two-hundred-a-year husband for his daughter Leonore. A crisis was rapidly rushing upon him, from which he knew he would emerge with neither money nor credit; all his recent ventures had fallen flat, and flattest of all had gone the wonderful new breakfast food, Pipenta, on the advertisement of which he had sunk such huge sums. It could scarcely be called a drug in the market; people bought drugs, but no one bought Pipenta.

'Would you marry Leonore if she were a poor man's daughter?' asked the man of phantom wealth.

'Yes,' said Mark, wisely avoiding the error of over-protestation. And to his astonishment Leonore's father not only gave his consent, but suggested a fairly early date for the wedding.

'I wish I could show my gratitude in some way,' said Mark with genuine emotion. 'I'm afraid it's rather like the mouse proposing to help the lion.'

'Get people to buy that beastly muck,' said Dullamy, nodding savagely at a poster of the despised Pipenta, 'and you'll have done more than any of my agents have been able to accomplish.'

'It wants a better name,' said Mark reflectively, 'and something distinctive in the poster line. Anyway, I'll have a shot at it.'

Three weeks later the world was advised of the coming of a new breakfast food, heralded under the resounding name of 'Filboid Studge'. Spayley put forth no pictures of massive babies springing up with fungus-like rapidity under its forcing influence, or of representatives of the leading nations of the world scrambling with fatuous eagerness for its possession. One huge sombre poster depicted the Damned in Hell suffering a new torment from their inability to get at the Filboid Studge which elegant young fiends held in transparent bowls just beyond their reach. The scene was rendered even more gruesome by a subtle suggestion of the features of leading men and women of the day in the portrayal of the Lost Souls; prominent individuals of both political parties, Society hostesses, well-known dramatic authors and novelists, and distinguished aeroplanists were dimly recognizable in that doomed throng; noted lights of the musical-comedy stage flickered wanly in the shades of the Inferno, smiling still from force of habit, but with the fearsome smiling rage of baffled effort. The poster bore no fulsome allusions to the merits of the new breakfast food, but a single grim statement ran in bold letters along its base: 'They cannot buy it now.'

Spayley had grasped the fact that people will do things from a sense of duty which they would never attempt as a pleasure. There are thousands of respectable middle-class men who, if you found them unexpectedly in a Turkish bath, would explain in all sincerity that a doctor had ordered them to take Turkish baths; if you told them in return that you went there because you liked it, they would stare in pained wonder at the frivolity of your motive. In the same way, whenever a massacre of Armenians is reported from Asia Minor, everyone assumes that it has been carried out 'under orders' from somewhere or another; no one seems to think that there are people who might *like* to kill their neighbours now and then.

And so it was with the new breakfast food. No one would have eaten Filboid Studge as a pleasure, but the grim austerity of its advertisement drove housewives in shoals to the grocers' shops to clamour for an immediate supply. In small kitchens solemn pig-tailed daughters helped depressed mothers to perform the primitive ritual of its preparation. On the breakfast-tables of cheerless parlours it was partaken of in silence. Once the women-folk discovered that it was thoroughly unpalatable, their zeal in forcing it on their households knew no bounds. 'You haven't eaten your Filboid Studge!' would be screamed at the appetiteless clerk as he hurried wearily from the breakfast-table, and his evening meal would be prefaced by a warmed-up mess which would be explained as 'your Filboid Studge that you didn't eat this morning'. Those strange fanatics who ostentatiously mortify themselves, inwardly and outwardly, with health biscuits and health garments, battened aggressively on the new food. Earnest spectacled young men devoured it on the steps of the National Liberal Club. A bishop who did not believe in a future state preached against the poster, and a peer's daughter died from eating too much of the compound. A further advertisement was obtained when an infantry regiment mutinied and shot its officers rather than eat the nauseous mess; fortunately, Lord Birrell of Blatherstone, who was War Minister at the moment, saved the situation by his happy epigram, that 'Discipline to be effective must be optional'.

Filboid Studge had become a household word, but Dullamy wisely realized that it was not necessarily the last word in breakfast dietary; its supremacy would be challenged as soon as some yet more unpalatable food should be put on the market. There might even be a reaction in favour of something tasty and appetizing, and the Puritan austerity of the moment might be banished from domestic cookery. At an opportune moment, therefore, he sold out his interests in the article which had brought him in colossal wealth at a critical juncture, and placed his financial reputation beyond the reach of cavil. As for Leonore, who was now an heiress on a far greater scale than ever before, he naturally found her something a vast deal higher in the husband market than a two-hundred-a-year poster designer. Mark Spayley, the brainmouse who had helped the financial lion with such untoward effect, was left to curse the day he produced the wonder-working poster.

The Peace of Mowsle Barton

Crefton Lockyer sat at his ease, an ease alike of body and soul, in the little patch of ground, half-orchard and half-garden, that abutted on the farmyard at Mowsle Barton. After the stress and noise of long years of city life, the repose and peace of the hill-begirt homestead struck on his senses with an almost dramatic intensity. Time and space seemed to lose their meaning and their abruptness; the minutes slid away into hours, and the meadows and fallows sloped away into middle distance, softly and imperceptibly. Wild weeds of the hedgerow straggled into the flower-garden, and wallflowers and garden bushes made counter-raids into farmyard and lane. Sleepy-looking hens and solemn preoccupied ducks were equally at home in yard, orchard, or roadway; nothing seemed to belong definitely to anywhere; even the gates were not necessarily to be found on their hinges. And over the whole scene brooded the sense of a peace that had almost a quality of magic in it. In the afternoon you felt that it had always been afternoon, and must always remain afternoon; in the twilight you knew that it could never have been anything else but twilight. Crefton Lockyer sat at his ease in the rustic seat beneath an old medlar tree, and decided that here was the life-anchorage that his mind had so fondly pictured and that latterly his tired and jarred senses had so often pined for. He would make a permanent lodging-place among these simple friendly people, gradually increasing the modest comforts with which he would like to surround himself, but falling in as much as possible with their manner of living.

As he slowly matured this resolution in his mind an elderly woman came hobbling with uncertain gait through the orchard. He recognized her as a member of the farm household, the mother or possibly the mother-in-law of Mrs Spurfield, his present landlady, and hastily formulated some pleasant remark to make to her. She forestalled him.

'There's a bit of writing chalked up on the door over yonder. What is it?'

She spoke in a dull impersonal manner, as though the question had been on her lips for years and had best be got rid of. Her eyes, however, looked impatiently over Crefton's head at the door of a small barn which formed the outpost of a straggling line of farm buildings.

'Martha Pillamon is an old witch' was the announcement that met Crefton's inquiring scrutiny, and he hesitated a moment before giving the statement wider publicity. For all he knew to the contrary, it might be Martha herself to whom he was speaking. It was possible that Mrs Spurfield's maiden name had been Pillamon. And the gaunt, withered old dame at his side might certainly fulfil local conditions as to the outward aspect of a witch.

'It's something about someone called Martha Pillamon,' he explained cautiously.

'What does it say?'

'It's very disrespectful,' said Crefton; 'it says she's a witch. Such things ought not to be written up.'

'It's true, every word of it,' said his listener with considerable satisfaction, adding as a special descriptive note of her own, 'the old toad.'

And as she hobbled away through the farmyard she shrilled out in her cracked voice, 'Martha Pillamon is an old witch!'

'Did you hear what she said?' mumbled a weak, angry voice somewhere behind Crefton's shoulder. Turning hastily, he beheld another old crone, thin and yellow and wrinkled, and evidently in a high state of displeasure. Obviously this was Martha Pillamon in person. The orchard seemed to be a favourite promenade for the aged women of the neighbourhood.

' 'Tis lies, 'tis sinful lies,' the weak voice went on. ' 'Tis Betsy Croot is the old witch. She an' her daughter, the dirty rat. I'll put a spell on 'em, the old nuisances.'

As she limped slowly away her eye caught the chalk inscription on the barn door.

'What's written up there?' she demanded, wheeling round on Crefton.

'Vote for Soarker,' he responded, with the craven boldness of the practised peacemaker.

The old woman grunted, and her mutterings and her faded red shawl lost themselves gradually among the tree-trunks. Crefton rose presently and made his way towards the farm-house. Somehow a good deal of the peace seemed to have slipped out of the atmosphere.

The cheery bustle of tea-time in the old farm kitchen, which Crefton had found so agreeable on previous afternoons, seemed to have soured today into a certain uneasy melancholy. There was a dull, dragging silence around the board, and the tea itself, when Crefton came to taste it, was a flat, lukewarm concoction that would have driven the spirit of revelry out of a carnival.

'It's no use complaining of the tea,' said Mrs Spurfield hastily, as her guest stared with an air of polite inquiry at his cup. 'The kettle won't boil, that's the truth of it.'

Crefton turned to the hearth, where an unusually fierce fire was banked up under a big black kettle which sent a thin wreath of steam from its spout, but seemed otherwise to ignore the action of the roaring blaze beneath it.

'It's been there more than an hour, an' boil it won't,' said Mrs Spurfield, adding, by way of complete explanation, 'we're bewitched.'

'It's Martha Pillamon as has done it,' chimed in the old mother; 'I'll be even with the old toad. I'll put a spell on her.'

'It must boil in time,' protested Crefton, ignoring the suggestions of foul influences. 'Perhaps the coal is damp.'

'It won't boil in time for supper, nor for breakfast tomorrow morning, not if you was to keep the fire a-going all night for it,' said Mrs Spurfield. And it didn't. The household subsisted on fried and baked dishes, and a neighbour obligingly brewed tea and sent it across in a moderately warm condition.

'I suppose you'll be leaving us, now that things has turned up uncomfortable,' Mrs Spurfield observed at breakfast; 'there are folks as deserts one as soon as trouble comes.'

Crefton hurriedly disclaimed any immediate change of plans; he observed, however, to himself that the earlier heartiness of manner had in a large measure deserted the household. Suspicious looks, sulky silences, or sharp speeches had become the order of the day. As for the old mother, she sat about the kitchen or the garden all day, murmuring threats and spells against Martha Pillamon. There was something alike terrifying and piteous in the spectacle of these frail old morsels of humanity consecrating their last flickering energies to the task of making each other wretched. Hatred seemed to be the one faculty which had survived in undiminished vigour and intensity where all else was dropping into ordered and symmetrical decay. And the uncanny part of it was that some horrid unwholesome power seemed to be distilled from their spite and their cursings. No amount of sceptical explanation could remove the undoubted fact that neither kettle nor saucepan would come to boiling-point over the hottest fire. Crefton clung as long as possible to the theory of some defect in the coals, but a wood fire gave the same result, and when a small spirit-lamp kettle, which he ordered out by carrier, showed the same obstinate refusal to allow its contents to boil he felt that he had come suddenly into contact with some unguessed-at and very evil aspect of hidden forces. Miles away, down through an opening in the hills, he could catch glimpses of a road where motor-cars sometimes passed, and yet here, so little removed from the arteries of the latest civilization, was a bat-haunted old homestead, where something unmistakably like witchcraft seemed to hold a very practical sway.

Passing out through the farm garden on his way to the lanes beyond, where he hoped to recapture the comfortable sense of peacefulness that was so lacking around house and hearth – especially hearth – Crefton came across the old mother, sitting mumbling to herself in the seat beneath the medlar tree. 'Let un sink as swims, let un sink as swims,' she was repeating over and over again, as a child repeats a half-learned lesson. And now and then she would break off into a shrill laugh, with a note of malice in it that was not pleasant to hear. Crefton was glad when he found himself out of earshot, in the quiet and seclusion of the deep overgrown lanes that seemed to lead away to nowhere; one, narrower and deeper than the rest, attracted his footsteps, and he was almost annoyed when he found that it really did act as a miniature roadway to a human dwelling. A forlorn-looking cottage with a scrap of ill-tended cabbage garden and a few aged apple trees stood at an angle where a swift-flowing stream widened out for a space into a decent-sized pond before hurrying away again through the willows that had checked its course. Crefton leaned against a tree-trunk and looked across the swirling eddies of the pond at the humble little homestead opposite him; the only sign of life came from a small procession of dingy-looking ducks that marched in single file down to the water's edge. There is always something rather taking in the way a duck changes itself in an instant from a slow, clumsy waddler of the earth to a graceful, buoyant swimmer of the waters, and Crefton waited with a certain arrested attention to watch the leader of the file launch itself on to the surface of the pond. He was aware at the same time of a curious warning instinct that something strange and unpleasant was about to happen. The duck flung itself confidently forward into the water, and rolled immediately under the surface. Its head appeared for a moment and went under again, leaving a train of bubbles in its wake, while wings and legs churned the water in a helpless swirl of flapping and kicking. The bird was obviously drowning. Crefton thought at first that it had caught itself in some weeds, or was being attacked from below by a pike or water-rat. But no blood floated to the surface, and the wildly bobbing body made the circuit of the pond current without hindrance from any entanglement. A second duck had by this time launched itself into the pond, and a second struggling body rolled and twisted under the surface. There was something peculiarly piteous in the sight of the gasping beaks that showed now and again above the water, as though in terrified protest at this treachery of a trusted and familiar element. Crefton gazed with something like horror as a third duck poised itself on the bank and splashed in, to share the fate of the other two. He felt almost relieved when the remainder of the flock, taking tardy alarm from the commotion of the slowly drowning bodies, drew themselves up with tense outstretched necks, and sidled away from the scene of danger, quacking a deep note of disquietude as they went. At the same moment Crefton became aware that he was not the only human witness of the scene; a bent and withered old woman, whom he recognized at once as Martha Pillamon, of sinister reputation, had limped down the cottage path to the water's edge, and was gazing fixedly at the gruesome whirligig of dying birds that went in horrible procession round the pool. Presently her voice rang out in a shrill note of quavering rage:

' 'Tis Betsy Croot adone it, the old rat. I'll put a spell on her, see if I don't.'

Crefton slipped quietly away, uncertain whether or no the old woman had noticed his presence. Even before she had proclaimed the guiltiness of Betsy Croot, the latter's muttered incantation 'Let us sink as swims' had flashed uncomfortably across his mind. But it was the final threat of a retaliatory spell which crowded his mind with misgiving to the exclusion of all other thoughts or fancies. His reasoning powers could no longer afford to dismiss these old-wives' threats as empty bickerings. The household at Mowsle Barton lay under the displeasure of a vindictive old woman who seemed able to materialize her personal spites in a very practical fashion, and there was no saying what form her revenge for three drowned ducks might not take. As a member of the household Crefton might find himself involved in some general and highly disagreeable visitation of Martha Pillamon's wrath. Of course he knew that he was giving way to absurd fancies, but the behaviour of the spirit-lamp kettle and the subsequent scene at the pond had considerably unnerved him. And the vagueness of his alarm added to its terrors; when once you have taken the Impossible into your calculations its possibilities become practically limitless.

Crefton rose at his usual early hour the next morning, after one of the least restful nights he had spent at the farm. His sharpened senses quickly detected that subtle atmosphere of things-being-not-altogether well that hangs over a stricken household. The cows had been milked, but they stood huddled about in the yard, waiting impatiently to be driven out afield, and the poultry kept up an importunate querulous reminder of deferred feeding-time; the yard pump, which usually made discordant music at frequent intervals during the early morning, was today ominously silent. In the house itself there was a coming and going of scuttering footsteps, a rushing and dying away of hurried voices, and long, uneasy stillnesses. Crefton finished his dressing and made his way to the head of a narrow staircase. He could hear a dull, complaining voice, a voice into which an awed hush had crept, and recognized the speaker as Mrs Spurfield.

'He'll go away, for sure,' the voice was saying; 'there are those as runs away from one as soon as real misfortune shows itself.'

Crefton felt that he probably was one of 'those', and that there were moments when it was advisable to be true to type.

He crept back to his room, collected and packed his few belongings, placed the money due for his lodgings on a table, and made his way out by a back door into the yard. A mob of poultry surged expectantly towards him; shaking off their interested attentions he hurried along under cover of cowstall, piggery, and hayricks till he reached the lane at the back of the farm. A few minutes' walk, which only the burden of his portmanteaux restrained from developing into an undisguised run, brought him to a main road, where the early carrier soon overtook him and sped him onward to the neighbouring town. At a bend of the road he caught a last glimpse of the farm; the old gabled roofs and thatched barns, the straggling orchard, and the medlar tree, with its wooden seat, stood out with an almost spectral clearness in the early morning light, and over it all brooded that air of magic possession which Crefton had once mistaken for peace.

The bustle and roar of Paddington Station smote on his ears with a welcome protective greeting.

'Very bad for our nerves, all this rush and hurry,' said a fellow-traveller; 'give me the peace and quiet of the country.'

Crefton mentally surrendered his share of the desired commodity. A crowded, brilliantly over-lighted music-hall, where an exuberant rendering of '1812' was being given by a strenuous orchestra, came nearest to his ideal of a nerve sedative.

Hermann the Irascible – A Story of the Great Weep

It was in the second decade of the twentieth century, after the Great Plague had devastated England, that Hermann the Irascible, nicknamed also the Wise, sat on the British throne. The Mortal Sickness had swept away the entire Royal Family, unto the third and fourth generations, and thus it came to pass that Hermann the Fourteenth of Saxe-Drachsen-Wachtelstein, who had stood thirtieth in the order of succession, found himself one day ruler of the British dominions within and beyond the seas. He was one of the unexpected things that happen in politics, and he happened with great thoroughness. In many ways he was the most progressive monarch who had sat on an important throne; before people knew where they were, they were somewhere else. Even his Ministers, progressive though they were by tradition, found it difficult to keep pace with his legislative suggestions.

'As a matter of fact,' admitted the Prime Minister, 'we are hampered by these votes-for-women creatures; they disturb our meetings throughout the country, and they try to turn Downing Street into a sort of political picnic-ground.'

'They must be dealt with,' said Hermann.

'Dealt with,' said the Prime Minister; 'exactly, just so; but how?'

'I will draft you a Bill', said the King, sitting down at his typewriting machine, 'enacting that women shall vote at all future elections. *Shall* vote, you observe; or, to put it plainer, must. Voting will remain optional, as before, for male electors; but every woman between the ages of twenty-one and seventy will be obliged to vote, not only at elections for Parliament, county councils, district boards, parish councils, and municipalities, but for coroners, school inspectors, churchwardens, curators of museums, sanitary authorities, police-court interpreters, swimming-bath instructors, contractors, choir-masters, market superintendents, art-school teachers, cathedral vergers, and other local functionaries whose names I will add as they occur to me. All these offices will become elective, and failure to vote at any election falling within her area of residence will involved the female elector in a penalty of £10. Absence, unsupported by an adequate medical certificate, will not be accepted as an excuse. Pass this Bill through the two Houses of Parliament and bring it to me for signature the day after tomorrow.'

From the very outset the Compulsory Female Franchise produced little or no elation even in circles which had been loudest in demanding the vote. The bulk of the women of the country had been indifferent or hostile to the franchise agitation, and the most fanatical Suffragettes began to wonder what they had found so attractive in the prospect of putting ballot-papers into a box. In the country districts the task of carrying out the provisions of the new Act was irksome enough; in the towns and cities it became an incubus. There seemed no end to the elections. Laundresses and seamstresses had to hurry away from their work to vote, often for a candidate whose name they hadn't heard before, and whom they selected at haphazard; female clerks and waitresses got up extra early to get their voting done before starting off to their places of business. Society women found their arrangements impeded and upset by the continual necessity for attending the polling stations, and week-end parties and summer holidays became gradually a masculine luxury. As for Cairo and the Riviera, they were possible only for genuine invalids or people of enormous wealth, for the accumulation of £10 fines during a prolonged absence was a contingency that even ordinarily wealthy folk could hardly afford to risk.

It was not wonderful that the female disfranchisement agitation became a formidable movement. The No-Votes-for-Women League numbered its feminine adherents by the million; its colours, citron and old Dutch-madder, were flaunted everywhere, and its battle hymn, 'We don't want to Vote', became a popular refrain. As the Government showed no signs of being impressed by peaceful persuasion, more violent methods came into vogue. Meetings were disturbed, Ministers were mobbed, policemen were bitten, and ordinary prison fare rejected, and on the eve of the anniversary of Trafalgar women bound themselves in tiers up the entire length of the Nelson column so that its customary floral decoration had to be abandoned. Still the Government obstinately adhered to its conviction that women ought to have the vote.

Then, as a last resort, some woman wit hit upon an expedient which it was strange that no one had thought of before. The Great Weep was organized. Relays of women, ten thousand at a time, wept continuously in the public places of the Metropolis. They wept in railway stations, in tubes and omnibuses, in the National Gallery, at the Army and Navy Stores, in St James's Park, at ballad concerts, at Prince's and in the Burlington Arcade. The hitherto unbroken success of the brilliant farcical comedy 'Henry's Rabbit' was imperilled by the presence of drearily weeping women in stalls and circle and gallery, and one of the brightest divorce cases that had been tried for many years was robbed of much of its sparkle by the lachrymose behaviour of a section of the audience.

'What are we to do?' asked the Prime Minister, whose cook had wept into all the breakfast dishes and whose nursemaid had gone out, crying quietly and miserably, to take the children for a walk in the Park.

'There is a time for everything,' said the King; 'there is a time to yield. Pass a measure through the two Houses depriving women of the right to vote, and bring it to me for the Royal assent the day after tomorrow.'

As the Minister withdrew, Hermann the Irascible, who was also nicknamed the Wise, gave a profound chuckle.

'There are more ways of killing a cat than by choking it with cream,' he quoted, 'but I'm not sure', he added, 'that it's not the best way.'

The Parting

(From *The Unbearable Bassington*)

On a conveniently secluded bench facing the Northern Pheasantry in the Zoological Society's Gardens, Regent's Park, Courtenay Youghal sat immersed in mature flirtation with a lady, who, though certainly young in fact and appearance, was some four or five years his senior. When he was a schoolboy of sixteen, Molly McQuade had personally conducted him to the Zoo and stood him dinner afterwards at Kettner's, and whenever the two of them happened to be in town on the anniversary of that bygone festivity they religiously repeated the programme in its entirety. Even the menu of the dinner was adhered to as nearly as possible; the original selection of food and wine that schoolboy exuberance, tempered by schoolboy shyness, had pitched on those many years ago, confronted Youghal on those occasions, as a drowning man's past life is said to rise up and parade itself in his last moments of consciousness.

The flirtation which was thus perennially restored to its old-time footing owed its longevity more to the enterprising solicitude of Miss McQuade than to any conscious sentimental effort on the part of Youghal himself. Molly McQuade was known to her neighbours in a minor hunting shire as a hard-riding conventionally unconventional type of young woman, who came naturally into the classification, 'a good sort'. She was just sufficiently good-looking, sufficiently reticent about her own illnesses, when she had any, and sufficiently appreciative of her neighbour's gardens, children and hunters to be generally popular. Most men liked her, and the percentage of women who disliked her was not inconveniently high. One of these days, it was assumed, she would marry a brewer or a Master of Otter Hounds, and, after a brief interval, be known to the world as the mother of a boy or two at Malvern or some similar seat of learning. The romantic side of her nature was altogether unguessed by the countryside.

Her romances were mostly in serial form, and suffered perhaps in fervour from their disconnected course what they gained in length of days. Her affectionate interest in the several young men who figured in her affairs of the heart was perfectly honest, and she certainly made no attempt either to conceal their separate existences, or to play them off one against the other. Neither could it be said that she was a husband hunter; she had made up her mind what sort of man she was likely to marry, and her forecast did not differ very widely from that formed by her local acquaintances. If her married life were eventually to turn out a failure, at least she looked forward to it with very moderate expectations. Her love affairs she put on a very different footing, and apparently they were the all-absorbing element in her life. She possessed the happily constituted temperament which enables a man or woman to be a 'pluralist', and to observe the sage precaution of not putting all one's eggs into one basket. Her demands were not exacting: she required of her affinity that he should be young, good-looking, and at least moderately amusing; she would have preferred him to be invariably faithful, but, with her own example before her, she was prepared for the probability, bordering on certainty, that he would be nothing of the sort. The philosophy of the 'Garden of Kama' was the compass by which she steered her barque, and thus far, if she had encountered some storms and buffeting, she had at least escaped being either shipwrecked or becalmed.

Courtenay Youghal had not been designed by Nature to fulfil the role of an ardent or devoted lover, and he scrupulously respected the limits which Nature had laid down. For Molly, however, he had a certain responsive affection. She had always obviously admired him, and at the same time she never beset him with crude flattery; the principal reason why the flirtation had stood the test of so many years was the fact that it only flared into active existence at convenient intervals. In an age when the telephone has undermined almost every fastness of human privacy, and the sanctity of one's seclusion depends often on the ability for tactful falsehood shown by a club page-boy, Youghal was duly appreciative of the circumstance that his lady fair spent a large part of the year pursuing foxes, in lieu of pursuing him. Also the honestly admitted fact that, in her human hunting, she rode after more than one quarry, made the inevitable break-up of the affair a matter to which both could look forward without a sense of coming embarrassment and recrimination. When the time for gathering ye rose-buds should be over, neither of them could accuse the other of having wrecked his or her entire life. At the most they would only have disorganized a week-end.

On this particular afternoon, when old reminiscences had been gone through, and the intervening gossip of past months duly recounted, a lull in the conversation made itself rather obstinately felt. Molly had already guessed that matters were about to slip into a new phase; the affair had reached maturity long ago, and a new phase must be in the nature of a wane.

'You're a clever brute,' she said suddenly, with an air of affectionate regret; 'I always knew you'd get on in the House, but I hardly expected you to come to the front so soon.'

'I'm coming to the front,' admitted Youghal judicially; 'the problem is, shall I be able to stay there? Unless something happens in the financial line before long, I don't see how I'm to stay in Parliament at all. Economy is out of the question. It would open people's eyes, I fancy, if they knew how little I exist on as it is. And I'm living so far beyond my income that we may almost be said to be living apart.'

'It will have to be a rich wife, I suppose,' said Molly slowly; 'that's the worst of success, it imposes so many conditions. I rather knew, from something in your manner, that you were drifting that way.'

Youghal said nothing in the way of contradiction; he gazed steadfastly at the aviary in front of him as though exotic pheasants were for the moment the most absorbing study in the world. As a matter of fact, his mind was centered on the image of Elaine de Frey, with her clear untroubled eyes and her Leonardo da Vinci air. He was wondering whether he was likely to fall into a frame of mind concerning her which would be in the least like falling in love.

'I shall mind horribly,' continued Molly, after a pause, 'but, of course, I have always known that something of the sort would have to happen one of these days. When a man goes into politics he can't call his soul his own, and I suppose his heart becomes an impersonal possession in the same way.'

'Most people who know me would tell you that I haven't got a heart,' said Youghal.

'I've often felt inclined to agree with them,' said Molly; 'and then, now and again, I think you have a heart tucked away somewhere.'

'I hope I have,' said Youghal, 'because I'm trying to break to you the fact that I think I'm falling in love with somebody.'

Molly McQuade turned sharply to look at her companion, who still fixed his gaze on the pheasant run in front of him.

'Don't tell me you're losing your head over somebody useless, someone without money,' she said; 'I don't think I could stand that.'

For the moment she feared that Courtenay's selfishness might have taken an unexpected turn, in which ambition had given way to the fancy of the hour; he might be going to sacrifice his Parliamentary career for a life of stupid lounging in momentarily attractive company. He quickly undeceived her.

'She's got heaps of money.'

Molly gave a grunt of relief. Her affection for Courtenay had produced the anxiety which underlay her first question; a natural jealousy prompted the next one.

'Is she young and pretty and all that sort of thing, or is she just a good sort with a sympathetic manner and nice eyes? As a rule that's the kind that goes with a lot of money.'

'Young and quite good-looking in her way, and a distinct style of her own. Some people would call her beautiful. As a political hostess I should think she'd be splendid. I imagine I'm rather in love with her.'

'And is she in love with you?'

Youghal threw back his head with the slight assertive movement that Molly knew and liked.

'She's a girl who I fancy would let judgment influence her a lot. And without being stupidly conceited I think I may say she might do worse than throw herself away on me. I'm young and quite good-looking, and I'm making a name for myself in the House; she'll be able to read all sorts of nice and horrid things about me in the papers at breakfast-time. I can be brilliantly amusing at times, and I understand the value of silence; there is no fear that I shall ever degenerate into that fearsome thing – a cheerful talkative husband. For a girl with money and social ambitions I should think I was rather a good thing.'

'You are certainly in love, Courtenay,' said Molly, 'but it's the old love and not a new one. I'm rather glad. I should have hated to have you head-over-heels in love with a pretty woman, even for a short time. You'll be much happier as it is. And I'm going to put all my feelings in the background, and tell you to go in and win. You've got to marry a rich woman, and if she's nice and will make a good hostess, so much the better for everybody. You'll be happier in your married life than I shall be in mine, when it comes; you'll have other interests to absorb you. I shall just have the garden and dairy and nursery and lending library, as like as two peas to all the gardens and dairies and nurseries for hundreds of miles round. You won't care for your wife enough to be worried every time she has a finger-ache, and you'll like her well enough to be pleased to meet her sometimes at your own house. I shouldn't wonder if you were quite happy. She will probably be miserable, but any woman who married you would be.'

There was a short pause; they were both staring at the pheasant cages. Then Molly spoke again, with the swift nervous tone of a general who is hurriedly altering the disposition of his forces for a strategic retreat.

'When you are safely married and honeymooned and all that sort of thing, and have put your wife through her paces as a political hostess, some time, when the House isn't sitting, you must come down by yourself, and do a little hunting with us. Will you? It won't be quite the same as old times, but it will be something to look forward to when I'm reading the endless paragraphs about your fashionable political wedding.'

'You're looking forward pretty far,' laughed Youghal; 'the lady may take your view as to the probable unhappiness of a future shared with me, and I may have to content myself with penurious political bachelorhood. Anyhow, the present is still with us. We dine at Kettner's tonight, don't we?'

'Rather,' said Molly, 'though it will be more or less a throat-lumpy feast as far as I am concerned. We shall have to drink to the health of the future Mrs Youghal. By the way, it's rather characteristic of you that you haven't told me who she is, and of me that I haven't asked. And now, like a dear boy, trot away and leave me. I haven't got to say good-bye to you yet, but I'm going to take a quiet farewell of the Pheasantry. We've had some jolly good talks, you and I, sitting on this seat, haven't we? And I know, as well as I know anything, that this is the last of them. Eight o'clock tonight, as punctually as possible.'

She watched his retreating figure with eyes that grew slowly misty; he had been such a jolly, comely boy-friend, and they had had such good times together. The mist deepened on her lashes as she looked round at the familiar rendezvous where they had so often kept tryst since the day when they had first come there together, he a schoolboy and she but lately out of her teens. For the moment she felt herself in the thrall of very real sorrow.

Then, with the admirable energy of one who is only in town for a fleeting fortnight, she raced away to have tea with a world-faring naval admirer at his club. Pluralism is a merciful narcotic.

The She-Wolf

Leonard Bilsiter was one of those people who have failed to find this world attractive or interesting, and who have sought compensation in an 'unseen world' of their own experience or imagination – or invention. Children do that sort of thing successfully, but children are content to convince themselves, and do not vulgarize their beliefs by trying to convince other people. Leonard Bilsiter's beliefs were for 'the few', that is to say, anyone who would listen to him.

His dabblings in the unseen might not have carried him beyond the customary platitudes of the drawing-room visionary if accident had not reinforced his stock-in-trade of mystical lore. In company with a friend, who was interested in a Ural mining concern, he had made a trip across Eastern Europe at a moment when the great Russian railway strike was developing from a threat to a reality; its outbreak caught him on the return journey, somewhere on the further side of Perm, and it was while waiting for a couple of days at a wayside station in a state of suspended locomotion that he made the acquaintance of a dealer in harness and metalware, who profitably whiled away the tedium of the long halt by initiating his English travelling companion in a fragmentary system of folk-lore that he had picked up from Trans-Baikal traders and natives. Leonard returned to his home circle garrulous about his Russian strike experiences, but oppressively reticent about certain dark mysteries, which he alluded to under the resounding title of Siberian Magic. The reticence wore off in a week or two under the influence of an entire lack of general curiosity, and Leonard began to make more detailed allusions to the enormous powers which this new esoteric force, to use his own description of it, conferred on the initiated few who knew how to wield it. His aunt, Cecilia Hoops, who loved sensation perhaps rather better than she loved the truth, gave him as clamorous an advertisement as anyone could wish for by retailing an account of how he had turned a vegetable marrow into a wood-pigeon before her very eyes. As a manifestation of the possession of supernatural powers, the story was discounted in some quarters by the respect accorded to Mrs Hoops' powers of imagination.

However divided opinion might be on the question of Leonard's status as a wonderworker or a charlatan, he certainly arrived at Mary Hampton's house-party with a reputation for pre-eminence in one or other of those professions, and he was not disposed to shun such publicity as might fall to his share. Esoteric forces and unusual powers figured largely in whatever conversation he or his aunt had a share in, and his own performances, past and potential, were the subject of mysterious hints and dark avowals.

'I wish you would turn me into a wolf, Mr Bilsiter,' said his hostess at luncheon the day after his arrival.

'My dear Mary,' said Colonel Hampton, 'I never knew you had a craving in that direction.'

'A she-wolf, of course,' continued Mrs Hampton; 'it would be too confusing to change one's sex as well as one's species at a moment's notice.'

'I don't think one should jest on these subjects,' said Leonard.

'I'm not jesting, I'm quite serious, I assure you. Only don't do it today; we have only eight available bridge players, and it would break up one of our tables. Tomorrow we shall be a larger party. Tomorrow night, after dinner –'

'In our present imperfect understanding of these hidden forces I think one should approach them with humbleness rather than mockery,' observed Leonard, with such severity that the subject was forthwith dropped.

Clovis Sangrail had sat unusually silent during the discussion on the possibilities of Siberian Magic; after lunch he side-tracked Lord Pabham into the comparative seclusion of the billiard-room and delivered himself of a searching question.

'Have you such a thing as a she-wolf in your collection of wild animals? A she-wolf of moderately good temper?'

Lord Pabham considered. 'There is Louisa,' he said, 'a rather fine specimen of the timber-wolf. I got her two years ago in exchange for some Arctic foxes. Most of my animals get to be fairly tame before they've been with me very long; I think I can say Louisa has an angelic temper, as she-wolves go. Why do you ask?'

'I was wondering whether you would lend her to me for tomorrow night,' said Clovis, with the careless solicitude of one who borrows a collar stud or a tennis racquet.

'Tomorrow night?'

'Yes, wolves are nocturnal animals, so the late hours won't hurt her,' said Clovis, with the air of one who has taken everything into consideration; 'one of your men could bring her over from Pabham Park after dusk, and with a little help he ought to be able to smuggle her into the conservatory at the same moment that Mary Hampton makes an unobtrusive exit.'

Lord Pabham stared at Clovis for a moment in pardonable bewilderment; then his face broke into a wrinkled network of laughter.

'Oh, that's your game, is it? You are going to do a little Siberian Magic on your own account. And is Mrs Hampton willing to be a fellow-conspirator?'

'Mary is pledged to see me through with it, if you will guarantee Louisa's temper.'

'I'll answer for Louisa,' said Lord Pabham.

By the following day the house-party had swollen to larger proportions, and Bilsiter's instinct for self-advertisement expanded duly under the stimulant of an increased audience. At dinner that evening he held forth at length on the subject of unseen forces and untested powers, and his flow of impressive eloquence continued unabated while coffee was being served in the drawing-room preparatory to a general migration to the card-room. His aunt ensured a respectful hearing for his utterances, but her sensation-loving soul hankered after something more dramatic than mere vocal demonstration.

'Won't you do something to *convince* them of your powers, Leonard?' she pleaded; 'change something into another shape. He can, you know, if he only chooses to,' she informed the company.

'Oh, do,' said Mavis Pellington earnestly, and her request was echoed by nearly everyone present. Even those who were not open to conviction were perfectly willing to be entertained by an exhibition of amateur conjuring.

Leonard felt that something tangible was expected of him.

'Has anyone present,' he asked, 'got a threepenny bit or some small object of no particular value —'

'You're surely not going to make coins disappear, or something primitive of that sort?' said Clovis contemptuously.

'I think it very unkind of you not to carry out my suggestion of turning me into a wolf,' said Mary Hampton, as she crossed over to the conservatory to give her macaws their usual tribute from the dessert dishes.

'I have already warned you of the danger of treating these powers in a mocking spirit,' said Leonard solemnly.

'I don't believe you can do it,' laughed Mary provocatively from the conservatory; 'I dare you to do it if you can. I defy you to turn me into a wolf.'

As she said this she was lost to view behind a clump of azaleas.

'Mrs Hampton –' began Leonard with increased solemnity, but he got no further. A breath of chill air seemed to rush across the room, and at the same time the macaws broke forth into ear-splitting screams.

'What on earth is the matter with those confounded birds, Mary?' exclaimed Colonel Hampton; at the same moment an even more piercing scream from Mavis Pellington stampeded the entire company from their seats. In various attitudes of helpless horror or instinctive defence they confronted the evil-looking grey beast that was peering at them from amid a setting of fern and azalea.

Mrs Hoops was the first to recover from the general chaos of fright and bewilderment.

'Leonard!' she screamed shrilly to her nephew, 'turn it back into Mrs Hampton at once! It may fly at us at any moment. Turn it back!'

'I – I don't know how to,' faltered Leonard, who looked more scared and horrified than anyone.

'What!' shouted Colonel Hampton, 'you've taken the abominable liberty of turning my wife into a wolf, and now you stand there calmly and say you can't turn her back again!'

To do strict justice to Leonard, calmness was not a distinguishing feature of his attitude at the moment.

'I assure you I didn't turn Mrs Hampton into a wolf; nothing was farther from my intentions,' he protested.

'Then where is she, and how came that animal into the conservatory?' demanded the Colonel.

'Of course we must accept your assurance that you didn't turn Mrs Hampton into a wolf,' said Clovis politely, 'but you will agree that appearances are against you.'

'Are we to have all these recriminations with that beast standing there ready to tear us to pieces?' wailed Mavis indignantly.

'Lord Pabham, you know a good deal about wild beasts –' suggested Colonel Hampton.

'The wild beasts that I have been accustomed to', said Lord Pabham, 'have come with proper credentials from well-known dealers, or have been bred in my own menagerie. I've never before been confronted with an animal that walks unconcernedly out of an azalea bush, leaving a charming and popular hostess unaccounted for. As far as one can judge from *outward* characteristics,' he continued, 'it has the appearance of a well-grown female of the North American timber-wolf, a variety of the common species *canis lupus*.'

'Oh, never mind its Latin name,' screamed Mavis, as the beast came a step or two further into the room; 'can't you entice it away with food, and shut it up where it can't do any harm?'

'If it is really Mrs Hampton, who has just had a very good dinner, I don't suppose food will appeal to it very strongly,' said Clovis.

'Leonard,' beseeched Mrs Hoops tearfully, 'even if this *is* none of your doing can't you use your great powers to turn this dreadful beast into something harmless before it bites us all – a rabbit or something?'

'I don't suppose Colonel Hampton would care to have his wife turned into a succession of fancy animals as though we were playing a round game with her,' interposed Clovis.

'I absolutely forbid it,' thundered the Colonel.

'Most wolves that I've had anything to do with have been inordinately fond of sugar,' said Lord Pabham; 'if you like I'll try the effect on this one.'

He took a piece of sugar from the saucer of his coffee cup and flung it to the expectant Louisa, who snapped it in mid-air. There was a sigh of relief from the company; a wolf that ate sugar when it might at the least have been employed in tearing macaws to pieces had already shed some of its terrors. The sigh deepened to a gasp of thanksgiving when Lord Pabham decoyed the animal out of the room by a pretended largesse of further sugar. There was an instant rush to the vacated conservatory. There was no trace of Mrs Hampton except the plate containing the macaws' supper.

'The door is locked on the inside!' exclaimed Clovis, who had deftly turned the key as he affected to test it.

Everyone turned towards Bilsiter.

'If you haven't turned my wife into a wolf,' said Colonel Hampton, 'will you kindly explain where she has disappeared to, since she obviously could not have gone through a locked door? I will not press you for an explanation of how a North American timber-wolf suddenly appeared in the conservatory, but I think I have some right to inquire what has become of Mrs Hampton.

Bilsiter's reiterated disclaimer was met with a general murmur of impatient disbelief.

'I refuse to stay another hour under this roof,' declared Mavis Pellington.

'If our hostess has really vanished out of human form,' said Mrs Hoops, 'none of the ladies of the party can very well remain. I absolutely decline to be chaperoned by a wolf!'

'It's a she-wolf,' said Clovis soothingly.

The correct etiquette to be observed under the unusual circumstances received no further elucidation. The sudden entry of Mary Hampton deprived the discussion of its immediate interest.

'Someone has mesmerized me,' she exclaimed crossly; 'I found myself in the game larder, of all places, being fed with sugar by Lord Pabham. I hate being mesmerized, and the doctor has forbidden me to touch sugar.'

The situation was explained to her, as far as it permitted of anything that could be called explanation.

'Then you *really* did turn me into a wolf, Mr Bilsiter?' she exclaimed excitedly.

But Leonard had burned the boat in which he might now have embarked on a sea of glory. He could only shake his head feebly.

'It was I who took that liberty,' said Clovis; 'you see, I happen to have lived for a couple of years in North-Eastern Russia, and I have more than a tourist's acquaintance with the magic craft of that region. One does not care to speak about these strange powers, but once in a way, when one hears a lot of nonsense being talked about them, one is tempted to show what Siberian magic can accomplish in the hands of someone who really understands it. I yielded to that temptation. May I have some brandy? The effort has left me rather faint.'

If Leonard Bilsiter could at that moment have transformed Clovis into a cockroach and then have stepped on him he would gladly have performed both operations.

The Boar-Pig

'There is a back way on to the lawn,' said Mrs Philidore Stossen to her daughter, 'through a small grass paddock and then through a walled fruit garden full of gooseberry bushes. I went all over the place last year when the family were away. There is a door that opens from the fruit garden into a shrubbery, and once we emerge from there we can mingle with the guests as if we had come in by the ordinary way. It's much safer than going in by the front entrance and running the risk of coming bang up against the hostess; that would be so awkward when she doesn't happen to have invited us.'

'Isn't it a lot of trouble to take for getting admittance to a garden party?'

'To a garden party, yes; to *the* garden party of the season, certainly not. Everyone of any consequence in the county, with the exception of ourselves, has been asked to meet the Princess, and it would be far more troublesome to invent explanations as to why we weren't there than to get in by a roundabout way. I stopped Mrs Cuvering in the road yesterday and talked very pointedly about the Princess. If she didn't choose to take the hint and send me an invitation it's not my fault, is it? Here we are: we just cut across the grass and through that little gate into the garden.'

Mrs Stossen and her daughter, suitably arrayed for a county garden party function with an infusion of Almanack de Gotha, sailed through the narrow grass paddock and the ensuing gooseberry garden with the air of state barges making an unofficial progress along a rural trout stream. There was a certain amount of furtive haste mingled with the stateliness of their advance as though hostile searchlights might be turned on them at any moment; and, as a matter of fact, they were not unobserved. Matilda Cuvering, with the alert eyes of thirteen years old and the added advantage of an exalted position in the branches of a medlar tree, had enjoyed a good view of the Stossen flanking movement and had foreseen exactly where it would break down in execution.

'They'll find the door locked, and they'll jolly well have to go back the way they came,' she remarked to herself. 'Serves them right for not coming in by the proper entrance. What a pity Tarquin Superbus isn't loose in the paddock. After all, as everyone else is enjoying themselves, I don't see why Tarquin shouldn't have an afternoon out.

Matilda was of an age when thought is action; she slid down from the branches of the medlar tree, and when she clambered back again, Tarquin, the huge white Yorkshire boar-pig, had exchanged the narrow limits of his sty for the wider range of the grass paddock. The discomfited Stossen expedition, returning in recriminatory but otherwise orderly retreat from the unyielding obstacle of the locked door, came to a sudden halt at the gate dividing the paddock from the gooseberry garden.

'What a villainous-looking animal,' exclaimed Mrs Stossen; 'it wasn't there when we came in.'

'It's there now, anyhow,' said her daughter. 'What on earth are we to do? I wish we had never come.'

The boar-pig had drawn nearer to the gate for a closer inspection of the human intruders, and stood champing his jaws and blinking his small red eyes in a manner that was doubtless intended to be disconcerting, and, as far as the Stossens were concerned, thoroughly achieved that result.

'Shoo! Hish! Hish! Shoo!' cried the ladies in chorus.

'If they think they're going to drive him away by reciting lists of the kings of Israel and Judah they're laying themselves out for disappointment,' observed Matilda from her seat in the medlar tree. As she made the observation aloud Mrs Stossen became for the first time aware of her presence. A moment or two earlier she would have been anything but pleased at the discovery that the garden was not as deserted as it looked, but now she hailed the fact of the child's presence on the scene with absolute relief.

'Little girl, can you find someone to drive away –' she began hopefully.

'*Comment? Comprends pas*,' was the response.

'Oh, are you French? *Êtes vous française?*'

'*Pas de tous. 'Suis anglaise.*'

'Then why not talk English? I want to know if –'

'*Permettez-moi expliquer.* You see, I'm rather under a cloud,' said Matilda. 'I'm staying with my aunt, and I was told I must behave particularly well today, as lots of people were coming for a garden party, and I was told to imitate Claude, that's my young cousin, who never does anything wrong except by accident, and then is always apologetic about it. It seems they thought I ate too much raspberry trifle at lunch, and they said Claude never eats too much raspberry trifle. Well, Claude always goes to sleep for half an hour after lunch, because he's told to, and I waited till he was asleep, and tied his hands and started forcible feeding with a whole bucketful of raspberry trifle that they were keeping for the garden party. Lots of it went on to his sailor-suit and some of it on to the bed, but a good deal went down Claude's throat, and they can't say again that he has never been known to eat too much raspberry trifle. That is why I am not allowed to go to the party, and as an additional punishment I must speak French all the afternoon. I've had to tell you all this in English, as there were words like "forcible feeding" that I didn't know the French for; of course I could have invented them, but if I had said *nourriture obligatoire* you wouldn't have had the least idea what I was talking about. *Mais maintenant, nous parlons français.*'

'Oh, very well, *très bien*,' said Mrs Stossen reluctantly; in moments of flurry such French as she knew was not under very good control. '*Là, à l'autre côté de la porte, est un cochon* –'

'*Un cochon? Ah, le petit charmant!*' exclaimed Matilda with enthusiasm.

'*Mais non, pas du tout petit, et pas du tout charmant; un bête féroce* –'

'*Une bête*,' corrected Matilda; 'a pig is masculine as long as you call it a pig, but if you lose your temper with it and call it a ferocious beast it becomes one of us at once. French is a dreadfully unsexing language.'

'For goodness' sake let us talk English then,' said Mrs Stossen. 'Is there any way out of this garden except through the paddock where the pig is?'

'I always go over the wall, by way of the plum tree,' said Matilda.

'Dressed as we are we could hardly do that,' said Mrs Stossen; it was difficult to imagine her doing it in any costume.

'Do you think you could go and get someone who would drive the pig away?' asked Miss Stossen.

'I promised my aunt I would stay here till five o'clock; it's not four yet.'

'I am sure, under the circumstances, your aunt would permit –'

'My conscience would not permit,' said Matilda with cold dignity.

'We can't stay here till five o'clock,' exclaimed Mrs Stossen with growing exasperation.

'Shall I recite to you to make the time pass quicker?' asked Matilda obligingly. ' "Belinda, the little Breadwinner," is considered my best piece, or, perhaps, it ought to be something in French. Henri Quatre's address to his soldiers is the only thing I really know in that language.'

'If you will go and fetch someone to drive that animal away I will give you something to buy yourself a nice present,' said Mrs Stossen.

Matilda came several inches lower down the medlar tree.

'That is the most practical suggestion you have made yet for getting out of the garden,' she remarked cheerfully; 'Claude and I are collecting money for the Children's Fresh Air Fund, and we are seeing which of us can collect the biggest sum.'

'I shall be very glad to contribute half a crown, very glad indeed,' said Mrs Stossen, digging that coin out of the depths of a receptacle which formed a detached outwork of her toilet.

'Claude is a long way ahead of me at present,' continued Matilda, taking no notice of the suggested offering; 'you see, he's only eleven, and has golden hair, and those are enormous advantages when you're on the collecting job. Only the other day a Russian lady gave him ten shillings. Russians understand the art of giving far better than we do. I expect Claude will net quite twenty-five shillings this afternoon; he'll have the field to himself, and he'll be able to do the pale, fragile, not-long-for-this-world business to perfection after his raspberry trifle experience. Yes, he'll be *quite* two pounds ahead of me by now.'

With much probing and plucking and many regretful murmurs the beleaguered ladies managed to produce seven-and-sixpence between them.

'I am afraid this is all we've got,' said Mrs Stossen.

Matilda showed no sign of coming down either to the earth or to their figure.

'I could not do violence to my conscience for anything less than ten shillings,' she announced stiffly.

Mother and daughter muttered certain remarks under their breath, in which the word 'beast' was prominent, and probably had no reference to Tarquin.

'I find I *have* got another half-crown,' said Mrs Stossen in a shaking voice; 'here you are. Now please fetch someone quickly.'

Matilda slipped down from the tree, took possession of the donation, and proceeded to pick up a handful of over-ripe medlars from the grass at her feet. Then she climbed over the gate and addressed herself affectionately to the boar-pig.

'Come, Tarquin, dear old boy; you know you can't resist medlars when they're rotten and squashy.'

Tarquin couldn't. By dint of throwing the fruit in front of him at judicious intervals Matilda decoyed him back to his sty, while the delivered captives hurried across the paddock.

'Well, I never! The little minx!' exclaimed Mrs Stossen when she was safely on the high road. 'The animal wasn't savage at all, and as for the ten shillings, I don't believe the Fresh Air Fund will see a penny of it!'

There she was unwarrantably harsh in her judgment. If you examine the books of the fund you will find the acknowledgment: 'Collected by Miss Matilda Cuvering, 2s.6d.'

The Cobweb

The farmhouse kitchen probably stood where it did as a matter of accident or haphazard choice; yet its situation might have been planned by a master-strategist in farmhouse architecture. Dairy and poultry-yard, and herb garden, and all the busy places of the farm seemed to lead by easy access into its wide flagged haven, where there was room for everything and where muddy boots left traces that were easily swept away. And yet, for all that it stood so well in the centre of human bustle, its long, latticed window, with the wide window-seat, built into an embrasure beyond the huge fireplace, looked out on a wild spreading view of hill and heather and wooded combe. The window nook made almost a little room in itself, quite the pleasantest room in the farm as far as situation and capabilities went. Young Mrs Ladbruk, whose husband had just come into the farm by way of inheritance, cast covetous eyes on this snug corner, and her fingers itched to make it bright and cosy with chintz curtains and bowls of flowers, and a shelf or two of old china. The musty farm parlour, looking out to a prim, cheerless garden imprisoned within high, blank walls, was not a room that lent itself readily either to comfort or decoration.

'When we are more settled I shall work wonders in the way of making the kitchen habitable,' said the young woman to her occasional visitors. There was an unspoken wish in those words, a wish which was unconfessed as well as unspoken. Emma Ladbruk was the mistress of the farm; jointly with her husband she might have her say, and to a certain extent her way, in ordering its affairs. But she was not mistress of the kitchen.

On one of the shelves of an old dresser, in company with chipped sauce-boats, pewter jugs, cheese-graters, and paid bills, rested a worn and ragged Bible, on whose front page was the record, in faded ink, of a baptism dated ninety-four years ago. 'Martha Crale' was the name written on that yellow page. The yellow, wrinkled old dame who hobbled and muttered about the kitchen, looking like a dead autumn leaf which the winter winds still pushed hither and thither, had once been Martha Crale; for seventy odd years she had been Martha Mountjoy. For longer than anyone could remember she had pattered to and fro between oven and wash-house and dairy, and out to chicken-run and garden, grumbling and muttering and scolding, but working unceasingly. Emma Ladbruk, of whose coming she took as little notice as she would of a bee wandering in at a window on a summer's day, used at first to watch her with a kind of frightened curiosity. She was so old and so much a part of the place, it was difficult to think of her exactly as a living thing. Old Shep, the white-nozzled, stiff-limbed collie, waiting for his time to die, seemed almost more human than the withered, dried-up old woman. He had been a riotous, roystering puppy, mad with the joy of life, when she was already a tottering, hobbling dame; now he was just a blind, breathing carcase, nothing more, and she still worked with frail energy, still swept and baked and washed, fetched and carried. If there were something in these wise old dogs that did not perish utterly with death, Emma used to think to herself, what generations of ghost-dogs there must be out on those hills, that Martha had reared and fed and tended and spoken a last good-bye word to in that old kitchen. And what memories she must have of human generations that had passed away in her time. It was difficult for anyone, let alone a stranger like Emma, to get her to talk of the days that had been; her shrill, quavering speech was of doors that had been left unfastened, pails that had got mislaid, calves whose feeding-time was overdue, and the various little faults and lapses that chequer a farmhouse routine. Now and again, when election time came round, she would unstore her recollections of the old names round which the fight had waged in the days gone by. There had been a Palmerston, that had been a name down Tiverton way; Tiverton was not a far journey as the crow flies, but to Martha it was almost a foreign country. Later there had been Northcotes and Aclands, and many other newer names that she had forgotten; the names changed, but it was always Libruls and Toories, Yellows and Blues. And they always quarrelled and shouted as to who was right and who was wrong. The one they quarrelled about most was a fine old gentleman with an angry face – she had seen his picture on the walls. She had seen it on the floor too, with a rotten apple squashed over it, for the farm had changed its politics from time to time. Martha had never been on one side or the other; none of 'they' had ever done the farm a stroke of good. Such was her sweeping verdict, given with all a peasant's distrust of the outside world.

When the half-frightened curiosity had somewhat faded away, Emma Ladbruk was uncomfortably conscious of another feeling towards the old woman. She was a quaint old tradition, lingering about the place, she was part and parcel of the farm itself, she was something at once pathetic and picturesque – but she was dreadfully in the way. Emma had come to the farm full of plans for little reforms and improvements, in part the result of training in the newest ways and methods, in part the outcome of her own ideas and fancies. Reforms in the kitchen region, if those deaf old ears could have been induced to give them even a hearing, would have met with short shrift and scornful rejection, and the kitchen region spread over the zone of dairy and market business and half the work of the household. Emma, with the latest science of dead-poultry dressing at her fingertips, sat by, an unheeded watcher, while old Martha trussed the chickens for the market-stall as she had trussed them for nearly four-score years – all leg and no breast. And the hundred hints anent effective cleaning and labour-lightening and the things that make for wholesomeness which the young woman was ready to impart or to put into action dropped away into nothingness before that wan, muttering, unheeding presence. Above all, the coveted window corner, that was to be a dainty, cheerful oasis in the gaunt old kitchen, stood now choked and lumbered with a litter of odds and ends that Emma, for all her nominal authority, would not have dared or cared to displace; over them seemed to be spun the protection of something that was like a human cobweb. Decidedly Martha was in the way. It would have been an unworthy meanness to have wished to see the span of that brave old life shortened by a few paltry months, but as the days sped by Emma was conscious that the wish was there, disowned though it might be, lurking at the back of her mind.

She felt the meanness of the wish come over her with a qualm of self-reproach one day when she came into the kitchen and found an unaccustomed state of things in that usually busy quarter. Old Martha was not working. A basket of corn was on the floor by her side, and out in the yard the poultry were beginning to clamour a protest of overdue feeding-time. But Martha sat huddled in a shrunken bunch on the window seat, looking out with her dim old eyes as though she saw something stranger than the autumn landscape.

'Is anything the matter, Martha?' asked the young woman.

' 'Tis death, 'tis death a-coming,' answered the quavering voice; 'I knew 'twere coming. I knew it. 'Tweren't for nothing that old Shep's been howling all morning. An' last night I heard the screech-owl give the death-cry, and there were something white as run across the yard yesterday; 'tweren't a cat nor a stoat, 'twere something. The fowls knew 'twere something; they all drew off to one side. Ay, there's been warnings. I knew it were a-coming.'

The young woman's eyes clouded with pity. The old thing sitting there so white and shrunken had once been a merry, noisy child, playing about in lanes and hay-lofts and farmhouse garrets; that had been eighty odd years ago, and now she was just a frail old body cowering under the approaching chill of the death that was coming at last to take her. It was not probable that much could be done for her, but Emma hastened away to get assistance and counsel. Her husband, she knew, was down at a tree-felling some little distance off, but she might find some other intelligent soul who knew the old woman better than she did. The farm, she soon found out, had that faculty common to farmyards of swallowing up and losing its human population. The poultry followed her in interested fashion, the swine grunted interrogations at her from behind the bars of their styes, but barnyard and rickyard, orchard and stables and dairy, gave no reward to her search. Then, as she retraced her steps towards the kitchen, she came suddenly on her cousin, young Mr Jim, as everyone called him, who divided his time between amateur horse-dealing, rabbit-shooting, and flirting with the farm maids.

'I'm afraid old Martha is dying,' said Emma. Jim was not the sort of person to whom one had to break news gently.

'Nonsense,' he said; 'Martha means to live to a hundred. She told me so, and she'll do it.'

'She may be actually dying at this moment, or it may just be the beginning of the break-up,' persisted Emma, with a feeling of contempt for the slowness and dullness of the young man.

A grin spread over his good-natured features.

'It don't look like it,' he said, nodding towards the yard. Emma turned to catch the meaning of his remark. Old Martha stood in the middle of a mob of poultry scattering handfuls of grain around her. The turkey-cock, with the bronzed sheen of his feathers and the purple-red of his wattles, the gamecock with the glowing metallic lustre of his Eastern plumage, the hens, with their ochres and buffs and umbers and their scarlet combs, and the drakes, with their bottle-green heads, made a medley of rich colour, in the centre of which the old woman looked like a withered stalk standing amid the riotous growth of gaily-hued flowers. But she threw the grain deftly amid the wilderness of beaks, and her quavering voice carried as far as the two people who were watching her. She was still harping on the theme of death coming to the farm.

'I knew 'twere a-coming. There's been signs an' warnings.'

'Who's dead, then, old Mother?' called out the young man.

' 'Tis young Mister Ladbruk,' she shrilled back; 'they've just a-carried his body in. Run out of the way of a tree that was coming down an' ran hisself on to an iron post. Dead when they picked un up. Aye, I knew 'twere coming.'

And she turned to fling a handful of barley at a belated group of guinea-fowl that came racing toward her.

The farm was a family property, and passed to the rabbit-shooting cousin as the next-of-kin. Emma Ladbruk drifted out of its history as a bee that had wandered in at an open window might flit its way out again. On a cold grey morning she stood waiting with her boxes already stowed in the farm cart, till the last of the market produce should be ready, for the train she was to catch was of less importance than the chickens and butter and eggs that were to be offered for sale. From where she stood she could see an angle of the long latticed window that was to have been cosy with curtains and gay with bowls of flowers. Into her mind came the thought that for months, perhaps for years, long after she had been utterly forgotten, a white, unheeding face would be seen peering out through those latticed panes, and a weak muttering voice would be heard quavering up and down those flagged passages. She made her way to a narrow barred casement that opened into the farm larder. Old Martha was standing at a table trussing a pair of chickens for the market stall as she had trussed them for nearly fourscore years.

The Elk

Teresa, Mrs Thropplestance, was the richest and most intractable old woman in the county of Woldshire. In her dealings with the world in general her manner suggested a blend between a Mistress of the Robes and a Master of Foxhounds, with the vocabulary of both. In her domestic circle she comported herself in the arbitrary style that one attributes, probably without the least justification, to an American political Boss in the bosom of his caucus. The late Theodore Thropplestance had left her, some thirty-five years ago, in absolute possession of a considerable fortune, a large landed property, and a gallery full of valuable pictures. In those intervening years she had outlived her son and quarrelled with her elder grandson, who had married without her consent or approval. Bertie Thropplestance, her younger grandson, was the heir-designate to her property, and as such he was a centre of interest and concern to some half-hundred ambitious mothers with daughters of marriageable age. Bertie was an amiable, easy-going young man, who was quite ready to marry anyone who was favourably recommended to his notice, but he was not going to waste his time in falling in love with anyone who would come under his grandmother's veto. The favourable recommendation would have to come from Mrs Thropplestance.

Teresa's house-parties were always rounded off with a plentiful garnishing of presentable young women and alert, attendant mothers, but the old lady was emphatically discouraging whenever any one of her girl guests became at all likely to outbid the others as a possible granddaughter-in-law. It was the inheritance of her fortune and estate that was in question, and she was evidently disposed to exercise and enjoy her powers of selection and rejection to the utmost. Bertie's preferences did not greatly matter; he was of the sort who can be stolidly happy with any kind of wife; he had cheerfully put up with his grandmother all his life, so he was not likely to fret and fume over anything that might befall him in the way of a helpmate.

The party that gathered under Teresa's roof in Christmas week of the year nineteen-hundred-and-something was of smaller proportions than usual, and Mrs Yonelet, who formed one of the party, was inclined to deduce hopeful augury from this circumstance. Dora Yonelet and Bertie were so obviously made for one another, she confided to the vicar's wife, and if the old lady were accustomed to seeing them about a lot together she might adopt the view that they would make a suitable married couple.

'People soon get used to an idea if it is dangled constantly before their eyes,' said Mrs Yonelet hopefully, 'and the more often Teresa sees those young people together, happy in each other's company, the more she will get to take a kindly interest in Dora as a possible and desirable wife for Bertie.'

'My dear,' said the vicar's wife resignedly, 'my own Sybil was thrown together with Bertie under the most romantic circumstances – I'll tell you about it some day – but it made no impression whatever on Teresa; she put her foot down in the most uncompromising fashion, and Sybil married an Indian civilian.'

'Quite right of her,' said Mrs Yonelet with vague approval; 'it's what any girl of spirit would have done. Still, that was a year or two ago, I believe; Bertie is older now, and so is Teresa. Naturally she must be anxious to see him settled.'

The vicar's wife reflected that Teresa seemed to be the one person who showed no immediate anxiety to supply Bertie with a wife, but she kept the thought to herself.

Mrs Yonelet was a woman of resourceful energy and generalship; she involved the other members of the house-party, the deadweight, so to speak, in all manner of exercises and occupations that segregated them from Bertie and Dora, who were left to their own devisings – that is to say, to Dora's devisings and Bertie's accommodating acquiescence. Dora helped in the Christmas decorations of the parish church, and Bertie helped her to help. Together they fed the swans, till the birds went on a dyspepsia-strike, together they played billiards, together they photographed the village almshouses, and, at a respectful distance, the tame elk that browsed in solitary aloofness in the park. It was 'tame' in the sense that it had long ago discarded the least vestige of fear of the human race; nothing in its record encouraged its human neighbours to feel a reciprocal confidence.

Whatever sport or exercise or occupation Bertie and Dora indulged in together was unfailingly chronicled and advertised by Mrs Yonelet for the due enlightenment of Bertie's grandmother.

'Those two inseparables have just come in from a bicycle ride,' she would announce; 'quite a picture they make, so fresh and glowing after their spin.'

'A picture needing words,' would be Teresa's private comment, and as far as Bertie was concerned she was determined that the words should remain unspoken.

On the afternoon after Christmas Day Mrs Yonelet dashed into the drawing-room, where her hostess was sitting amid a circle of guests and tea-cups and muffin dishes. Fate had placed what seemed like a trump-card in the hands of the patiently-manœuvring mother. With eyes blazing with excitement and a voice heavily escorted with exclamation marks she made a dramatic announcement.

'Bertie has saved Dora from the elk!'

In swift, excited sentences, broken with maternal emotion, she gave supplementary information as to how the treacherous animal had ambushed Dora as she was hunting for a strayed golf ball, and how Bertie had dashed to her rescue with a stable fork and driven the beast off in the nick of time.

'It was touch and go! She threw her niblick at it, but that didn't stop it. In another moment she would have been crushed beneath its hoofs,' panted Mrs Yonelet.

'The animal is not safe,' said Teresa, handing her agitated guest a cup of tea. 'I forget if you take sugar. I suppose the solitary life it leads has soured its temper. There are muffins in the grate. It's not my fault; I've tried to get it a mate for ever so long. You don't know of anyone with a lady elk for sale or exchange, do you?' she asked the company generally.

But Mrs Yonelet was in no humour to listen to talk of elk marriages. The mating of two human beings was the subject uppermost in her mind, and the opportunity for advancing her pet project was too valuable to be neglected.

'Teresa,' she exclaimed impressively, 'after those two young people have been thrown together so dramatically, nothing can be quite the same again between them. Bertie has done more than save Dora's life; he has earned her affection. One cannot help feeling that Fate has consecrated them for one another.'

'Exactly what the vicar's wife said when Bertie saved Sybil from the elk a year or two ago,' observed Teresa placidly; 'I pointed out to her that he had rescued Mirabel Hicks from the same predicament a few months previously, and that priority really belonged to the gardener's boy, who had been rescued in the January of that year. There is a good deal of sameness in country life, you know.'

'It seems to be a very dangerous animal,' said one of the guests.

'That's what the mother of the gardener's boy said,' remarked Teresa; 'she wanted me to have it destroyed, but I pointed out to her that she had eleven children and I had only one elk. I also gave her a black silk skirt; she said that though there hadn't been a funeral in her family, she felt as if there had been. Anyhow, we parted friends. I can't offer you a silk skirt, Emily, but you may have another cup of tea. As I have already remarked, there are muffins in the grate.'

Teresa closed the discussion, having deftly conveyed the impression that she considered the mother of the gardener's boy had shown a far more reasonable spirit than the parents of other elk-assaulted victims.

'Teresa is devoid of feeling,' said Mrs Yonelet afterwards to the vicar's wife; 'to sit there, talking of muffins, with an appalling tragedy only narrowly averted –'

'Of course you know whom she really intends Bertie to marry?'

asked the vicar's wife; 'I've noticed it for some time. The Bickelby's German governess.'

'A German governess! What an idea!' gasped Mrs Yonelet.

'She's of quite good family, I believe,' said the vicar's wife, 'and not at all the mouse-in-the-background sort of person that governesses are usually supposed to be. In fact, next to Teresa, she's about the most assertive and combative personality in the neighbourhood. She's pointed out to my husband all sorts of errors in his sermons, and she gave Sir Laurence a public lecture on how he ought to handle the hounds. You know how sensitive Sir Laurence is about any criticism of his Mastership, and to have a governess laying down the law to him nearly drove him into a fit. She's behaved like that to everyone, except, of course, Teresa, and everyone has been defensively rude to her in return. The Bickelbys are simply too afraid of her to get rid of her. Now isn't that exactly the sort of woman whom Teresa would take a delight in installing as her successor? Imagine the discomfort and awkwardness in the county if we suddenly found that she was to be the future hostess at the Hall. Teresa's only regret will be that she won't be alive to see it.'

'But', objected Mrs Yonelet, 'surely Bertie hasn't shown the least sign of being attracted in that quarter?'

'Oh, she's quite nice-looking in a way, and dresses well, and plays a good game of tennis. She often comes across the park with messages from the Bickelby mansion, and one of these days Bertie will rescue her from the elk, which has become almost a habit with him, and Teresa will say that Fate has consecrated them to one another. Bertie might not be disposed to pay much attention to the consecrations of Fate, but he would not dream of opposing his grandmother.'

The vicar's wife spoke with the quiet authority of one who has intuitive knowledge, and in her heart of hearts Mrs Yonelet believed her.

Six months later the elk had to be destroyed. In a fit of exceptional moroseness it had killed the Bickelby's German governess. It was an irony of its fate that it should achieve popularity in the last moments of its career; at any rate, it established the record of being the only living thing that had permanently thwarted Teresa

Thropplestance's plans.

Dora Yonelet broke off her engagement with an Indian civilian, and married Bertie three months after his grandmother's death – Teresa did not long survive the German governess fiasco. At Christmas time every year young Mrs Thropplestance hangs an extra large festoon of evergreens on the elk horns that decorate the hall.

'It was a fearsome beast,' she observes to Bertie, 'but I always feel that it was instrumental in bringing us together.'

Which, of course, was true.

The Stake

'Ronnie is a great trial to me,' said Mrs Attray plaintively. 'Only eighteen years old last February and already a confirmed gambler. I am sure I don't know where he inherits it from; his father never touched cards, and you know how little I play – a game of bridge on Wednesday afternoons in the winter, for threepence a hundred, and even that I shouldn't do if it wasn't that Edith always wants a fourth and could be certain to ask that detestable Jenkinham woman if she couldn't get me. I would much rather sit and talk any day than play bridge; cards are such a waste of time, I think. But as to Ronnie, bridge and baccarat and poker-patience are positively all that he thinks about. Of course I've done my best to stop it; I've asked the Norridrums not to let him play cards when he's over there, but you might as well ask the Atlantic Ocean to keep quiet for a crossing as expect them to bother about a mother's natural anxieties.'

'Why do you let him go there?' asked Eleanor Saxelby.

'My dear,' said Mrs Attray, 'I don't want to offend them. After all, they are my landlords and I have to look to them for anything I want done about the place; they were very accommodating about the new roof for the orchid house. And they lend me one of their cars when mine is out of order; you know how often it gets out of order.'

'I don't know how often,' said Eleanor, 'but it must happen very frequently. Whenever I want you to take me anywhere in your car I am always told that there is something wrong with it, or else that the chauffeur has got neuralgia and you don't like to ask him to go out.'

'He suffers quite a lot from neuralgia,' said Mrs Attray hastily. 'Anyhow,' she continued, 'you can understand that I don't want to offend the Norridrums. Their household is the most rackety one in the county, and I believe no one ever knows to an hour or two when any particular meal will appear on the table or what it will consist of when it does appear.'

Eleanor Saxelby shuddered. She liked her meals to be of regular occurrence and assured proportions.

'Still,' pursued Mrs Attray, 'whatever their own home life may be, as landlords and neighbours they are considerate and obliging, so I don't want to quarrel with them. Besides, if Ronnie didn't play cards there he'd be playing somewhere else.'

'Not if you were firm with him,' said Eleanor; 'I believe in being firm.'

'Firm? I am firm,' exclaimed Mrs Attray; 'I am more than firm – I am farseeing. I've done everything I can think of to prevent Ronnie from playing for money. I've stopped his allowance for the rest of the year, so he can't even gamble on credit, and I've subscribed a lump sum to the church offertory in his name instead of giving him instalments of small silver to put in the bag on Sundays. I wouldn't even let him have the money to tip the hunt servants with, but sent it by postal order. He was furiously sulky about it, but I reminded him of what happened to the ten shillings that I gave him for the Young Men's Endeavour League "Self-Denial Week".'

'What did happen to it?' asked Eleanor.

'Well, Ronnie did some preliminary endeavouring with it, on his own account, in connection with the Grand National. If it had come off, as he expressed it, he would have given the League twenty-five shillings and netted a comfortable commission for himself; as it was, that ten shillings was one of the things the League had to deny itself. Since then I've been careful not to let him have a penny piece in his hands.'

'He'll get round that in some way,' said Eleanor with quiet conviction; 'he'll sell things.'

'My dear, he's done all that is to be done in that direction already. He's got rid of his wrist-watch and his hunting flask and both his cigarette cases, and I shouldn't be surprised if he's wearing imitation-gold sleeve links instead of those his Aunt Rhoda gave him on his seventeenth birthday. He can't sell his clothes, of course, except his winter overcoat, and I've locked that up in the camphor cupboard on the pretext of preserving it from moth. I really don't see what else he can raise money on. I consider that I've been both firm and farseeing.'

'Has he been at the Norridrums lately?' asked Eleanor.

'He was there yesterday afternoon and stayed to dinner,' said Mrs Attray. 'I don't quite know when he came home, but I fancy it was late.'

'Then depend on it he was gambling,' said Eleanor, with the assured air of one who has few ideas and makes the most of them. 'Late hours in the country always mean gambling.'

'He can't gamble if he has no money and no chance of getting any,' argued Mrs Attray; 'even if one plays for small stakes one must have a decent prospect of paying one's losses.'

'He may have sold some of the Amherst pheasant chicks,' suggested Eleanor; 'they would fetch about ten or twelve shillings each, I dare say.'

'Ronnie wouldn't do such a thing,' said Mrs Attray; 'and anyhow I went and counted them this morning and they're all there. No,' she continued, with the quiet satisfaction that comes from a sense of painstaking and merited achievement, 'I fancy that Ronnie had to content himself with the role of onlooker last night, as far as the card-table was concerned.'

'Is that clock right?' asked Eleanor, whose eyes had been straying restlessly towards the mantelpiece for some little time; 'lunch is usually so punctual in your establishment.'

'Three minutes past the half-hour,' exclaimed Mrs Attray; 'cook must be preparing something unusually sumptuous in your honour. I am not in the secret; I've been out all the morning, you know.'

Eleanor smiled forgivingly. A special effort by Mrs Attray's cook was worth waiting a few minutes for.

As a matter of fact, the luncheon fare, when it made its tardy appearance, was distinctly unworthy of the reputation which the justly-treasured cook had built up for herself. The soup alone would have sufficed to cast a gloom over any meal that it had inaugurated, and it was not redeemed by anything that followed. Eleanor said little, but when she spoke there was a hint of tears in her voice that was far more eloquent than outspoken denunciation would have been, and even the insouciant Ronald showed traces of depression when he tasted the rognons Saltikoff.

'Not quite the best luncheon I've enjoyed in your house,' said Eleanor at last, when her final hope had flickered out with the savoury.

'My dear, it's the worst meal I've sat down to for years,' said her hostess; 'that last dish tasted principally of red pepper and wet toast. I'm awfully sorry. Is anything the matter in the kitchen, Pellin?' she asked of the attendant maid.

'Well, ma'am, the new cook hadn't hardly time to see to things properly, coming in so sudden –' commenced Pellin by way of explanation.

'The *new* cook!' screamed Mrs Attray.

'Colonel Norridrum's cook, ma'am,' said Pellin.

'What on earth do you mean? What is Colonel Norridrum's cook doing in my kitchen – and where is *my* cook?'

'Perhaps I can explain better than Pellin can,' said Ronald hurriedly; 'the fact is, I was dining at the Norridrums' yesterday, and they were wishing they had a swell cook like yours, just for today and tomorrow, while they've got some gourmet staying with them; their own cook is no earthly good – well, you've seen what she turns out when she's at all flurried. So I thought it would be rather sporting to play them at baccarat for the loan of our cook against a money stake, and I lost, that's all. I have had rotten luck at baccarat all this year.'

The remainder of his explanation, of how he had assured the cooks that the temporary transfer had his mother's sanction, and had smuggled the one out and the other in during the maternal absence, was drowned in the outcry of scandalized upbraiding.

'If I had sold the woman into slavery there couldn't have been a bigger fuss about it,' he confided afterwards to Bertie Norridrum, 'and Eleanor Saxelby raged and ramped the louder of the two. I tell you what, I'll bet you two of the Amherst pheasants to five shillings that she refuses to have me as a partner at the croquet tournament. We're drawn together, you know.'

This time he won his bet.

The Name-Day

Adventures, according to the proverb, are to the adventurous. Quite as often they are to the non-adventurous, to the retiring, to the constitutionally timid. John James Abbleway had been endowed by Nature with the sort of disposition that instinctively avoids Carlist intrigues, slum crusades, the tracking of wounded wild beasts, and the moving of hostile amendments at political meetings. If a mad dog or a Mad Mullah had come his way he would have surrendered the way without hesitation. At school he had unwillingly acquired a thorough knowledge of the German tongue out of deference to the plainly-expressed wishes of a foreign-languages master, who, though he taught modern subjects, employed old-fashioned methods in driving his lessons home. It was this enforced familiarity with an important commercial language which thrust Abbleway in later years into strange lands where adventures were less easy to guard against than in the ordered atmosphere of an English country town. The firm that he worked for saw fit to send him one day on a prosaic business errand to the far city of Vienna, and, having sent him there, continued to keep him there, still engaged in humdrum affairs of commerce, but with the possibilities of romance and adventure, or even misadventure, jostling at his elbow. After two and a half years of exile, however, John James Abbleway had embarked on only one hazardous undertaking, and that was of a nature which would assuredly have overtaken him sooner or later if he had been leading a sheltered, stay-at-home existence at Dorking or Huntingdon. He fell placidly in love with a placidly lovable English girl, the sister of one of his commercial colleagues, who was improving her mind by a short trip to foreign parts, and in due course he was formally accepted as the young man she was engaged to. The further step by which she was to become Mrs John Abbleway was to take place a twelvemonth hence in a town in the English midlands, by which time the firm that employed John James would have no further need for his presence in the Austrian capital.

It was early in April, two months after the installation of Abbleway as the young man Miss Penning was engaged to, when he received a letter from her, written from Venice. She was still peregrinating under the wing of her brother, and as the latter's business arrangements would take him across to Fiume for a day or two, she had conceived the idea that it would be rather jolly if John could obtain leave of absence and run down to the Adriatic coast to meet them. She had looked up the route on the map, and the journey did not appear likely to be expensive. Between the lines of her communication there lay a hint that if he really cared for her –

Abbleway obtained leave of absence and added a journey to Fiume to his life's adventures. He left Vienna on a cold, cheerless day. The flower shops were full of spring blooms, and the weekly organs of illustrated humour were full of spring topics, but the skies were heavy with clouds that looked like cotton-wool that has been kept over long in a shop window.

'Snow comes,' said the train official to the station officials; and they agreed that snow was about to come. And it came, rapidly, plenteously. The train had not been more than an hour on its journey when the cotton-wool clouds commenced to dissolve in a blinding downpour of snowflakes. The forest trees on either side of the line were speedily coated with a heavy white mantle, the telegraph wires became thick glistening ropes, the line itself was buried more and more completely under a carpeting of snow, through which the not very powerful engine ploughed its way with increasing difficulty. The Vienna-Fiume line is scarcely the best equipped of the Austrian State railways, and Abbleway began to have serious fears for a breakdown. The train had slowed down to a painful and precarious crawl and presently came to a halt at a spot where the drifting snow had accumulated in a formidable barrier. The engine made a special effort and broke through the obstruction, but in the course of another twenty minutes it was again held up. The process of breaking through was renewed and the train doggedly resumed its way, encountering and surmounting fresh hindrances at frequent intervals. After a standstill of unusually long duration in a particularly deep drift the compartment in which Abbleway was sitting gave a huge jerk and a lurch, and then seemed to remain stationary; it undoubtedly was not moving, and yet he could hear the puffing of the engine and the slow rumbling and jolting of wheels. The puffing and rumbling grew fainter, as though it were dying away through the agency of intervening distance. Abbleway suddenly gave vent to an exclamation of scandalized alarm, opened the window, and peered out into the snowstorm. The flakes perched on his eyelashes and blurred his vision, but he saw enough to help him to realize what had happened. The engine had made a mighty plunge through the drift and had gone merrily forward, lightened of the load of its rear carriage, whose coupling had snapped under the strain. Abbleway was alone, or almost alone, with a derelict railway waggon, in the heart of some Styrian or Croatian forest. In the third-class compartment next to his own he remembered to have seen a peasant woman, who had entered the train at a small wayside station. 'With the exception of that woman,' he exclaimed dramatically to himself, 'the nearest living beings are probably a pack of wolves.'

Before making his way to the third-class compartment to acquaint his fellow-traveller with the extent of the disaster Abbleway hurriedly pondered the question of the woman's nationality. He had acquired a smattering of Slavonic tongues during his residence in Vienna, and felt competent to grapple with several racial possibilities.

'If she is Croat or Serb or Bosniak I shall be able to make her understand,' he promised himself. 'If she is Magyar, heaven help me! We shall have to converse entirely by signs.'

He entered the carriage and made his momentous announcement in the best approach to Croat speech that he could achieve.

'The train has broken away and left us!'

The woman shook her head with a movement that might be intended to convey resignation to the will of heaven, but probably meant noncomprehension. Abbleway repeated his information with variations of Slavonic tongues and generous displays of pantomime.

'Ah,' said the woman at last in German dialect, 'the train has gone? We are left. Ah, so.'

She seemed about as much interested as though Abbleway had told her the result of the municipal elections in Amsterdam.

'They will find out at some station, and when the line is clear of snow they will send an engine. It happens that way sometimes.'

'We may be here all night!' exclaimed Abbleway.

The woman looked as though she thought it possible.

'Are there wolves in these parts?' asked Abbleway hurriedly.

'Many,' said the woman; 'just outside this forest my aunt was devoured three years ago, as she was coming home from market. The horse and a young pig that was in the cart were eaten too. The horse was a very old one, but it was a beautiful young pig, oh, so fat. I cried when I heard that it was taken. They spare nothing.'

'They may attack us here,' said Abbleway tremulously; 'they could easily break in, these carriages are like matchwood. We may both be devoured.'

'You, perhaps,' said the woman calmly; 'not me.'

'Why not you?' demanded Abbleway.

'It is the day of Saint Mariä Kleophä, my name-day. She would not allow me to be eaten by wolves on her day. Such a thing could not be thought of. You, yes, but not me.'

Abbleway changed the subject.

'It is only afternoon now; if we are to be left here till morning we shall be starving.'

'I have here some good eatables,' said the woman tranquilly; 'on my festival day it is natural that I should have provision with me. I have five good blood-sausages; in the town shops they cost twenty-five heller each. Things are dear in the town shops.'

'I will give you fifty heller apiece for a couple of them,' said Abbleway with some enthusiasm.

'In a railway accident things become very dear,' said the woman; 'these blood-sausages are four kronen apiece.'

'Four kronen!' exclaimed Abbleway; 'four kronen for a blood sausage!'

'You cannot get them any cheaper on this train,' said the woman, with relentless logic, 'because there aren't any others to get. In Agram you can buy them cheaper, and in Paradise no doubt they will be given to us for nothing, but here they cost four kronen each. I have a small piece of Emmenthaler cheese and a honey-cake and a piece of bread that I can let you have. That will be another three kronen, eleven kronen in all. There is a piece of ham, but that I cannot let you have on my name-day.'

Abbleway wondered to himself what price she would have put on the ham, and hurried to pay her the eleven kronen before her emergency tariff expanded into a famine tariff. As he was taking possession of his modest store of eatables he suddenly heard a noise which set his heart thumping in a miserable fever of fear. There was a scraping and shuffling as of some animal or animals trying to climb up to the footboard. In another moment, through the snow-encrusted glass of the carriage window, he saw a gaunt prick-eared head, with gaping jaw and lolling tongue and gleaming teeth; a second later another head shot up.

'There are hundreds of them,' whispered Abbleway; 'they have scented us. They will tear the carriage to pieces. We shall be devoured.'

'Not me, on my name-day. The holy Mariä Kleophä would not permit it,' said the woman with provoking calm.

The heads dropped down from the window and an uncanny silence fell on the beleaguered carriage. Abbleway neither moved nor spoke. Perhaps the brutes had not clearly seen or winded the human occupants of the carriage, and had prowled away on some other errand of rapine.

The long torture-laden minutes passed slowly away.

'It grows cold,' said the woman suddenly, crossing over to the far end of the carriage, where the heads had appeared. 'The heating apparatus does not work any longer. See, over there beyond the trees, there is a chimney with smoke coming from it. It is not far, and the snow has nearly stopped. I shall find a path through the forest to that house with the chimney.'

'But the wolves!' exclaimed Abbleway; 'they may –'

'Not on my name-day,' said the woman obstinately, and before he could stop her she had opened the door and climbed down into the snow. A moment later he hid his face in his hands; two gaunt lean figures rushed upon her from the forest. No doubt she had courted her fate, but Abbleway had no wish to see a human being torn to pieces and devoured before his eyes.

When he looked at last a new sensation of scandalized astonishment took possession of him. He had been straitly brought up in a small English town, and he was not prepared to be the witness of a miracle. The wolves were not doing anything worse to the woman than drench her with snow as they gambolled round her.

A short, joyous bark revealed the clue to the situation.

'Are those – dogs?' he called weakly.

'My cousin Karl's dogs, yes,' she answered; 'that is his inn, over beyond the trees. I knew it was there, but I did not want to take you there; he is always grasping with strangers. However, it grows too cold to remain in the train. Ah, ah, see what comes!'

A whistle sounded, and a relief engine made its appearance, snorting its way sulkily through the snow. Abbleway did not have the opportunity for finding out whether Karl was really avaricious.

'Down Pens'

'Have you written to thank the Froplinsons for what they sent us?' asked Egbert.

'No,' said Janetta, with a note of tired defiance in her voice; 'I've written eleven letters today expressing surprise and gratitude for sundry unmerited gifts, but I haven't written to the Froplinsons.'

'Someone will have to write to them,' said Egbert.

'I don't dispute the necessity, but I don't think the someone should be me,' said Janetta. 'I wouldn't mind writing a letter of angry recrimination or heartless satire to some suitable recipient; in fact, I should rather enjoy it, but I've come to the end of my capacity for expressing servile amiability. Eleven letters today and nine yesterday, all couched in the same strain of ecstatic thankfulness: really, you can't expect me to sit down to another. There is such a thing as writing oneself out.'

'I've written nearly as many,' said Egbert, 'and I've had my usual business correspondence to get through too. Besides, I don't know what it was that the Froplinsons sent us.'

'A William the Conqueror calendar,' said Janetta, 'with a quotation of one of his great thoughts for every day of the year.'

'Impossible,' said Egbert; 'he didn't have three hundred and sixty-five thoughts in the whole of his life, or, if he did, he kept them to himself. He was a man of action, not of introspection.'

'Well, it was William Wordsworth, then,' said Janetta; 'I know William came into it somewhere.'

'That sounds more probable,' said Egbert; 'well, let's collaborate on this letter of thanks and get it done. I'll dictate, and you can scribble it down. "Dear Mrs Froplinson – thank you and your husband so much for the very pretty calender you sent us. It was very good of you to think of us," '

'You can't possibly say that,' said Janetta, laying down her pen.

'It's what I always do say, and what everyone says to me,' protested Egbert.

'We sent them something on the twenty-second,' said Janetta, 'so they simply *had* to think of us. There was no getting away from it.'

'What did we send them?' asked Egbert gloomily.

'Bridge-markers,' said Janetta, 'in a cardboard case, with some inanity about "digging for fortune with a royal spade" emblazoned on the cover. The moment I saw it in the shop I said to myself "Froplinsons" and to the attendant "How much?" When he said "Ninepence", I gave him their address, jabbed our card in, paid tenpence or elevenpence to cover the postage, and thanked heaven. With less sincerity and infinitely more trouble they eventually thanked me.'

'The Froplinsons don't play bridge,' said Egbert.

'One is not supposed to notice social deformities of that sort,' said Janetta; 'it wouldn't be polite. Besides, what trouble did they take to find out whether we read Wordsworth with gladness? For all they knew or cared we might be frantically embedded in the belief that all poetry begins and ends with John Masefield, and it might infuriate or depress us to have a daily sample of Wordsworthian products flung at us.'

'Well, let's get on with the letter of thanks,' said Egbert.

'Proceed,' said Janetta.

' "How clever of you to guess that Wordsworth is our favourite poet," ' dictated Egbert.

Again Janetta laid down her pen.

'Do you realize what that means?' she asked; 'a Wordsworth booklet next Christmas, and another calendar the Christmas after, with the same problem of having to write suitable letters of thankfulness. No, the best thing to do is to drop all further allusion to the calendar and switch off on to some other topic.'

'But what other topic?'

'Oh, something like this: "What do you think of the New Year Honours List? A friend of ours made such a clever remark when he read it." Then you can stick in any remark that comes into your head; it needn't be clever. The Froplinsons won't know whether it is or isn't.'

'We don't even know on which side they are in politics,' objected Egbert; 'and anyhow you can't suddenly dismiss the subject of the calendar. Surely there must be some intelligent remark that can be made about it.'

'Well, we can't think of one,' said Janetta wearily; 'the fact is, we've both written ourselves out. Heavens! I've just remembered Mrs Stephen Ludberry. I haven't thanked her for what she sent.'

'What did she send?'

'I forget; I think it was a calendar.'

There was a long silence, the forlorn silence of those who are bereft of hope and have almost ceased to care.

Presently Egbert started from his seat with an air of resolution. The light of battle was in his eyes.

'Let me come to the writing-table,' he exclaimed.

'Gladly,' said Janetta. 'Are you going to write to Mrs Ludberry or the Froplinsons?'

'To neither,' said Egbert, drawing a stack of notepaper towards him; 'I'm going to write to the editor of every enlightened and influential newspaper in the Kingdom. I'm going to suggest that there should be a sort of epistolary Truce of God during the festivities of Christmas and New Year. From the twenty-fourth of December to the third or fourth of January it shall be considered an offence against good sense and good feeling to write or expect any letter or communication that does not deal with the necessary events of the moment. Answers to invitations, arrangements about trains, renewal of club subscriptions, and, of course, all the ordinary everyday affairs of business, sickness, engaging new cooks, and so forth, these will be dealt with in the usual manner as something inevitable, a legitimate part of our daily life. But all the devastating accretions of correspondence, incident to the festive season, these should be swept away to give the season a chance of being really festive, a time of untroubled, unpunctuated peace and good will.'

'But you would have to make some acknowledgment of presents received,' objected Janetta; 'otherwise people would never know whether they had arrived safely.'

'Of course, I have thought of that,' said Egbert; 'every present that was sent off would be accompanied by a ticket bearing the date of dispatch and the signature of the sender, and some conventional hieroglyphic to show that it was intended to be a Christmas or New Year gift; there would be a counterfoil with space for the recipient's name and the date of arrival, and all you would have to do would be to sign and date the counterfoil, add a conventional hieroglyphic indicating heartfelt thanks and gratified surprise, put the thing into an envelope and post it.'

'It sounds delightfully simple,' said Janetta wistfully, 'but people would consider it too cut-and-dried, too perfunctory.'

'It is not a bit more perfunctory than the present system,' said Egbert; 'I have only the same conventional language of gratitude at my disposal with which to thank dear old Colonel Chuttle for his perfectly delicious Stilton, which we shall devour to the last morsel, and the Froplinsons for their calendar, which we shall never look at. Colonel Chuttle knows that we are grateful for the Stilton, without having to be told so, and the Froplinsons know that we are bored with their calendar, whatever we may say to the contrary, just as we know that they are bored with the bridge-markers in spite of their written assurance that they thanked us for our charming little gift. What is more, the Colonel knows that even if we had taken a sudden aversion to Stilton or been forbidden it by the doctor, we should still have written a letter of hearty thanks around it. So you see the present system of acknowledgment is just as perfunctory and conventional as the counterfoil business would be, only ten times more tiresome and brain-racking.'

'Your plan would certainly bring the ideal of a Happy Christmas a step nearer realization,' said Janetta.

'There are exceptions, of course,' said Egbert, 'people who really try to infuse a breath of reality into their letters of acknowledgment. Aunt Susan, for instance, who writes: "Thank you very much for the ham; not such a good flavour as the one you sent last year, which itself was not a particularly good one. Hams are not what they used to be." It would be a pity to be deprived of her Christmas comments, but that loss would be swallowed up in the general gain.'

'Meanwhile,' said Janetta, 'what *am* I to say to the Froplinsons?'

On Approval

Of all the genuine Bohemians who strayed from time to time into the would-be-Bohemian circle of the Restaurant Nuremberg, Owl Street, Soho, none was more interesting and more elusive than Gebhard Knopfschrank. He had no friends, and though he treated all the restaurant frequenters as acquaintances he never seemed to wish to carry the acquaintanceship beyond the door that led into Owl Street and the outer world. He dealt with them all rather as a market woman might deal with chance passers-by, exhibiting her wares and chattering about the weather and the slackness of business, occasionally about rheumatism, but never showing a desire to penetrate into their daily lives or to dissect their ambitions.

He was understood to belong to a family of peasant farmers, somewhere in Pomerania; some two years ago, according to all that was known of him, he had abandoned the labours and responsibilities of swine tending and goose rearing to try his fortune as an artist in London.

'Why London and not Paris or Munich?' he had been asked by the curious.

Well, there was a ship that left Stolpmünde for London twice a month, that carried few passengers, but carried them cheaply; the railway fares to Munich or Paris were not cheap. Thus it was that he came to select London as the scene of his great adventure.

The question that had long and seriously agitated the frequenters of the Nuremberg was whether this goose-boy migrant was really a soul-driven genius, spreading his wings to the light, or merely an enterprising young man who fancied he could paint and was pardonably anxious to escape from the monotony of rye bread diet and the sandy, swine-bestrewn plains of Pomerania. There was reasonable ground for doubt and caution; the artistic groups that foregathered at the little restaurant contained so many young women with short hair and so many young men with long hair, who supposed themselves to be abnormally gifted in the domain of music, poetry, painting, or stagecraft, with little or nothing to support the supposition, that a self-announced genius of any sort in their midst was inevitably suspect. On the other hand, there was the ever-imminent danger of entertaining, and snubbing, an angel unawares. There had been the lamentable case of Sledonti, the dramatic poet, who had been belittled and cold-shouldered in the Owl Street hall of judgment, and had been afterwards hailed as a master singer by the Grand Duke Constantine Constantinovitch – 'the most educated of the Romanoffs', according to Sylvia Strubble, who spoke rather as one who knew every individual member of the Russian imperial family; as a matter of fact, she knew a newspaper correspondent, a young man who ate *bortsch* with the air of having invented it. Sledonti's 'Poems of Death and Passion' were now being sold by the thousand in seven European languages, and were about to be translated into Syrian, a circumstance which made the discerning critics of the Nuremberg rather shy of maturing their future judgments too rapidly and too irrevocably.

As regards Knopfschrank's work, they did not lack opportunity for inspecting and appraising it. However resolutely he might hold himself aloof from the social life of his restaurant acquaintances, he was not minded to hide his artistic performances from their inquiring gaze. Every evening, or nearly every evening, at about seven o'clock, he would make his appearance, sit himself down at his accustomed table, throw a bulky black portfolio on to the chair opposite him, nod round indiscriminately at his fellow-guests, and commence the serious business of eating and drinking. When the coffee stage was reached he would light a cigarette, draw the portfolio over to him, and begin to rummage among its contents. With slow deliberation he would select a few of his more recent studies and sketches, and silently pass them round from table to table, paying especial attention to any new diners who might be present. On the back of each sketch was marked in plain figures the announcement 'Price ten shillings'.

If his work was not obviously stamped with the hall-mark of genius, at any rate it was remarkable for its choice of an unusual and unvarying theme. His pictures always represented some well-known street or public place in London, fallen into decay and denuded of its human population, in the place of which there roamed a wild fauna, which, from its wealth of exotic species, must have originally escaped from Zoological Gardens and travelling beast shows. 'Giraffes drinking at the fountain pools, Trafalgar Square', was one of the most notable and characteristic of his studies, while even more sensational was the gruesome picture of 'Vultures attacking dying camel in Upper Berkeley Street'. There were also photographs of the large canvas on which he had been engaged for some months, and which he was now endeavouring to sell to some enterprising dealer or adventurous amateur. The subject was 'Hyænas asleep in Euston Station', a composition that left nothing to be desired in the way of suggesting unfathomed depths of desolation.

'Of course it may be immensely clever, it may be something epoch-making in the realm of art,' said Sylvia Strubble to her own particular circle of listeners, 'but, on the other hand, it may be merely mad. One mustn't pay too much attention to the commercial aspect of the case, of course, but still, if some dealer would make a bid for that hyæna picture, or even for some of the sketches, we should know better how to place the man and his work.'

'We may all be cursing ourselves one of these days', said Mrs Nougat-Jones, 'for not having bought up his entire portfolio of sketches. At the same time, when there is so much real talent going about, one does not feel like planking down ten shillings for what looks like a bit of whimsical oddity. Now that picture that he showed us last week, "Sandgrouse roosting on the Albert Memorial", was very impressive, and of course I could see there was good workmanship in it and breadth of treatment; but it didn't in the least convey the Albert Memorial to me, and Sir James Beanquest tells me that sandgrouse don't roost, they sleep on the ground.'

Whatever talent or genius the Pomeranian artist might possess, it certainly failed to receive commercial sanction. The portfolio remained bulky with unsold sketches, and the 'Euston Siesta', as the wits of the Nuremberg nicknamed the large canvas, was still in the market. The outward and visible signs of financial embarrassment began to be noticeable; the half-bottle of cheap claret at dinner-time gave way to a small glass of lager, and this in turn was displaced by water. The one-and-sixpenny set dinner receded from an everyday event to a Sunday extravagance; on ordinary days the artist contented himself with a sevenpenny omelette and some bread and cheese, and there were evenings when he did not put in an appearance at all. On the rare occasions when he spoke of his own affairs it was observed that he began to talk more about Pomerania and less about the great world of art.

'It is a busy time there now with us,' he said wistfully; 'the schwines are driven out into the fields after harvest, and must be looked after. I could be helping to look after if I was there. Here it is difficult to live; art is not appreciate.'

'Why don't you go home on a visit?' someone asked tactfully.

'Ah, it cost money! There is the ship passage to Stolpmünde, and there is money that I owe at my lodgings. Even here I owe a few schillings. If I could sell some of my sketches –'

'Perhaps,' suggested Mrs Nougat-Jones, 'if you were to offer them for a little less, some of us would be glad to buy a few. Ten shillings is always a consideration, you know, to people who are not over well off. Perhaps if you were to ask six or seven shillings –'

Once a peasant, always a peasant. The mere suggestion of a bargain to be struck brought a twinkle of awakened alertness into the artist's eyes, and hardened the lines of his mouth.

'Nine schilling nine pence each,' he snapped, and seemed disappointed that Mrs Nougat-Jones did not pursue the subject further. He had evidently expected her to offer seven-and-fourpence.

The weeks sped by, and Knopfschrank came more rarely to the restaurant in Owl Street, while his meals on those occasions became more and more meagre. And then came a triumphal day, when he appeared early in the evening in a high state of elation, and ordered an elaborate meal that scarcely stopped short of being a banquet. The ordinary resources of the kitchen were supplemented by an imported dish of smoked goosebreast, a Pomeranian delicacy that was luckily procurable at a firm of *delikatessen* merchants in Coventry Street, while a long-necked bottle of Rhine wine gave a finishing touch of festivity and good cheer to the crowded table.

'He has evidently sold his masterpiece,' whispered Sylvia Strubble to Mrs Nougat-Jones, who had come in late.

'Who has bought it?' she whispered back.

'Don't know; he hasn't said anything yet, but it must be some American. Do you see, he has got a little American flag on the dessert dish, and he has put pennies in the music box three times, once to play the "Star-spangled Banner", then a Sousa march, and then the "Star-spangled Banner" again. It must be an American millionaire, and he's evidently got a big price for it; he's just beaming and chuckling with satisfaction.'

'We must ask him who has bought it,' said Mrs Nougat-Jones.

'Hush! no, don't. Let's buy some of his sketches, quick, before we are supposed to know that he's famous; otherwise he'll be doubling the prices. I *am* so glad he's had a success at last. I always believed in him, you know.'

For the sum of ten shillings each Miss Strubble acquired the drawings of the camel dying in Upper Berkeley Street and of the giraffes quenching their thirst in Trafalgar Square; at the same price Mrs Nougat-Jones secured the study of roosting sand-grouse. A more ambitious picture, 'Wolves and wapiti fighting on the steps of the Athenæum Club', found a purchaser at fifteen shillings.

'And now what are your plans?' asked a young man who contributed occasional paragraphs to an artistic weekly.

'I go back to Stolpmünde as soon as the ship sails,' said the artist, 'and I do not return. Never.'

'But your work? Your career as a painter?'

'Ah, there is nossing in it. One starves. Till today I have sold not one of my sketches. Tonight you have bought a few, because I am going away from you, but at other times, not one.'

'But has not some American –?

'Ah, the rich American,' chuckled the artist. 'God be thanked. He dash his car right into our herd of schwines as they were being driven out to the fields. Many of our best schwines he killed, but he paid all damages. He paid perhaps more than they were worth, many times more than they would have fetched in the market after a month of fattening, but he was in a hurry to get on to Dantzig. When one is in a hurry one must pay what one is asked. God be thanked for rich Americans, who are always in a hurry to get somewhere else. My father and mother, they have now so plenty of money; they send me some to pay my debts and come home. I start on Monday for Stolpmünde and I do not come back. Never.'

'But your picture, the hyænas?'

'No good. It is too big to carry to Stolpmünde. I burn it.'

In time he will be forgotten, but at present Knopfschrank is almost as sore a subject as Sledonti with some of the frequenters of the Nuremberg Restaurant, Owl Street, Soho.

The Wolves of Cernogratz

'Are there any old legends attached to the castle?' asked Conrad of his sister. Conrad was a prosperous Hamburg merchant, but he was the one poetically-dispositioned member of an eminently practical family.

The Baroness Gruebel shrugged her plump shoulders.

'There are always legends hanging about these old places. They are not difficult to invent and they cost nothing. In this case there is a story that when anyone dies in the castle all the dogs in the village and the wild beasts in the forest howl the night long. It would not be pleasant to listen to, would it?'

'It would be weird and romantic,' said the Hamburg merchant.

'Anyhow, it isn't true,' said the Baroness complacently; 'since we bought the place we have had proof that nothing of the sort happens. When the old mother-in-law died last springtime we all listened, but there was no howling. It is just a story that lends dignity to the place without costing anything.'

'The story is not as you have told it,' said Amalie, the grey old governess. Everyone turned and looked at her in astonishment. She was wont to sit silent and prim and faded in her place at table, never speaking unless someone spoke to her, and there were few who troubled themselves to make conversation with her. Today a sudden volubility had descended on her; she continued to talk, rapidly and nervously, looking straight in front of her and seeming to address no one in particular.

'It is not when *any one* dies in the castle that the howling is heard. It was when one of the Cernogratz family died here that the wolves came from far and near and howled at the edge of the forest just before the death hour. There were only a few couple of wolves that had their lairs in this part of the forest, but at such a time the keepers say there would be scores of them, gliding about in the shadows and howling in chorus, and the dogs of the castle and the village and all the farms round would bay and howl in fear and anger at the wolf chorus, and as the soul of the dying one left its body a tree would crash down in the park. That is what happened when a Cernogratz died in his family castle. But for a stranger dying here, of course no wolf would howl and no tree would fall. Oh, no.'

There was a note of defiance, almost of contempt, in her voice as she said the last words. The well-fed, much-too-well dressed Baroness stared angrily at the dowdy old woman who had come forth from her usual and seemly position of effacement to speak so disrespectfully.

'You seem to know quite a lot about the von Cernogratz legends, Fräulein Schmidt,' she said sharply; 'I did not know that family histories were among the subjects you are supposed to be proficient in.'

The answer to her taunt was even more unexpected and astonishing than the conversational outbreak which had provoked it.

'I am a von Cernogratz myself,' said the old woman, 'that is why I know the family history.'

'You a von Cernogratz? You!' came in an incredulous chorus.

'When we became very poor,' she explained, 'and I had to go out and give teaching lessons, I took another name; I thought it would be more in keeping. But my grandfather spent much of his time as a boy in this castle, and my father used to tell me many stories about it, and, of course, I knew all the family legends and stories. When one has nothing left to one but memories, one guards and dusts them with especial care. I little thought when I took service with you that I should one day come with you to the old home of my family. I could wish it had been anywhere else.'

There was silence when she finished speaking, and then the Baroness turned the conversation to a less embarrassing topic than family histories. But afterwards, when the old governess had slipped away quietly to her duties, there arose a clamour of derision and disbelief.

'It was an impertinence,' snapped out the Baron, his protruding eyes taking on a scandalized expression; 'fancy the woman talking like that at our table. She almost told us we were nobodies, and I don't believe a word of it. She is just Schmidt and nothing more. She has been talking to some of the peasants about the old Cernogratz family, and raked up their history and their stories.'

'She wants to make herself out of some consequence,' said the Baroness; 'she knows she will soon be past work and she wants to appeal to our sympathies. Her grandfather, indeed!'

The Baroness had the usual number of grandfathers, but she never, never boasted about them.

'I dare say her grandfather was a pantry boy or something of the sort in the castle,' sniggered the Baron; 'that part of the story may be true.'

The merchant from Hamburg said nothing; he had seen tears in the old woman's eyes when she spoke of guarding her memories – or, being of an imaginative disposition, he thought he had.

'I shall give her notice to go as soon as the New Year festivities are over,' said the Baroness; 'till then I shall be too busy to manage without her.'

But she had to manage without her all the same, for in the cold biting weather after Christmas, the old governess fell ill and kept to her room.

'It is most provoking,' said the Baroness, as her guests sat round the fire on one of the last evenings of the dying year; 'all the time that she has been with us I cannot remember that she was ever seriously ill, too ill to go about and do her work, I mean. And now, when I have the house full, and she could be useful in so many ways, she goes and breaks down. One is sorry for her, of course, she looks so withered and shrunken, but it is intensely annoying all the same.'

'Most annoying,' agreed the banker's wife, sympathetically; 'it is the intense cold, I expect, it breaks the old people up. It has been unusually cold this year.'

'The frost is the sharpest that has been known in December for many years,' said the Baron.

'And, of course, she is quite old,' said the Baroness; 'I wish I had given her notice some weeks ago, then she would have left before this happened to her. Why, Wappi, what is the matter with you?'

The small, woolly lapdog had leapt suddenly down from its cushion and crept shivering under the sofa. At the same moment an outburst of angry barking came from the dogs in the castle-yard, and other dogs could be heard yapping and barking in the distance.

'What is disturbing the animals?' asked the Baron.

And then the humans, listening intently, heard the sound that had roused the dogs to their demonstrations of fear and rage; heard a long-drawn whining howl, rising and falling, seeming at one moment leagues away, at others sweeping across the snow until it appeared to come from the foot of the castle walls. All the starved, cold misery of a frozen world, all the relentless hunger-fury of the wild, blended with other forlorn and haunting melodies to which one could give no name, seemed concentrated in that wailing cry.

'Wolves!' cried the Baron.

Their music broke forth in one raging burst, seeming to come from everywhere.

'Hundreds of wolves,' said the Hamburg merchant, who was a man of strong imagination.

Moved by some impulse which she could not have explained, the Baroness left her guests and made her way to the narrow, cheerless room where the old governess lay watching the hours of the dying year slip by. In spite of the biting cold of the winter night, the window stood open. With a scandalized exclamation on her lips, the Baroness rushed forward to close it.

'Leave it open,' said the old woman in a voice that for all its weakness carried an air of command such as the Baroness had never heard before from her lips.

'But you will die of cold!' she expostulated.

'I am dying in any case,' said the voice, 'and I want to hear their music. They have come from far and wide to sing the death-music of my family. It is beautiful that they have come; I am the last von Cernogratz that will die in our old castle, and they have come to sing to me. Hark, how loud they are calling!'

The cry of the wolves rose on the still winter air and floated round the castle walls in long-drawn piercing wails; the old woman lay back on her couch with a look of long-delayed happiness on her face.

'Go away,' she said to the Baroness; 'I am not lonely any more. I am one of a great old family . . .'

'I think she is dying,' said the Baroness when she had rejoined her guests; 'I suppose we must send for a doctor. And that terrible howling! Not for much money would I have such death-music.'

'That music is not to be bought for any amount of money,' said Conrad.

'Hark! What is that other sound?' asked the Baron, as a noise of splitting and crashing was heard.

It was a tree falling in the park.

There was a moment of constrained silence, and then the banker's wife spoke.

'It is the intense cold that is splitting the trees. It is also the cold that has brought the wolves out in such numbers. It is many years since we have had such a cold winter.'

The Baroness eagerly agreed that the cold was responsible for these things. It was the cold of the open window, too, which caused the heart failure that made the doctor's ministrations unnecessary for the old Fräulein. But the notice in the newspapers looked very well –

> 'On December 29th, at Schloss Cernogratz, Amalie von Cernogratz, for many years the valued friend of Baron and Baroness Gruebel.'

The Guests

'The landscape seen from our windows is certainly charming,' said Annabel; 'those cherry orchards and green meadows, and the river winding along the valley, and the church tower peeping out among the elms, they all make a most effective picture. There's something dreadfully sleepy and languorous about it, though; stagnation seems to be the dominant note. Nothing ever happens here; seedtime and harvest, an occasional outbreak of measles or a mildly destructive thunderstorm, and a little election excitement about once in five years, that is all that we have to modify the monotony of our existence. Rather dreadful, isn't it?'

'On the contrary,' said Matilda, 'I find it soothing and restful; but then, you see, I've lived in countries where things do happen, ever so many at a time, when you're not ready for them happening all at once.'

'That, of course, makes a difference,' said Annabel.

'I have never forgotten', said Matilda, 'the occasion when the Bishop of Bequar paid us an unexpected visit; he was on his way to lay the foundation-stone of a mission-house or something of the sort.'

'I thought that out there you were always prepared for emergency guests turning up,' said Annabel.

'I was quite prepared for half a dozen Bishops,' said Matilda, 'but it was rather disconcerting to find out after a little conversation that this particular one was a distant cousin of mine, belonging to a branch of the family that had quarrelled bitterly and offensively with our branch about a Crown Derby dessert service; they got it, and we ought to have got it, in some legacy, or else we got it and they thought they ought to have it, I forget which; anyhow, I know they behaved disgracefully. Now here was one of them turning up in the odour of sanctity, so to speak, and claiming the traditional hospitality of the East.'

'It was rather trying, but you could have left your husband to do most of the entertaining.'

'My husband was fifty miles up-country, talking sense, or what he imagined to be sense, to a village community that fancied one of their leading men was a were-tiger.'

'A what tiger?'

'A were-tiger; you've heard of were-wolves, haven't you, a mixture of wolf and human being and demon? Well, in those parts they have were-tigers, or think they have, and I must say that in this case, so far as sworn and uncontested evidence went, they had every ground for thinking so. However, as we gave up witchcraft prosecutions about three hundred years ago, we don't like to have other people keeping on our discarded practices; it doesn't seem respectful to our mental and moral position.'

'I hope you weren't unkind to the Bishop,' said Annabel.

'Well, of course he was my guest, so I had to be outwardly polite to him, but he was tactless enough to take up the incidents of the old quarrel, and to try to make out that there was something to be said for the way his side of the family had behaved; even if there was, which I don't for a moment admit, my house was not the place in which to say it. I didn't argue the matter, but I gave my cook a holiday to go and visit his aged parents some ninety miles away. The emergency cook was not a specialist in curries, in fact, I don't think cooking in any shape or form could have been one of his strong points. I believe he originally came to us in the guise of a gardener, but as we never pretended to have anything that could be considered a garden he was utilized as assistant goat-herd, in which capacity, I understand, he gave every satisfaction. When the Bishop heard that I had sent away the cook on a special and unnecessary holiday he saw the inwardness of the manœuvre, and from that moment we were scarcely on speaking terms. If you have ever had a Bishop with whom you were not on speaking terms staying in your house, you will appreciate the situation.'

Annabel confessed that her life-story had never included such a disturbing experience.

'Then,' continued Matilda, 'to make matters more complicated, the Gwadlipichee overflowed its banks, a thing it did every now and then when the rains were unduly prolonged, and the lower part of the house and all the out-buildings were submerged. We managed to get the ponies loose in time, and the syce swam the whole lot of them off to the nearest rising ground. A goat or two, the chief goat-herd, the chief goat-herd's wife, and several of their babies came to anchorage in the verandah. All the rest of the available space was filled up with wet, bedraggled-looking hens and chickens; one never really knows how many fowls one possesses till the servants' quarters are flooded out. Of course, I had been through something of the sort in previous floods, but never before had I had a houseful of goats and babies and half-drowned hens, supplemented by a Bishop with whom I was hardly on speaking terms.'

'It must have been a trying experience,' commented Annabel.

'More embarrassments were to follow. I wasn't going to let a mere ordinary flood wash out the memory of that Crown Derby dessert service, and I intimated to the Bishop that his large bedroom, with a writing table in it, and his small bath-room, with a sufficiency of cold-water jars in it, was his share of the premises, and that space was rather congested under the existing circumstances. However, at about three o'clock in the afternoon, when he had awakened from his midday sleep, he made a sudden incursion into the room that was normally the drawing-room, but was now dining-room, store-house, saddle-room, and half a dozen other temporary premises as well. From the condition of my guest's costume he seemed to think it might also serve as his dressing-room.

' "I'm afraid there is nowhere for you to sit," I said coldly; "the verandah is full of goats."

' "There is a goat in my bedroom,' he observed with equal coldness, and more than a suspicion of sardonic reproach.

' "Really," I said, "another survivor? I thought all the other goats were done for."

' "This particular goat is quite done for,' he said, "it is being devoured by a leopard at the present moment. That is why I left the room; some animals resent being watched while they are eating."

'The leopard, of course, was easily explained; it had been hanging round the goat sheds when the flood came, and had clambered up by the outside staircase leading to the Bishop's bath-room, thoughtfully bringing a goat with it. Probably it found the bath-room too damp and shut-in for its taste, and transferred its banqueting operations to the bedroom while the Bishop was having his nap.'

'What a frightful situation!' exclaimed Annabel; 'fancy having a ravening leopard in the house, with a flood all round you.'

'Not in the least ravening,' said Matilda; 'it was full of goat, had any amount of water at its disposal if it felt thirsty, and probably had no more immediate wish than a desire for uninterrupted sleep. Still, I think anyone will admit that it was an embarrassing predicament to have your only available guest-room occupied by a leopard, the verandah choked up with goats and babies and wet hens, and a Bishop with whom you were scarcely on speaking terms planted down in your only sitting-room. I really don't know how I got through those crawling hours, and of course mealtimes only made matters worse. The emergency cook had every excuse for sending in watery soup and sloppy rice, and as neither the chief goat-herd nor his wife were expert divers, the cellar could not be reached. Fortunately the Gwadlipichee subsides as rapidly as it rises, and just before dawn the syce came splashing back, with the ponies only fetlock deep in water. Then there arose some awkwardness from the fact that the Bishop wished to leave sooner than the leopard did, and as the latter was ensconced in the midst of the former's personal possessions there was an obvious difficulty in altering the order of departure. I pointed out to the Bishop that a leopard's habits and tastes are not those of an otter, and that it naturally preferred walking to wading, and that in any case a meal of an entire goat, washed down with tub-water, justified a certain amount of repose; if I had had guns fired to frighten the animal away, as the Bishop suggested, it would probably merely have left the bedroom to come into the already over-crowded drawing-room. Altogether it was rather a relief when they both left. Now, perhaps, you can understand my appreciation of a sleepy countryside where things don't happen.'

The Penance

Octavian Ruttle was one of those lively cheerful individuals on whom amiability had set its unmistakable stamp, and, like most of his kind, his soul's peace depended in large measure on the unstinted approval of his fellows. In hunting to death a small tabby cat he had done a thing of which he scarcely approved himself, and he was glad when the gardener had hidden the body in its hastily dug grave under a lone oak-tree in the meadow, the same tree that the hunted quarry had climbed as a last effort towards safety. It had been a distasteful and seemingly ruthless deed, but circumstances had demanded the doing of it. Octavian kept chickens; at least he kept some of them; others vanished from his keeping, leaving only a few bloodstained feathers to mark the manner of their going. The tabby cat from the large grey house that stood with its back to the meadow had been detected in many furtive visits to the hen-coops, and after due negotiation with those in authority at the grey house a sentence of death had been agreed on. 'The children will mind, but they need not know,' had been the last word on the matter.

The children in question were a standing puzzle to Octavian; in the course of a few months he considered that he should have known their names, ages, the dates of their birthdays, and have been introduced to their favourite toys. They remained, however, as non-committal as the long blank wall that shut them off from the meadow, a wall over which their three heads sometimes appeared at odd moments. They had parents in India – that much Octavian had learned in the neighbourhood; the children, beyond grouping themselves garment-wise into sexes, a girl and two boys, carried their life-story no further on his behoof. And now it seemed he was engaged in something which touched them closely, but must be hidden from their knowledge.

The poor helpless chickens had gone one by one to their doom, so it was meet that their destroyer should come to a violent end, yet Octavian felt some qualms when his share of the violence was ended. The little cat, headed off from its wonted tracks of safety, had raced unfriended from shelter to shelter, and its end had been rather piteous. Octavian walked through the long grass of the meadow with a step less jaunty than usual. And as he passed beneath the shadow of the high blank wall he glanced up and became aware that his hunting had had undesired witnesses. Three white set faces were looking down at him, and if ever an artist wanted a threefold study of cold human hate, impotent yet unyielding, raging yet masked in stillness, he would have found it in the triple gaze that met Octavian's eye.

'I'm sorry, but it had to be done,' said Octavian, with genuine apology in his voice.

'Beast!'

The answer came from three throats with startling intensity.

Octavian felt that the blank wall would not be more impervious to his explanations than the bunch of human hostility that peered over its coping; he wisely decided to withhold his peace overtures till a more hopeful occasion.

Two days later he ransacked the best sweet shop in the neighbouring market town for a box of chocolates that by its size and contents should fitly atone for the dismal deed done under the oak tree in the meadow. The first two specimens that were shown him he hastily rejected; one had a group of chickens pictured on its lid, the other bore the portrait of a tabby kitten. A third sample was more simply bedecked with a spray of painted poppies, and Octavian hailed the flowers of forgetfulness as a happy omen. He felt distinctly more at ease with his surroundings when the imposing package had been sent across to the grey house, and a message returned to say that it had been duly given to the children. The next morning he sauntered with purposeful steps past the long blank wall on his way to the chicken-run and piggery that stood at the bottom of the meadow. The three children were perched at their accustomed look-out, and their range of sight did not seem to concern itself with Octavian's presence. As he became depressingly aware of the aloofness of their gaze he also noted a strange variegation in the herbage at his feet; the greensward for a considerable space around was strewn and speckled with chocolate-coloured hail, enlivened here and there with gay tinsel-like wrappings or the glistening mauve of crystallised violets. It was as though the fairy paradise of a greedy-minded child had taken shape and substance in the vegetation of the meadow. Octavian's blood-money had been flung back at him in scorn.

To increase his discomfiture the march of events tended to shift the blame of ravaged chicken-coops from the supposed culprit who had already paid full forfeit; the young chicks were still carried off, and it seemed highly probable that the cat had only haunted the chicken-run to prey on the rats which harboured there. Through the flowing channels of servant talk the children learned of this belated revision of verdict, and Octavian one day picked up a sheet of copy-book paper on which was painstakingly written: 'Beast. Rats eated your chickens.' More ardently than ever did he wish for an opportunity for sloughing off the disgrace that enwrapped him, and earning some happier nickname from his three unsparing judges.

And one day a chance inspiration came to him. Olivia, his two-year-old daughter, was accustomed to spend the hour from high noon till one o'clock with her father while the nursemaid gobbled and digested her dinner and novelette. About the same time the blank wall was usually enlivened by the presence of its three small wardens. Octavian, with seeming carelessness of purpose, brought Olivia well within hail of the watchers and noted with hidden delight the growing interest that dawned in that hitherto sternly hostile quarter. His little Olivia, with her sleepy placid ways, was going to succeed where he, with his anxious well-meant overtures, had so signally failed. He brought her a large yellow dahlia, which she grasped tightly in one hand and regarded with a stare of benevolent boredom, such as one might bestow on amateur classical dancing performed in aid of a deserving charity. Then he turned shyly to the group perched on the wall and asked with affected carelessness, 'Do you like flowers?' Three solemn nods rewarded his venture.

'Which sorts do you like best?' he asked, this time with a distinct betrayal of eagerness in his voice.

'Those with all the colours, over there.' Three chubby arms pointed to a distant tangle of sweet-pea. Child-like, they had asked for what lay farthest from hand, but Octavian trotted off gleefully to obey their welcome behest. He pulled and plucked with unsparing hand, and brought every variety of tint that he could see into his bunch that was rapidly becoming a bundle. Then he turned to retrace his steps, and found the blank wall blanker and more deserted than ever, while the foreground was void of all trace of Olivia. Far down the meadow three children were pushing a go-cart at the utmost speed they could muster in the direction of the piggeries; it was Olivia's go-cart and Olivia sat in it, somewhat bumped and shaken by the pace at which she was being driven, but apparently retaining her wonted composure of mind. Octavian stared for a moment at the rapidly moving group, and then started in hot pursuit, shedding as he ran sprays of blossom from the mass of sweet-pea that he still clutched in his hands. Fast as he ran the children had reached the piggery before he could overtake them, and he arrived just in time to see Olivia, wondering but unprotesting, hauled and pushed up to the roof of the nearest sty. They were old buildings in some need of repair, and the rickety roof would certainly not have borne Octavian's weight if he had attempted to follow his daughter and her captors on their new vantage ground.

'What are you going to do with her?' he panted. There was no mistaking the grim trend of mischief in those flushed but sternly composed young faces.

'Hang her in chains over a slow fire,' said one of the boys. Evidently they had been reading English history.

'Frow her down and the pigs will d'vour her, every bit 'cept the palms of her hands,' said the other boy. It was also evident that they had studied Biblical history.

The last proposal was the one which most alarmed Octavian, since it might be carried into effect at a moment's notice; there had been cases, he remembered, of pigs eating babies.

'You surely wouldn't treat my poor little Olivia in that way?' he pleaded.

'You killed our little cat,' came in stern reminder from three throats.

'I'm very sorry I did,' said Octavian, and if there is a standard of measurement in truths Octavian's statement was assuredly a large nine.

'We shall be very sorry when we've killed Olivia,' said the girl, 'but we can't be sorry till we've done it.'

The inexorable child-logic rose like an unyielding rampart before Octavian's scared pleadings. Before he could think of any fresh line of appeal his energies were called out in another direction. Olivia had slid off the roof and fallen with a soft, unctuous splash into a morass of muck and decaying straw. Octavian scrambled hastily over the pigsty wall to her rescue, and at once found himself in a quagmire that engulfed his feet. Olivia, after the first shock of surprise at her sudden drop through the air, had been mildly pleased at finding herself in close and unstinted contact with the sticky element that oozed around her, but as she began to sink gently into the bed of slime a feeling dawned on her that she was not after all very happy, and she began to cry in the tentative fashion of the normally good child. Octavian, battling with the quagmire, which seemed to have learned the rare art of giving way at all points without yielding an inch, saw his daughter slowly disappearing in the engulfing slush, her smeared face further distorted with the contortions of whimpering wonder, while from their perch on the pigsty roof the three children looked down with the cold unpitying detachment of the Parcæ Sisters.

'I can't reach her in time,' gasped Octavian, 'she'll be choked in the muck. Won't you help her?'

'No one helped our cat,' came the inevitable reminder.

'I'll do anything to show you how sorry I am about that,' cried Octavian, with a further desperate flounder, which carried him scarcely two inches forward.

'Will you stand in a white sheet by the grave?'

'Yes,' screamed Octavian.

'Holding a candle?'

'An' saying "I'm a miserable Beast"?'

Octavian agreed to both suggestions.

'For a long, long time?'

'For half an hour,' said Octavian. There was an anxious ring in his voice as he named the time-limit; was there not the precedent of a German king who did open-air penance for several days and nights at Christmas-time clad only in his shirt? Fortunately the children did not appear to have read German history, and half an hour seemed long and goodly in their eyes.

'All right,' came with threefold solemnity from the roof, and a moment later a short ladder had been laboriously pushed across to Octavian, who lost no time in propping it against the low pigsty wall. Scrambling gingerly along its rungs he was able to lean across the morass that separated him from his slowly foundering offspring and extract her like an unwilling cork from its slushy embrace. A few minutes later he was listening to the shrill and repeated assurances of the nursemaid that her previous experience of filthy spectacles had been on a notably smaller scale.

That same evening when twilight was deepening into darkness Octavian took up his position as penitent under the lone oak-tree, having first carefully undressed the part. Clad in a zephyr shirt, which on this occasion thoroughly merited its name, he held in one hand a lighted candle and in the other a watch, into which the soul of a dead plumber seemed to have passed. A box of matches lay at his feet and was resorted to on the fairly frequent occasions when the candle succumbed to the night breezes. The house loomed inscrutable in the middle distance, but as Octavian conscientiously repeated the formula of his penance he felt certain that three pairs of solemn eyes were watching his moth-shared vigil.

And the next morning his eyes were gladdened by a sheet of copy-book paper lying beside the blank wall, on which was written the message 'Un-Beast'.

Mark

Augustus Mellowkent was a novelist with a future; that is to say, a limited but increasing number of people read his books, and there seemed good reason to suppose that if he steadily continued to turn out novels year by year a progressively increasing circle of readers would acquire the Mellowkent habit, and demand his works from the libraries and bookstalls. At the instigation of his publisher he had discarded the baptismal Augustus and taken the front name of Mark.

'Women like a name that suggests someone strong and silent, able but unwilling to answer questions. Augustus merely suggests idle splendour, but such a name as Mark Mellowkent, besides being alliterative, conjures up a vision of someone strong and beautiful and good, a sort of blend of Georges Carpentier and the Reverend What's-his-name.'

One morning in December Augustus sat in his writing-room, at work on the third chapter of his eighth novel. He had described at some length, for the benefit of those who could not imagine it, what a rectory garden looks like in July; he was now engaged in describing at greater length the feelings of a young girl, daughter of a long line of rectors and archdeacons, when she discovers for the first time that the postman is attractive.

'Their eyes met, for a brief moment, as he handed her two circulars and the fat wrapper-bound bulk of the *East Essex News*. Their eyes met, for the merest fraction of a second, yet nothing could ever be quite the same again. Cost what it might she felt that she must speak, must break the intolerable, unreal silence that had fallen on them. "How is your mother's rheumatism?" she said.'

The author's labours were cut short by the sudden intrusion of a maidservant.

'A gentleman to see you, sir,' said the maid, handing a card with the name Caiaphas Dwelf inscribed on it; 'says it's important.'

Mellowkent hesitated and yielded; the importance of the visitor's mission was probably illusory, but he had never met anyone with the name Caiaphas before. It would be at least a new experience.

Mr Dwelf was a man of indefinite age; his high, narrow forehead, cold grey eyes, and determined manner bespoke an unflinching purpose. He had a large book under his arm, and there seemed every probability that he had left a package of similar volumes in the hall. He took a seat before it had been offered him, placed the book on the table, and began to address Mellowkent in the manner of an 'open letter'.

'You are a literary man, the author of several well-known books –'

'I am engaged on a book at the present moment – rather busily engaged,' said Mellowkent, pointedly.

'Exactly,' said the intruder; 'time with you is a commodity of considerable importance. Minutes, even, have their value.'

'They have,' agreed Mellowkent, looking at his watch.

'That', said Caiaphas, 'is why this book that I am introducing to your notice is not a book that you can afford to be without. *Right Here* is indispensable for the writing man; it is no ordinary encyclopædia, or I should not trouble to show it to you. It is an inexhaustible mine of concise information –'

'On a shelf at my elbow,' said the author, 'I have a row of reference books that supply me with all the information I am likely to require.'

'Here,' persisted the would-be salesman, 'you have it all in one compact volume. No matter what the subject may be which you wish to look up, or the fact you desire to verify, *Right Here* gives you all that you want to know in the briefest and most enlightening form. Historical reference, for instance; career of John Huss, let us say. Here we are: "Huss, John, celebrated religious reformer. Born 1369, burned at Constance 1415. The Emperor Sigismund universally blamed." '

'If he had been burnt in these days everyone would have suspected the Suffragettes,' observed Mellowkent.

'Poultry-keeping, now,' resumed Caiaphas, 'that's a subject that might crop up in a novel dealing with English country life. Here we have all about it: "The Leghorn as egg-producer. Lack of maternal instinct in the Minorca. Gapes in chickens, its cause and cure. Ducklings for the early market, how fattened." There, you see, there it all is, nothing lacking.'

'Except the maternal instinct in the Minorca, and that you could hardly be expected to supply.'

'Sporting records, that's important, too; now how many men, sporting men even, are there who can say off-hand what horse won the Derby in any particular year? Now it's just a little thing of that sort –'

'My dear sir,' interrupted Mellowkent, 'there are at least four men in my club who can not only tell me what horse won in any given year, but what horse ought to have won and why it didn't. If your book could supply a method for protecting one from information of that sort it would do more than anything you have yet claimed for it.'

'Geography,' said Caiaphas, imperturbably; 'that's a thing that a busy man, writing at high pressure, may easily make a slip over. Only the other day a well-known author made the Volga flow into the Black Sea instead of the Caspian; now, with this book –'

'On a polished rose-wood stand behind you there reposes a reliable and up-to-date atlas,' said Mellowkent; 'and now I must really ask you to be going.'

'An atlas', said Caiaphas, 'gives merely the chart of the river's course, and indicates the principal towns that it passes. Now *Right Here* gives you the scenery, traffic, ferry-boat charges, the prevalent types of fish, boatmen's slang terms, and hours of sailing of the principal river steamers. It gives you –'

Mellowkent sat and watched the hard-featured, resolute, pitiless salesman, as he sat doggedly in the chair wherein he had installed himself, unflinchingly extolling the merits of his undesired wares. A spirit of wistful emulation took possession of the author; why could he not live up to the cold stern name he had adopted? Why must he sit here weakly and listen to this weary, unconvincing tirade, why could he not be Mark Mellowkent for a few brief moments, and meet this man on level terms?

A sudden inspiration flashed across him.

'Have you read my last book, *The Cageless Linnet*?' he asked.

'I don't read novels,' said Caiaphas tersely.

'Oh, but you ought to read this one, everyone ought to,' exclaimed Mellowkent, fishing the book down from a shelf; 'published at six shillings, you can have it at four-and-six. There is a bit in chapter five that I feel sure you would like, where Emma is alone in the birch copse waiting for Harold Huntingdon – that is the man her family want her to marry. She really wants to marry him, too, but she does not discover that till chapter fifteen. Listen: "Far as the eye could stretch rolled the mauve and purple billows of heather, lit up here and there with the glowing yellow of gorse and broom, and edged round with the delicate greys and silver and green of the young birch trees. Tiny blue and brown butterflies fluttered above the fronds of heather, revelling in the sunlight, and overhead the larks were singing as only larks can sing. It was a day when all Nature –'

'In *Right Here* you have full information on all branches of Nature study,' broke in the book-agent, with a tired note sounding in his voice for the first time; 'forestry, insect life, bird migration, reclamation of waste lands. As I was saying, no man who has to deal with the varied interests of life –'

'I wonder if you would care for one of my earlier books, *The Reluctance of Lady Cullumpton*,' said Mellowkent, hunting again through the book-shelf; 'some people consider it my best novel. Ah, here it is. I see there are one or two spots on the cover, so I won't ask more than three-and-ninepence for it. Do let me read you how it opens:

' "Beatrice Lady Cullumpton entered the long, dimly-lit drawing-room, her eyes blazing with a hope that she guessed to be groundless, her lips trembling with a fear that she could not disguise. In her hand she carried a small fan, a fragile toy of lace and satinwood. Something snapped as she entered the room; she had crushed the fan into a dozen pieces."

'There, what do you think of that for an opening? It tells you at once that there's something afoot.'

'I don't read novels,' said Caiaphas sullenly.

'But just think what a resource they are', exclaimed the author, 'on long winter evenings, or perhaps when you are laid up with a strained ankle – a thing that might happen to anyone; or if you were staying in a house-party with persistent wet weather and a stupid hostess and insufferably dull fellow-guests, you would just make an excuse that you had letters to write, go to your room, light a cigarette, and for three-and-ninepence you could plunge into the society of Beatrice Lady Cullumpton and her set. No one ought to travel without one or two of my novels in their luggage as a stand-by. A friend of mine said only the other day that he would as soon think of going into the tropics without quinine as of going on a visit without a couple of Mark Mellowkents in his kit-bag. Perhaps sensation is more in your line. I wonder if I've got a copy of *The Python's Kiss*.'

Caiaphas did not wait to be tempted with selections from that thrilling work of fiction. With a muttered remark about having no time to waste on monkey-talk, he gathered up his slighted volume and departed. He made no audible reply to Mellowkent's cheerful 'Good morning', but the latter fancied that a look of respectful hatred flickered in the cold, grey eyes.

Canossa

Demosthenes Platterbaff, the eminent Unrest Inducer, stood on his trial for a serious offence, and the eyes of the political world were focused on the jury. The offence, it should be stated, was serious for the Government rather than for the prisoner. He had blown up the Albert Hall on the eve of the great Liberal Federation Tango Tea, the occasion on which the Chancellor of the Exchequer was expected to propound his new theory: 'Do partridges spread infectious diseases?' Platterbaff had chosen his time well; the Tango Tea had been hurriedly postponed, but there were other political fixtures which could not be put off under any circumstances. The day after the trial there was to be a by-election at Nemesis-on-Hand, and it had been openly announced in the division that if Platterbaff were languishing in gaol on polling day the Government candidate would be 'outed' to a certainty. Unfortunately, there could be no doubt or misconception as to Platterbaff's guilt. He had not only pleaded guilty, but had expressed his intention of repeating his escapade in other directions as soon as circumstances permitted; throughout the trial he was busy examining a small model of the Free Trade Hall in Manchester. The jury could not possibly find that the prisoner had not deliberately and intentionally blown up the Albert Hall; the question was: Could they find any extenuating circumstances which would permit of an acquittal? Of course any sentence which the law might feel compelled to inflict would be followed by an immediate pardon, but it was highly desirable, from the Government's point of view, that the necessity for such an exercise of clemency should not arise. A headlong pardon, on the eve of a by-election, with threats of a heavy voting defection if it were withheld or even delayed, would not necessarily be a surrender, but it would look like one. Opponents would be only too ready to attribute ungenerous motives. Hence the anxiety in the crowded Court, and in the little groups gathered round the tape-machines in Whitehall and Downing Street and other affected centres.

The jury returned from considering their verdict; there was a flutter, an excited murmur, a death-like hush. The foreman delivered his message:

'The jury find the prisoner guilty of blowing up the Albert Hall. The jury wish to add a rider drawing attention to the fact that a by-election is pending in the Parliamentary division of Nemesis-on-Hand.'

'That, of course,' said the Government Prosecutor, springing to his feet, 'is equivalent to an acquittal?'

'I hardly think so,' said the Judge, coldly; 'I feel obliged to sentence the prisoner to a week's imprisonment.'

'And may the Lord have mercy on the poll,' a Junior Counsel exclaimed irreverently.

It was a scandalous sentence, but then the Judge was not on the Ministerial side in politics.

The verdict and sentence were made known to the public at twenty minutes past five in the afternoon; at half-past five a dense crowd was massed outside the Prime Minister's residence lustily singing, to the air of 'Trelawney':

'And should our Hero rot in gaol,
  For e'en a single day,
There's Fifteen Hundred Voting Men
  Will vote the other way.'

'Fifteen hundred,' said the Prime Minister, with a shudder; 'it's too horrible to think of. Our majority last time was only a thousand and seven.'

'The poll opens at eight tomorrow morning,' said the Chief

Organizer; 'we must have him out by 7 a.m.'

'Seven-thirty,' amended the Prime Minister; 'we must avoid any appearance of precipitancy.'

'Not later than seven-thirty, then,' said the Chief Organizer; 'I have promised the agent down there that he shall be able to display posters announcing "Platterbaff is Out", before the poll opens. He said it was our only chance of getting a telegram "Radprop is In" tonight.'

At half-past seven the next morning the Prime Minister and the Chief Organizer sat at breakfast, making a perfunctory meal, and awaiting the return of the Home Secretary, who had gone in person to superintend the releasing of Platterbaff. Despite the earliness of the hour a small crowd had gathered in the street outside, and the horrible menacing Trelawney refrain of the 'Fifteen Hundred Voting Men' came in a steady, monotonous chant.

'They will cheer presently when they hear the news,' said the Prime Minister hopefully; 'hark! They are booing someone now! That must be McKenna.'

The Home Secretary entered the room a moment later, disaster written on his face.

'He won't go!' he exclaimed.

'Won't go? Won't leave gaol?'

'He won't go unless he has a brass band. He says he never has left prison without a brass band to play him out, and he's not going to go without one now.'

'But surely that sort of thing is provided by his supporters and admirers?' said the Prime Minister; 'we can hardly be supposed to supply a released prisoner with a brass band. How on earth could we defend it on the Estimates?'

'His supporters say it is up to us to provide the music,' said the Home Secretary; 'they say we put him in prison, and it's our affair to see that he leaves it in a respectable manner. Anyway, he won't go unless he has a band.'

The telephone squealed shrilly; it was a trunk call from Nemesis.

'Poll opens in five minutes. Is Platterbaff out yet? In Heaven's name, why –'

The Chief Organizer rang off.

'This is not a moment for standing on dignity,' he observed bluntly; 'musicians must be supplied at once. Platterbaff must have his band.'

'Where are you going to find the musicians?' asked the Home Secretary wearily; 'we can't employ a military band, in fact, I don't think he'd have one if we offered it, and there aren't any others. There's a musicians' strike on, I suppose you know.'

'Can't you get a strike permit?' asked the Organizer.

'I'll try,' said the Home Secretary, and went to the telephone.

Eight o'clock struck. The crowd outside chanted with an increasing volume of sound:

'Will vote the other way.'

A telegram was brought in. It was from the central committee rooms at Nemesis. 'Losing twenty votes per minute,' was its brief message.

Ten o'clock struck. The Prime Minister, the Home Secretary, the Chief Organizer, and several earnest helpful friends were gathered in the inner gateway of the prison, talking volubly to Demosthenes Platterbaff, who stood with folded arms and squarely planted feet, silent in their midst. Golden-tongued legislators whose eloquence had swayed the Marconi Inquiry Committee, or at any rate the greater part of it, expended their arts of oratory in vain on this stubborn unyielding man. Without a band he would not go; and they had no band.

A quarter past ten, half-past. A constant stream of telegraph boys poured in through the prison gates.

'Yamley's factory hands just voted you can guess how,' ran a despairing message, and the others were all of the same tenor. Nemesis was going the way of Reading.

'Have you any band instruments of an easy nature to play?' demanded the Chief Organizer of the Prison Governor; 'drums, cymbals, those sort of things?'

'The warders have a private band of their own,' said the Governor, 'but of course I couldn't allow the men themselves –'

'Lend us the instruments,' said the Chief Organizer.

One of the earnest helpful friends was a skilled performer on the cornet, the Cabinet Ministers were able to clash cymbals more or less in tune, and the Chief Organizer had some knowledge of the drum.

'What tune would you prefer?' he asked Platterbaff.

'The popular song of the moment,' replied the Agitator after a moment's reflection.

It was a tune they had all heard hundreds of times, so there was no difficulty in turning out a passable imitation of it. To the improvised strains of 'I didn't want to do it' the prisoner strode forth to freedom. The words of the song had reference, it was understood, to the incarcerating Government and not to the destroyer of the Albert Hall.

The seat was lost, after all, by a narrow majority. The local Trade Unionists took offence at the fact of Cabinet Ministers having personally acted as strike-breakers, and even the release of Platterbaff failed to pacify them.

The seat was lost, but Ministers had scored a moral victory. They had shown that they knew when and how to yield.

The Infernal Parliament

In an age when it has become increasingly difficult to accomplish anything new or original, Bavton Bidderdale interested his generation by dying of a new disease. 'We always knew he would do something remarkable one of these days,' observed his aunts; 'he has justified our belief in him.' But there is a section of humanity ever ready to refuse recognition to meritorious achievement, and a large and influential school of doctors asserted their belief that Bidderdale was not really dead. The funeral arrangements had to be held over until the matter was settled one way or the other, and the aunts went provisionally into half-mourning.

Meanwhile, Bidderdale remained in Hell as a guest pending his reception on a more regular footing. 'If you are not really supposed to be dead,' said the authorities of that region, 'we don't want to seem in an indecent hurry to grab you. The theory that Hell is in serious need of population is a thing of the past. Why, to take your family alone, there are any number of Bidderdales on our books, as you may discover later. It is part of our system that relations should be encouraged to live together down here. From observations made in another world we have abundant evidence that it promotes the ends we have in view. However, while you are a guest we should like you to be treated with every consideration and be shown anything that specially interests you. Of course, you would like to see our Parliament?'

'Have you a Parliament in Hell?' asked Bidderdale in some surprise.

'Only quite recently. Of course we've always had chaos, but not under Parliamentary rules. Now, however, that Parliaments are becoming the fashion, in Turkey and Persia, and I suppose before long in Afghanistan and China, it seemed rather ostentatious to stand outside the movement. That young Fiend just going by is the Member for East Brimstone; he'll be delighted to show you over the institution.'

'You will just be in time to hear the opening of a debate,' said the Member, as he led Bidderdale through a spacious outer lobby, decorated with frescoes representing the fall of man, the discovery of gold, the invention of playing cards, and other traditionally appropriate subjects. 'The Member for Nether Furnace is proposing a motion "that this House do arrogantly protest to the legislatures of earthly countries against the wrongful and injurious misuses of the word 'fiendish', in application to purely human misdemeanours, a misuse tending to create a false and detrimental impression concerning the Infernal Regions." '

A feature of the Parliament Chamber itself was its enormous size. The space allotted to Members was small and very sparsely occupied, but the public galleries stretched away tier on tier as far as the eye could reach, and were packed to their utmost capacity.

'There seems to be a very great public interest in the debate,' exclaimed Bidderdale.

'Members are excused from attending the debates if they so desire,' the Fiend proceeded to explain; 'it is one of their most highly valued privileges. On the other hand, constituents are compelled to listen throughout to all the speeches. After all, you must remember, we are in Hell.'

Bidderdale repressed a shudder and turned his attention to the debate.

'Nothing', the Fiend-Orator was observing, 'is more deplorable among the cultured races of the present day than the tendency to identify fiendhood, in the most sweeping fashion, with all manner of disreputable excesses, excesses which can only be alleged against us on the merest legendary evidence. Vices which are exclusively or predominatingly human are unblushingly described as inhuman, and, what is even more contemptible and ungenerous, as fiendish. If one investigates such statements as "inhuman treatment of pit ponies" or "fiendish cruelties in the Congo", so frequently to be heard in our brother Parliaments on earth, one finds accumulative and indisputable evidence that it is the human treatment of pit ponies and Congo natives that is really in question, and that no authenticated case of fiendish agency in these atrocities can be substantiated. It is, perhaps, a minor matter for complaint,' continued the orator, 'that the human race frequently pays us the doubtful compliment of describing as "devilish funny" jokes which are neither funny nor devilish.'

The orator paused, and an oppressive silence reigned over the vast chamber.

'What is happening?' whispered Bidderdale.

'Five minutes Hush,' explained his guide; 'it is a sign that the speaker was listened to in silent approval, which is the highest mark of appreciation that can be bestowed in Pandemonium. Let's come into the smoking-room.'

'Will the motion be carried?' asked Bidderdale, wondering inwardly how Sir Edward Grey would treat the protest if it reached the British Parliament; an *entente* with the Infernal Regions opened up a fascinating vista, in which the Foreign Secretary's imagination might hopelessly lose itself.

'Carried? Of course not,' said the Fiend; 'in the Infernal Parliament all motions are necessarily lost.'

'In earthly Parliaments nowadays nearly everything is found,' said Bidderdale, 'including salaries and travelling expenses.'

He felt that at any rate he was probably the first member of his family to make a joke in Hell.

'By the way,' he added, 'talking of earthly Parliaments, have you got the Party system down here?'

'In Hell? Impossible. You see we have no system of rewards. We have specialized so thoroughly on punishments that the other branch has been entirely neglected. And besides, Government by delusion, as you practise it in your Parliament, would be unworkable here. I should be the last person to say anything against temptation, naturally, but we have a proverb down here "in baiting a mouse-trap with cheese, always leave room for the mouse". Such a party-cry, for instance, as your "ninepence for fourpence" would be absolutely inoperative; it not only leaves no room for the mouse, it leaves no room for the imagination. You have a saying in your country I believe, "there's no fool like a damned fool"; all the fools down here are, necessarily, damned, but – you wouldn't get them to nibble at ninepence for fourpence.'

'Couldn't they be scolded and lectured into believing it, as a sort of moral and intellectual duty?' asked Bidderdale.

'We haven't all your facilities,' said the Fiend; 'we've nothing down here that exactly corresponds to the Master of Elibank.'

At this moment Bidderdale's attention was caught by an item on a loose sheet of agenda paper: 'Vote on account of special Hells.'

'Ah,' he said, 'I've often heard the expression "there is a special Hell reserved for such-and-such a type of person". Do tell me about them.'

'I'll show you one in course of preparation,' said the Fiend, leading him down the corridor. 'This one is designed to accommodate one of the leading playwrights of your nation. You may observe scores of imps engaged in pasting notices of modern British plays into a huge press-cutting book, each under the name of the author, alphabetically arranged. The book will contain nearly half a million notices, I suppose, and it will form the sole literature supplied to this specially doomed individual.'

Bidderdale was not altogether impressed.

'Some dramatic authors wouldn't so very much mind spending eternity poring over a book of contemporary press-cuttings,' he observed.

The Fiend, laughing unpleasantly, lowered his voice.

'The letter "S" is missing.'

For the first time Bidderdale realized that he was in Hell.

The Comments of Moung Ka

Moung Ka, cultivator of rice and philosophic virtues, sat on the raised platform of his cane-built house by the banks of the swiftly-flowing Irrawaddy. On two sides of the house there was a bright-green swamp, which stretched away to where the uncultivated jungle growth began. In the bright-green swamp, which was really a rice-field when you looked closely at it, bitterns and pond-herons and elegant cattle-egrets stalked and peered with the absorbed air of careful and conscientious reptile-hunters, who could never forget that, while they were undoubtedly useful, they were also distinctly decorative. In the tall reed growth by the river-side grazing buffaloes showed in patches of dark slaty blue, like plums fallen amid long grass, and in the tamarind trees that shaded Moung Ka's house the crows, restless, raucous-throated, and much-too-many, kept up their incessant afternoon din, saying over and over again all the things that crows have said since there were crows to say them.

Moung Ka sat smoking his enormous green-brown cigar, without which no Burmese man, woman, or child seems really complete, dispensing from time to time instalments of worldly information for the benefit and instruction of his two companions. The steamer which came up-river from Mandalay thrice a week brought Moung Ka a Rangoon news-sheet, in which the progress of the world's events was set forth in telegraphic messages and commented on in pithy paragraphs. Moung Ka, who read these things and retailed them as occasion served to his friends and neighbours, with philosophical additions of his own, was held in some esteem locally as a political thinker; in Burma it is possible to be a politician without ceasing to be a philosopher.

His friend Moung Thwa, dealer in teakwood, had just returned down river from distant Bhamo, where he had spent many weeks in dignified, unhurried chaffering with Chinese merchants; the first place to which he had naturally turned his steps, bearing with him his betel-box and fat cigar, had been the raised platform of Moung Ka's cane-built house under the tamarind trees. The youthful Moung Shoogalay, who had studied in the foreign schools at Mandalay and knew many English words, was also of the little group that sat listening to Moung Ka's bulletin of the world's health and ignoring the screeching of the crows.

There had been the usual preliminary talk of timber and the rice market and sundry local matters, and then the wider and remoter things of life came under review.

'And what has been happening away from here?' asked Moung Thwa of the newspaper reader.

'Away from here' comprised that considerable portion of the world's surface which lay beyond the village boundaries.

'Many things,' said Moung Ka reflectively, 'but principally two things of much interest and of an opposite nature. Both, however, concern the action of Governments.'

Moung Thwa nodded his head gravely, with the air of one who reverenced and distrusted all Governments.

'The first thing, of which you may have heard on your journeyings,' said Moung Ka, 'is an act of the Indian Government, which has annulled the not-long-ago accomplished partition of Bengal.'

'I heard something of this', said Moung Thwa, 'from a Madrassi merchant on the boat journey. But I did not learn the reasons that made the Government take this step. Why was the partition annulled?'

'Because', said Moung Ka, 'it was held to be against the wishes of the greater number of the people of Bengal. Therefore the Government made an end of it.'

Moung Thwa was silent for a moment. 'Is it a wise thing the

Government has done?' he asked presently.

'It is a good thing to consider the wishes of a people,' said Moung Ka. 'The Bengalis may be a people who do not always wish what is best for them. Who can say? But at least their wishes have been taken into consideration, and that is a good thing.'

'And the other matter of which you spoke?' questioned Moung Thwa, 'the matter of an opposite nature.'

'The other matter,' said Moung Ka, 'is that the British Government has decided on the partition of Britain. Where there has been one Parliament and one Government there are to be two Parliaments and two Governments, and there will be two treasuries and two sets of taxes.'

Moung Thwa was greatly interested at this news.

'And is the feeling of the people of Britain in favour of this partition?' he asked. 'Will they not dislike it, as the people of Bengal disliked the partition of their Province?'

'The feeling of the people of Britain has not been consulted, and will not be consulted,' said Moung Ka; 'the Act of Partition will pass through one Chamber where the Government rules supreme, and the other Chamber can only delay it a little while, and then it will be made into the Law of the Land.'

'But is it wise not to consult the feeling of the people?' asked Moung Thwa.

'Very wise,' answered Moung Ka, 'for if the people were consulted they would say 'No', as they have always said when such a decree was submitted to their opinion, and if the people said 'No' there would be an end of the matter, but also an end of the Government. Therefore, it is wise for the Government to shut its ears to what the people may wish.'

'But why must the people of Bengal be listened to and the people of Britain not listened to?' asked Moung Thwa; 'surely the partition of their country affects them just as closely. Are their opinions too silly to be of any weight?'

'The people of Britain are what is called a Democracy,' said Moung Ka.

'A Democracy?' questioned Moung Thwa; 'what is that?'

'A Democracy', broke in Moung Shoogalay eagerly, 'is a community that governs itself according to its own wishes and interests by electing accredited representatives who enact its laws and supervise and control their administration. Its aim and object is government of the community in the interests of the community.'

'Then,' said Moung Thwa, turning to his neighbour, 'if the people of Britain are a Democracy –'

'I never said they were a Democracy,' interrupted Moung Ka placidly.

'Surely we both heard you!' exclaimed Moung Thwa.

'Not correctly,' said Moung Ka; 'I said they are what is called a Democracy.'

The Gala Programme

An Unrecorded Episode in Roman History

It was an auspicious day in the Roman Calendar, the birthday of the popular and gifted young Emperor Placidus Superbus. Everyone in Rome was bent on keeping high festival, the weather was at its best, and naturally the Imperial Circus was crowded to its fullest capacity. A few minutes before the hour fixed for the commencement of the spectacle a loud fanfare of trumpets proclaimed the arrival of Cæsar, and amid the vociferous acclamations of the multitude the Emperor took his seat in the Imperial Box. As the shouting of the crowd died away an even more thrilling salutation could be heard in the near distance, the angry, impatient roaring and howling of the beasts caged in the Imperial menagerie.

'Explain the programme to me,' commanded the Emperor, having beckoned the Master of the Ceremonies to his side.

That eminent official wore a troubled look.

'Gracious Cæsar,' he announced, 'a most promising and entertaining programme has been devised and prepared for your august approval. In the first place there is to be a chariot contest of unusual brilliancy and interest; three teams that have never hitherto suffered defeat are to contend for the Herculaneum Trophy, together with the purse which your Imperial generosity has been pleased to add. The chances of the competing teams are accounted to be as nearly as possible equal, and there is much wagering among the populace. The black Thracians are perhaps the favourites –.'

'I know, I know,' interrupted Cæsar, who had listened to exhaustive talk on the same subject all the morning; 'what else is there on the programme?'

'The second part of the programme', said the Imperial Official, 'consists of a grand combat of wild beasts, specially selected for their strength, ferocity, and fighting qualities. There will appear simultaneously in the arena fourteen Nubian lions and lionesses, five tigers, six Syrian bears, eight Persian panthers, and three North African ditto, a number of wolves and lynxes from the Teutonic forests, and seven gigantic wild bulls from the same region. There will also be wild swine of unexampled savageness, a rhinoceros from the Barbary coast, some ferocious man-apes, and a hyæna, reputed to be mad.'

'It promises well,' said the Emperor.

'It *promised* well, O Cæsar,' said the official dolorously, 'it promised marvellously well; but between the promise and the performance a cloud has arisen.'

'A cloud? What cloud?' queried Cæsar, with a frown.

'The Suffragetæ,' explained the official; 'they threaten to interfere with the chariot race.'

'I'd like to see them do it!' exclaimed the Emperor indignantly.

'I fear your Imperial wish may be unpleasantly gratified,' said the Master of the Ceremonies; 'we are taking, of course, every possible precaution, and guarding all the entrances to the arena and the stables with a triple guard; but it is rumoured that at the signal for the entry of the chariots five hundred women will let themselves down with ropes from the public seats and swarm all over the course. Naturally no race could be run under such circumstances; the programme will be ruined.'

'On my birthday', said Placidus Superbus, 'they would not dare to do such an outrageous thing.'

'The more august the occasion, the more desirous they will be to advertise themselves and their cause,' said the harassed official; 'they do not scruple to make riotous interference even with the ceremonies in the temples.'

'Who *are* these Suffragetæ?' asked the Emperor. 'Since I came back from my Pannonian expedition I have heard of nothing else but their excesses and demonstrations.'

'They are a political sect of very recent origin, and their aim seems to be to get a big share of political authority into their hands. The means they are taking to convince us of their fitness to help in making and administering the laws consist of wild indulgence in tumult, destruction, and defiance of all authority. They have already damaged some of the most historically valuable of our public treasures, which can never be replaced.'

'Is it possible that the sex which we hold in such honour and for which we feel such admiration can produce such hordes of Furies?' asked the Emperor.

'It takes all sorts to make a sex,' observed the Master of the Ceremonies, who possessed a certain amount of worldly wisdom; 'also,' he continued anxiously, 'it takes very little to upset a gala programme.'

'Perhaps the disturbance that you anticipate will turn out to be an idle threat,' said the Emperor consolingly.

'But if they should carry out their intention,' said the official, 'the programme will be utterly ruined.'

The Emperor said nothing.

Five minutes later the trumpets rang out for the commencement of the entertainment. A hum of excited anticipation ran through the ranks of the spectators, and final bets on the issue of the great race were hurriedly shouted. The gates leading from the stables were slowly swung open, and a troop of mounted attendants rode round the track to ascertain that everything was clear for the momentous contest. Again the trumpets rang out, and then, before the foremost chariot had appeared, there arose a wild tumult of shouting, laughing, angry protests, and shrill screams of defiance. Hundreds of women were being lowered by their accomplices into the arena. A moment later they were running and dancing in frenzied troops across the track where the chariots were supposed to compete. No team of arena-trained horses would have faced such a frantic mob; the race was clearly an impossibility. Howls of disappointment and rage rose from the spectators, howls of triumph echoed back from the women in possession. The vain efforts of the circus attendants to drive out the invading horde merely added to the uproar and confusion; as fast as the Suffragetæ were thrust away from one portion of the track they swarmed on to another.

The Master of the Ceremonies was nearly delirious from rage and mortification. Placidus Superbus, who remained calm and unruffled as ever, beckoned to him and spoke a word or two in his ear. For the first time that afternoon the sorely-tried official was seen to smile.

A trumpet rang out from the Imperial Box: an instant hush fell over the excited throng. Perhaps the Emperor, as a last resort, was going to announce some concession to the Suffragetæ.

'Close the stable gates,' commanded the Master of the Ceremonies, 'and open all the menagerie dens. It is the Imperial pleasure that the second portion of the programme be taken first.'

It turned out that the Master of the Ceremonies had in no wise exaggerated the probable brilliancy of this portion of the spectacle. The wild bulls were really wild, and the hyæna reputed to be mad thoroughly lived up to its reputation.

Eve and the Forbidden Fruit

A Fragment of Incomplete History

In endeavouring to get Eve to eat the Forbidden Fruit, the Serpent elaborated all the arguments and inducements that he could think of and even improvised some new ones. But Eve's reply was unfailingly the same. Her mind was made up.

The Serpent gave a final petulant wiggle of its coils and slid out of the landscape with an unmistakable air of displeasure.

'You haven't tasted the Forbidden Fruit, I suppose?' said a pleasant but rather anxious voice at Eve's shoulder a few minutes later. It was one of the Archangels who was speaking.

'No,' said Eve placidly, 'Adam and I went into the matter very thoroughly last night and we came to the conclusion that we should be rather ill-advised in eating the fruit of that tree; after all, there are heaps of other trees and vegetables for us to feed on.'

'Of course it does great credit to your sense of obedience,' said the Archangel, with an entire lack of enthusiasm in his voice, 'but it will cause considerable disappointment in some quarters. There was an idea going about that you might be persuaded by specious arguments into tasting the Forbidden Fruit.'

'There *was* a Serpent here speaking about it the last few days,' said Eve; 'he seemed rather huffed that we didn't follow his advice, but Adam and I went into the whole matter last night and we came to t –'

'Yes, yes,' said the Archangel in an embarrassed voice, 'a very praiseworthy decision, of course. At the same time, well, it's not exactly what everyone anticipated. You see Sin has got to come into the world, somehow.'

'Yes?' said Eve, without any marked show of interest.

'And you are practically the only people who *can* introduce it.'

'I don't know anything about that,' said Eve placidly; 'Adam and I have got to think of our own interests. We went very thoroughly –'

'You see,' said the Archangel, 'the most elaborate arrangements have been foreordained on the assumption that you *would* yield to temptation. No end of pictures of the Fall of Man are destined to be painted and a poet is going one day to write an immortal poem called "Paradise L –" '

'Called what?' asked Eve as the Archangel suddenly pulled himself up.

' "Paradise Life." It's all about you and Adam eating the Forbidden Fruit. If you don't eat it I don't see how the poem can possibly be written.'

Eve is still dogged – says she has no appetite for more fruit.

'I had some figs and plantains and half a dozen medlars early this morning, and mulberries and a few mangosteens in the middle of today, and last night Adam and I feasted to repletion on young asparagus and parsley-tops with a sauce of pomegranate juice; and yesterday morning –'

'I must be going,' said the Archangel, adding rather sulkily, 'if I should see the Serpent would it be any use telling him to look round again –?'

'Not in the least,' said Eve. Her mind was made up.

'The trouble is,' said the Archangel as he folded his wings in a serener atmosphere and recounted his Eden experiences, 'there is too great a profusion of fruit in that garden; there isn't enough temptation to hunger after one special kind. Now if there was a partial crop failure –' The idea was acted on. Blight, mildew and caterpillars and untimely frosts worked havoc among trees and bushes and herbs; the plantains withered, the asparagus never sprouted, the pineapples never ripened, radishes were worm-eaten before they were big enough to pick. The Tree of Knowledge alone flaunted itself in undiminished luxuriance.

'We shall have to eat it after all,' said Adam, who had breakfasted sparsely on some mouldy tamarinds and the rind of yesterday's melon.

'We were told not to, and we're not going to,' said Eve stubbornly. Her mind was made up on the point –.

How William Came

(From *When William Came*)

'I was in the early stages of my fever when I got the first inkling of what was going on,' said Yeovil to the doctor, as they sat over their coffee in a recess of the big smoking-room; 'just able to potter about a bit in the daytime, fighting against depression and inertia, feverish as evening came on, and delirious in the night. My game tracker and my attendant were both Buriats, and spoke very little Russian, and that was the only language we had in common to converse in. In matters concerning food and sport we soon got to understand each other, but on other subjects we were not easily able to exchange ideas. One day my tracker had been to a distant trading-store to get some things of which we were in need; the store was eighty miles from the nearest point of railroad, eighty miles of terribly bad roads, but it was in its way a centre and transmitter of news from the outside world. The tracker brought back with him vague tidings of a conflict of some sort between the "Metskie Tsar" and the "Angliskie Tsar", and kept repeating the Russian word for defeat. The "Angliskie Tsar" I recognized, of course, as the King of England, but my brain was too sick and dull to read any further meaning into the man's reiterated gabble. I grew so ill just then that I had to give up the struggle against fever, and make my way as best I could towards the nearest point where nursing and doctoring could be had. It was one evening, in a lonely rest-hut on the edge of a huge forest, as I was waiting for my boy to bring the meal for which I was feverishly impatient, and which I knew I should loathe as soon as it was brought, that the explanation of the word "Metskie" flashed on me. I had thought of it as referring to some Oriental potentate, some rebellious rajah perhaps, who was giving trouble, and whose followers had possibly discomfited an isolated British force in some out-of-the-way corner of our Empire. And all of a sudden I knew that "Nemetskie Tsar', German Emperor, had been the name that the man had been trying to convey to me. I shouted for the tracker, and put him through a breathless cross-examination; he confirmed what my fears had told me. The "Metskie Tsar" was a big European ruler, he had been in conflict with the "Angliskie Tsar", and the latter had been defeated, swept away; the man spoke the word that he used for ships, and made energetic pantomime to express the sinking of a fleet. Holham, there was nothing for it but to hope that this was a false, groundless rumour, that had somehow crept to the confines of civilization. In my saner balanced moments it was possible to disbelieve it, but if you have ever suffered from delirium you will know what raging torments of agony I went through in the nights, how my brain fought and refought that rumoured disaster.'

The doctor gave a murmur of sympathetic understanding.

'Then', continued Yeovil, 'I reached the small Siberian town towards which I had been struggling. There was a little colony of Russians there, traders, officials, a doctor or two, and some army officers. I put up at the primitive hotel-restaurant, which was the general gathering-place of the community. I knew quickly that the news was true. Russians are the most tactful of any European race that I have ever met; they did not stare with insolent or pitying curiosity, but there was something changed in their attitude which told me that the travelling Briton was no longer in their eyes the interesting respect-commanding personality that he had been in past days. I went to my own room, where the samovar was bubbling its familiar tune and a smiling red-shirted Russian boy was helping my Buriat servant to unpack my wardrobe, and I asked for any back numbers of newspapers that could be supplied at a moment's notice. I was given a bundle of well-thumbed sheets, odd pieces of the *Novoe Vremya*, the *Moskovskie Viedomosti*, one or two complete numbers of local papers published at Perm and Tobolsk. I do not read Russian well, though I speak it fairly readily, but from the fragments of disconnected telegrams that I pieced together I gathered enough information to acquaint me with the extent of the tragedy that had been worked out in a few crowded hours in a corner of North-Western Europe. I searched frantically for telegrams of later dates that would put a better complexion on the matter, that would retrieve something from the ruin; presently I came across a page of the illustrated supplement that the *Novoe Vremya* publishes once a week. There was a photograph of a long-fronted building with a flag flying over it, labelled "The new standard floating over Buckingham Palace". The picture was not much more than a smudge, but the flag, possibly touched up, was unmistakable. It was the eagle of the Nemetskie Tsar. I have a vivid recollection of that plainly-furnished little room, with the inevitable gilt ikon in one corner, and the samovar hissing and gurgling on the table, and the thrumming music of a balalaika orchestra coming up from the restaurant below; the next coherent thing I can remember was weeks and weeks later, discussing in an impersonal detached manner whether I was strong enough to stand the fatigue of the long railway journey to Finland.

'Since then, Holham, I have been encouraged to keep my mind as much off the war and public affairs as possible, and I have been glad to do so. I knew the worst and there was no particular use in deepening my despondency by dragging out the details. But now I am more or less a live man again, and I want to fill in the gaps in my knowledge of what happened. You know how much I know, and how little; those fragments of Russian newspapers were about all the information that I had. I don't even know clearly how the whole thing started.'

Yeovil settled himself back in his chair with the air of a man who has done some necessary talking, and now assumes the role of listener.

'It started', said the doctor, 'with a wholly unimportant disagreement about some frontier business in East Africa; there was a slight attack of nerves in the stock markets, and then the whole thing seemed in a fair way towards being settled. Then the negotiations over the affair began to drag unduly, and there was a further flutter of nervousness in the money world. And then one morning the papers reported a highly menacing speech by one of the German Ministers, and the situation began to look black indeed. "He will be disavowed," everyone said over here, but in less than twenty-four hours those who knew anything knew that the crisis was on us – only their knowledge came too late. "War between two such civilized and enlightened nations is an impossibility," one of our leaders of public opinion had declared on the Saturday; by the following Friday the war had indeed become an impossibility, because we could no longer carry it on. It burst on us with calculated suddenness, and we were just not enough, everywhere where the pressure came. Our ships were good against their ships, our seamen were better than their seamen, but our ships were not able to cope with their ships plus their superiority in aircraft. Our trained men were good against their trained men, but they could not be in several places at once, and the enemy could. Our half-trained men and our untrained men could not master the science of war at a moment's notice, and a moment's notice was all they got. The enemy were a nation apprenticed in arms, we were not even the idle apprentice: we had not deemed apprenticeship worth our while. There was courage enough running loose in the land, but it was like unharnessed electricity, it controlled no forces, it struck no blows. There was no time for the heroism and the devotion which a drawn-out struggle, however hopeless, can produce; the war was over almost as soon as it had begun. After the reverses which happened with lightning rapidity in the first three days of warfare, the newspapers made no effort to pretend that the situation could be retrieved; editors and public alike recognized that these were blows over the heart, and that it was a matter of moments before we were counted out. One might liken the whole affair to a snap checkmate early in a game of chess; one side had thought out the moves, and brought the requisite pieces into play, the other side was hampered and helpless, with its resources unavailable, its strategy discounted in advance. That, in a nutshell, is the history of the war.'

Yeovil was silent for a moment or two, then he asked:

'And the sequel, the peace?'

'The collapse was so complete that I fancy even the enemy were hardly prepared for the consequences of their victory. No one had quite realized what one disastrous campaign would mean for an island nation with a closely packed population. The conquerors were in a position to dictate what terms they pleased, and it was not wonderful that their ideas of aggrandizement expanded in the hour of intoxication. There was no European combination ready to say them nay, and certainly no one Power was going to be rash enough to step in to contest the terms of the treaty that they imposed on the conquered. Annexation had probably never been a dream before the war; after the war it suddenly became temptingly practical. *Warum nicht?* became the theme of leader-writers in the German press; they pointed out that Britain, defeated and humiliated, but with enormous powers of recuperation, would be a dangerous and inevitable enemy for the Germany of tomorrow, while Britain incorporated within the Hohenzollern Empire would merely be a disaffected province, without a navy to make its disaffection a serious menace, and with great tax-paying capabilities, which would be available for relieving the burdens of the other Imperial States. Wherefore, why not annex? The *warum nicht?* party prevailed. Our King, as you know, retired with his Court to Delhi, as Emperor in the East, with most of his overseas dominions still subject to his sway. The British Isles came under the German Crown as a *Reichsland*, a sort of Alsace-Lorraine washed by the North Sea instead of the Rhine. We still retain our Parliament, but it is a clipped and pruned-down shadow of its former self, with most of its functions in abeyance; when the elections were held it was difficult to get decent candidates to come forward or to get people to vote. It makes one smile bitterly to think that a year or two ago we were seriously squabbling as to who should have votes. And, of course, the old party divisions have more or less crumbled away. The Liberals naturally are under the blackest of clouds, for having steered the country to disaster, though to do them justice it was no more their fault than the fault of any other party. In a democracy such as ours was the Government of the day must more or less reflect the ideas and temperament of the nation in all vital matters, and the British nation in those days could not have been persuaded in the urgent need for military apprenticeship or of the deadly nature of its danger. It was willing now and then to be half-frightened and to have half-measures, or, one might better say, quarter-measures taken to reassure it, and the governments of the day were willing to take them, but any political party or group of statesmen that had said "the danger is enormous and immediate, the sacrifices and burdens must be enormous and immediate", would have met with certain defeat at the polls. Still, of course, the Liberals, as the party that had held office for nearly a decade, incurred the odium of a people maddened by defeat and humiliation; one Minister, who had had less responsibility for military organization than perhaps any of them, was attacked and nearly killed at Newcastle, another was hiding for three days on Exmoor, and escaped in disguise.'

'And the Conservatives?'

'They are also under eclipse, but it is more or less voluntary in their case. For generations they had taken their stand as supporters of Throne and Constitution, and when they suddenly found the Constitution gone and the Throne filled by an alien dynasty, their political orientation had vanished. They are in much the same position as the Jacobites occupied after the Hanoverian accession. Many of the leading Tory families have emigrated to the British lands beyond the seas, others are shut up in their country houses, retrenching their expenses, selling their acres, and investing their money abroad. The Labour faction, again, are almost in as bad odour as the Liberals, because of having hob-nobbed too effusively and ostentatiously with the German democratic parties on the eve of the war, exploiting an evangel of universal brotherhood which did not blunt a single Teuton bayonet when the hour came. I suppose in time party divisions will reassert themselves in some form or other; there will be a Socialist Party, and the mercantile and manufacturing interests will evolve a sort of bourgeoise party, and the different religious bodies will try to get themselves represented –'

Yeovil made a movement of impatience.

'All these things that you forecast', he said, 'must take time, considerable time; is this nightmare, then, to go on for ever?'

'It is not a nightmare, unfortunately,' said the doctor, 'it is a reality.'

'But, surely – a nation such as ours, a virile, highly-civilized nation with an age-long tradition of mastery behind it, cannot be held under for ever by a few thousand bayonets and machine guns. We must surely rise up one day and drive them out.'

'Dear man,' said the doctor, 'we might, of course, at some given moment overpower the garrison that is maintained here, and seize the forts, and perhaps we might be able to mine the harbours; what then? In a fortnight or so we could be starved into unconditional submission. Remember, all the advantages of isolated position that told in our favour while we had the sea dominion, tell against us now that the sea dominion is in other hands. The enemy would not need to mobilize a single army corps or to bring a single battleship into action; a fleet of nimble cruisers and destroyers circling round our coasts would be sufficient to shut out our food supplies.'

'Are you trying to tell me that this is a final overthrow?' said Yeovil in a shaking voice; 'are we to remain a subject race like the Poles?'

'Let us hope for a better fate,' said the doctor. 'Our opportunity may come if the Master Power is ever involved in an unsuccessful naval war with some other nation, or perhaps in some time of European crisis, when everything hung in the balance, our latent hostility might have to be squared by a concession of independence. That is what we have to hope for and watch for. On the other hand, the conquerors have to count on time and tact to weaken and finally obliterate the old feelings of nationality; the middle-aged of today will grow old and acquiescent in the changed state of things; the young generations will grow up never having known anything different. It's a far cry to Delhi, as the old Indian proverb says, and the strange half-European, half-Asiatic Court out there will seem more and more a thing exotic and unreal. "The King across the water" was a rallying-cry once upon a time in our history, but a king on the further side of the Indian Ocean is a shadowy competitor for one who alternates between Potsdam and Windsor.'

'I want you to tell me everything,' said Yeovil, after another pause; 'tell me, Holham, how far has this obliterating process of "time and tact" gone? It seems to be pretty fairly started already. I bought a newspaper as soon as I landed, and I read it in the train coming up. I read things that puzzled and disgusted me. There were announcements of concerts and plays and first-nights and private views; there were even small dances. There were advertisements of house-boats and week-end cottages and string bands for garden parties. It struck me that it was rather like merry-making with a dead body lying in the house.'

'Yeovil,' said the doctor, 'you must bear in mind two things. First, the necessity for the life of the country going on as if nothing had happened. It is true that many thousands of our working men and women have emigrated and thousands of our upper and middle class too; they were the people who were not tied down by business, or who could afford to cut those ties. But those represent comparatively a few out of the many. The great businesses and the small businesses must go on, people must be fed and clothed and housed and medically treated, and their thousand-and-one wants and necessities supplied. Look at me, for instance; however much I loathe coming under a foreign domination and paying taxes to an alien government, I can't abandon my practice and my patients, and set up anew in Toronto or Allahabad, and if I could, some other doctor would have to take my place here. I or that other doctor must have our servants and motors and food and furniture and newspapers, even our sport. The golf links and the hunting field have been well-nigh deserted since the war, but they are beginning to get back their votaries because out-door sport has become a necessity, and a very rational necessity, with numbers of men who have to work otherwise under unnatural and exacting conditions. That is one factor of the situation. The other affects London more especially, but through London it influences the rest of the country to a certain extent. You will see around you here much that will strike you as indications of heartless indifference to the calamity that has befallen our nation. Well, you must remember that many things in modern life, especially in the big cities, are not national but international. In the world of music and art and the drama, for instance, the foreign names are legion, they confront you at every turn, and some of our British devotees of such arts are more acclimatized to the ways of Munich or Moscow than they are familiar with the life, say, of Stirling or York. For years they have lived and thought and spoken in an atmosphere and jargon of denationalized culture – even those of them who have never left our shores. They would take pains to be intimately familiar with the domestic affairs and views of life of some Galician gipsy dramatist, and gravely quote and discuss his opinions on debts and mistresses and cookery, while they would shudder at "D'ye ken John Peel?" as a piece of uncouth barbarity. You cannot expect a world of that sort to be permanently concerned or downcast because the Crown of Charlemagne takes its place now on the top of the Royal box in the theatres, or at the head of programmes at State concerts. And then there are the Jews.'

'There are many in the land, or at least in London,' said Yeovil.

'There are even more of them now than there used to be,' said Holham. 'I am to a great extent a disliker of Jews myself, but I will be fair to them, and admit that those of them who were in any genuine sense British have remained British and have stuck by us loyally in our misfortune; all honour to them. But of the others, the men who by temperament and everything else were far more

Teuton or Polish or Latin than they were British, it was not to be expected that they would be heartbroken because London had suddenly lost its place among the political capitals of the world, and became a cosmopolitan city. They had appreciated the free and easy liberty of the old days, under British rule, but there was a stiff insularity in the ruling race that they chafed against. Now, putting aside some petty Government restrictions that Teutonic bureaucracy has brought in, there is really, in their eyes, more licence and social adaptability in London than before. It has taken on some of the aspects of a No-Man's Land, and the Jew, if he likes, may almost consider himself as of the dominant race; at any rate he is ubiquitous. Pleasure, of the café and cabaret and boulevard kind, the sort of thing that gave Berlin the aspect of the gayest capital in Europe within the last decade, that is the insidious leaven that will help to denationalize London. Berlin will probably climb back to some of its old austerity and simplicity, a world-ruling city with a great sense of its position and its responsibilities, while London will become more and more the centre of what these people understand by life.'

Yeovil made a movement of impatience and disgust.

'I know, I know,' said the doctor, sympathetically; 'life and enjoyment mean to you the howl of a wolf in a forest, the call of a wild swan on the frozen tundras, the smell of a wood fire in some little inn among the mountains. There is more music to you in the quick thud, thud of hoofs on desert mud as a free-stepping horse is led up to your tent door than in all the dronings and flourishes that a highly-paid orchestra can reel out to an expensively fed audience. But the tastes of modern London, as we see them crystallized around us, lie in a very different direction. People of the world that I am speaking of, our dominant world at the present moment, herd together as closely packed to the square yard as possible, doing nothing worth doing, and saying nothing worth saying, but doing it and saying it over and over again, listening to the same melodies, watching the same artistes, echoing the same catchwords, ordering the same dishes in the same restaurants, suffering each other's cigarette smoke and perfumes and conversation, feverishly, anxiously making arrangements to meet each other again tomorrow, next week, and the week after next, and repeat the same gregarious experience. If they were not herded together in a corner of western London, watching each other with restless intelligent eyes, they would be herded together at Brighton or Dieppe, doing the same thing. Well, you will find that life of that sort goes forward just as usual, only it is even more prominent and noticeable now because there is less public life of other kinds.'

Yeovil said something which was possibly the Buriat word for the nether world.

Outside in the neighburing square a band had been playing at intervals during the evening. Now it struck up an air that Yeovil had already heard whistled several times since his landing, an air with a captivating suggestion of slyness and furtive joyousness running through it.

He rose and walked across to the window, opening it a little wider. He listened till the last notes had died away.

'What is that tune they have just played?' he asked.

'You'll hear it often enough,' said the doctor. 'A Frenchman writing in the *Matin* the other day called it the "National Anthem of the *fait accompli*".'

The Toys of Peace

'Harvey,' said Eleanor Bope, handing her brother a cutting from a London morning paper[1] of the 19th of March, 'just read this about children's toys, please; it exactly carries out some of our ideas about influence and upbringing.'

'In the view of the National Peace Council,' ran the extract, 'there are grave objections to presenting our boys with regiments of fighting men, batteries of guns, and squadrons of "Dread-

[1] An actual extract from a London paper of March 1914.

noughts". Boys, the Council admits, naturally love fighting and all the panoply of war . . . but that is no reason for encouraging, and perhaps giving permanent form to, their primitive instincts. At the Children's Welfare Exhibition, which opens at Olympia in three weeks' time, the Peace Council will make an alternative suggestion to parents in the shape of an exhibition of "peace toys". In front of a specially-painted representation of the Peace Palace at The Hague will be grouped, not miniature soldiers but miniature civilians, not guns but ploughs and the tools of industry. . . . It is hoped that manufacturers may take a hint from the exhibit, which will bear fruit in the toy shops.'

'The idea is certainly an interesting and very well-meaning one,' said Harvey; 'whether it would succeed well in practice –'

'We must try,' interrupted his sister; 'you are coming down to us at Easter, and you always bring the boys some toys, so that will be an excellent opportunity for you to inaugurate the new experiment. Go about in the shops and buy any little toys and models that have special bearing on civilian life in its more peaceful aspects. Of course you must explain the toys to the children and interest them in the new idea. I regret to say that the "Siege of Adrianople" toy, that their Aunt Susan sent them, didn't need any explanation; they knew all the uniforms and flags, and even the names of the respective commanders, and when I heard them one day using what seemed to be the most objectionable language they said it was Bulgarian words of command; of course it *may* have been, but at any rate I took the toy away from them. Now I shall expect your Easter gifts to give quite a new impulse and direction to the children's minds; Eric is not eleven yet, and Bertie is only nine-and-a-half, so they are really at a most impressionable age.'

'There is primitive instinct to be taken into consideration, you know,' said Harvey doubtfully, 'and hereditary tendencies as well. One of their great-uncles fought in the most intolerant fashion at Inkerman – he was specially mentioned in dispatches, I believe – and their great-grandfather smashed all his Whig neighbours' hothouses when the great Reform Bill was passed. Still, as you say, they are at an impressionable age. I will do my best.'

On Easter Saturday Harvey Bope unpacked a large, promising-looking red cardboard box under the expectant eyes of his nephews. 'Your uncle has brought you the newest things in toys,' Eleanor had said impressively, and youthful anticipation had been anxiously divided between Albanian soldiery and a Somali camel-corps. Eric was hotly in favour of the latter contingency. 'There would be Arabs on horseback,' he whispered; 'the Albanians have got jolly uniforms, and they fight all day long, and all night, too, when there's a moon, but the country's rocky, so they've got no cavalry.'

A quantity of crinkly paper shavings was the first thing that met the view when the lid was removed; the most exciting toys always began like that. Harvey pushed back the top layer and drew forth a square, rather featureless building.

'It's a fort!' exclaimed Bertie.

'It isn't, it's the palace of the Mpret of Albania,' said Eric, immensely proud of his knowledge of the exotic title; 'it's got no windows, you see, so that passers-by can't fire in at the Royal Family.'

'It's a municipal dust-bin,' said Harvey hurriedly; 'you see all the refuse and litter of a town is collected there, instead of lying about and injuring the health of the citizens.'

In an awful silence he disinterred a little lead figure of a man in black clothes.

'That', he said, 'is a distinguished civilian, John Stuart Mill. He was an authority on political economy.'

'Why?' asked Bertie.

'Well, he wanted to be; he thought it was a useful thing to be.'

Bertie gave an expressive grunt, which conveyed his opinion that there was no accounting for tastes.

Another square building came out, this time with windows and chimneys.

'A model of the Manchester branch of the Young Women's Christian Association,' said Harvey.

'Are there any lions?' asked Eric hopefully. He had been reading Roman history and thought that where you found Christians you might reasonably expect to find a few lions.

'There are no lions,' said Harvey. 'Here is another civilian, Robert Raikes, the founder of Sunday schools, and here is a model of a municipal wash-house. These little round things are loaves baked in a sanitary bakehouse. That lead figure is a sanitary inspector, this one is a district councillor, and this one is an official of the Local Government Board.'

'What does he do?' asked Eric wearily.

'He sees to things connected with his Department,' said Harvey. 'This box with a slit in it is a ballot-box. Votes are put into it at election times.'

'What is put into it at other times?' asked Bertie.

'Nothing. And here are some tools of industry, a wheelbarrow and a hoe, and I think these are meant for hop-poles. This is a model beehive, and that is a ventilator, for ventilating sewers. This seems to be another municipal dust-bin – no, it is a model of a school of art and a public library. This little lead figure is Mrs Hemans, a poetess, and this is Rowland Hill, who introduced the system of penny postage. This is Sir John Herschel, the eminent astrologer.'

'Are we to play with these civilian figures?' asked Eric.

'Of course,' said Harvey, 'these are toys; they are meant to be played with.'

'But how?'

It was rather a poser. 'You might make two of them contest a seat in Parliament,' said Harvey, 'and have an election –'

'With rotten eggs, and free fights, and ever so many broken heads!' exclaimed Eric.

'And noses all bleeding and everybody drunk as can be,' echoed Bertie, who had carefully studied one of Hogarth's pictures.

'Nothing of the kind,' said Harvey, 'nothing in the least like that. Votes will be put in the ballot-box, and the Mayor will count them – the district councillor will do for the Mayor – and he will say which has received the most votes, and then the two candidates will thank him for presiding, and each will say that the contest has been conducted throughout in the pleasantest and most straightforward fashion, and they part with expressions of mutual esteem. There's a jolly game for you boys to play. I never had such toys when I was young.'

'I don't think we'll play with them just now,' said Eric, with an entire absence of the enthusiasm that his uncle had shown; 'I think perhaps we ought to do a little of our holiday task. It's history this time; we've got to learn up something about the Bourbon period in France.'

'The Bourbon period,' said Harvey, with some disapproval in his voice.

'We've got to know something about Louis the Fourteenth,' continued Eric; 'I've learnt the names of all the principal battles already.'

This would never do. 'There were, of course, some battles fought during his reign,' said Harvey, 'but I fancy the accounts of them were much exaggerated; news was very unreliable in those days, and there were practically no war correspondents, so generals and commanders could magnify every little skirmish they engaged in till they reached the proportions of decisive battles. Louis was really famous, now, as a landscape gardener; the way he laid out Versailles was so much admired that it was copied all over Europe.'

'Do you know anything about Madame Du Barry?' asked Eric; 'didn't she have her head chopped off?'

'She was another great lover of gardening,' said Harvey, evasively; 'in fact, I believe the well-known rose Du Barry was named after her, and now I think you had better play for a little and leave your lessons till later.'

Harvey retreated to the library and spent some thirty or forty minutes in wondering whether it would be possible to compile a history, for use in elementary schools, in which there should be no prominent mention of battles, massacres, murderous intrigues, and violent deaths. The York and Lancaster period and the Napoleonic era would, he admitted to himself, present considerable difficulties, and the Thirty Years' War would entail something of a gap if you left it out altogether. Still, it would be something gained if, at a highly impressionable age, children could be got to fix their attention on the invention of calico printing instead of the Spanish Armada or the Battle of Waterloo.

It was time, he thought, to go back to the boys' room, and see how they were getting on with their peace toys. As he stood outside the door he could hear Eric's voice raised in command; Bertie chimed in now and again with a helpful suggestion.

'That is Louis the Fourteenth,' Eric was saying, 'that one in knee-breeches, that Uncle said invented Sunday schools. It isn't a bit like him, but it'll have to do.'

'We'll give him a purple coat from my paint-box by and by,' said Bertie.

'Yes, an' red heels. That is Madame de Maintenon, that one he called Mrs Hemans. She begs Louis not to go on this expedition, but he turns a deaf ear. He takes Marshal Saxe with him, and we must pretend that they have thousands of men with them. The watchword is *Qui vive?* and the answer is *L'état c'est moi* – that was one of his favourite remarks, you know. They land at Manchester in the dead of night, and a Jacobite conspirator gives them the keys of the fortress.'

Peeping in through the doorway Harvey observed that the municipal dustbin had been pierced with holes to accommodate the muzzles of imaginary cannon, and now represented the principal fortified position in Manchester; John Stuart Mill had been dipped in red ink, and apparently stood for Marshal Saxe.

'Louis orders his troops to surround the Young Women's Christian Association and seize the lot of them. "Once back at the Louvre and the girls are mine," he exclaims. We must use Mrs Hemans again for one of the girls; she says "Never," and stabs Marshal Saxe to the heart.'

'He bleeds dreadfully,' exclaimed Bertie, splashing red ink liberally over the façade of the Association building.

'The soldiers rush in and avenge his death with the utmost savagery. A hundred girls are killed' – here Bertie emptied the remainder of the red ink over the devoted building – 'and the surviving five hundred are dragged off to the French ships. "I have lost a Marshal," says Louis, "but I do not go back empty-handed." '

Harvey stole away from the room, and sought out his sister.

'Eleanor,' he said, 'the experiment –'

'Yes?'

'Has failed. We have begun too late.'

An Old Love

'I know nothing about war,' a boy of nineteen said to me two days ago, 'except, of course, that I've heard of its horrors; yet, somehow, in spite of the horrors, there seems to be something in it different to anything else in the world, something a little bit finer.'

He spoke wistfully, as one who feared that to him war would always be an unreal, distant, second-hand thing, to be read about in special editions, and peeped at through the medium of cinematograph shows. He felt that the thing that was a little bit finer than anything else in the world would never come into his life.

Nearly every red-blooded human boy has had war, in some shape or form, for his first love; if his blood has remained red and he has kept some of his boyishness in after life, that first love will never have been forgotten. No one could really forget those wonderful leaden cavalry soldiers; the horses were as sleek and prancing as though they had never left the parade-ground, and the uniforms were correspondingly spick and span, but the amount of campaigning and fighting they got through was prodigious. There are other unforgettable memories for those who had brothers to play with and fight with, of sieges and ambushes and pitched encounters, of the slaying of an entire garrison without quarter, or of chivalrous, punctilious courtesy to a defeated enemy. Then there was the slow unfolding of the long romance of actual war, particularly of European war, ghastly, devastating, heartrending in its effect, and yet somehow captivating to the imagination. The Thirty Years' War was one of the most hideously cruel wars ever waged, but, in conjunction with the subsequent campaigns of the Great Louis, it throws a glamour over the scene of the present struggle. The thrill that those far-off things call forth in us may be ethically indefensible, but it comes in the first place from something too deep to be driven out; the magic region of the Low Countries is beckoning to us again, as it beckoned to our forefathers, who went campaigning there almost from force of habit.

One must admit that we have in these Islands a variant from the red-blooded type. One or two young men have assured me that they are not in the least interested in the war – 'I'm not at all patriotic, you know,' they announce, as one might announce that one was not a vegetable or did not use a safety-razor. There are others whom I have met within the recent harrowing days who had no place for the war crisis in their thoughts and conversations; they would talk by the hour about chamber-music, Greek folk-dances, Florentine art, and the difficulty of getting genuine old oak furniture, but the national honour and the national danger were topics that bored them. One felt that the war would affect them chiefly as involving a possible shortage in the supply of eau-de-Cologne or by debarring them from visiting some favourite art treasure at a Munich gallery. It is inconceivable that these persons were ever boys, they have certainly not grown up into men; one cannot call them womanish – the women of our race are made of different stuff. They belong to no sex and it seems a pity that they should belong to any nation; other nations probably have similar encumbrances, but we seem to have more of them than we either desire or deserve.

There are other men among us who are patriotic, one supposes, but with a patriotism that one cannot understand; it must be judged by a standard that we should never care to set up. It seems to place a huckstering interpretation on honour, to display sacred things in a shop window, marked in plain figures. 'If we remained neutral,' as a leading London morning paper once pleaded, 'we should be, from the commercial point of view, in precisely the same position as the United States. We should be able to trade with all the belligerents (so far as war allows of trade with them); we should be able to capture the bulk of their trade in neutral markets; we should keep our expenditure down; we should keep out of debt; we should have healthy finances.'

A question was buzzing in my head by the time I had finished reading those alluring arguments:

'Some men of noble stock were made;
Some glory in the murder-blade:
Some praise a science or an art,
But I like honourable trade.

The poet has given a satiric meaning to the last word but one in those lines; perhaps that is why they flashed so readily to the mind.

One remembers with some feeling of relief the spectacle last August of boys and youths marching and shouting through the streets in semi-disciplined mobs, waving the flags of France and Britain. There is perhaps nothing very patriotic in shouting and flag-waving, but it is the only way these youngsters had of showing their feelings.

The C.O.C.

A leading French newspaper a few years ago published an imaginary account of the difficulties experienced by Noah in mobilizing birds and beasts and creeping things for embarkation in the Ark. The arctic animals were the chief embarrassment; the polar bears persistently ate the seals long before the consignment had reached the rendezvous, and while a fresh supply was being sent for certain South American insects, which only live for a few hours, had to be kept alive by artificial respiration. When everything seemed at length to have been got ready, and the last bale of hay and the last hundredweight of bird-seed had been taken on board, someone asked, with cold reproach, 'I suppose you know you've forgotten the Australian animals?'

The job of Company Orderly Corporal resembles in some respects the labours of Noah; one can never safely flatter oneself at any given moment that one has got to a temporary end of it. When one has drawn the milk and doled out the margarine, and distributed the letters and parcels, and seen to the whereabouts of migratory tea-pails and flat-pans and paraded defaulters and off-duty men under the cold scrutiny of the canteen sergeant – and disentangled recruits from messes to which they do not belong – and induced unwilling hut-orderlies to saddle themselves with buckets full of unpeeled potatoes which they neither desire nor deserve – and has begun to think that the moment has arrived in which one may indulge in a cigarette and read a letter – then some detestably thoughtful friend will sidle up to one and say, 'I suppose you know there's the watercress waiting at the cook-house?'

There are at least two distinct styles in use by those who hold the office of Company Orderly Corporal. One is to stalk at the head of one's hut-orderlies like a masterful rainproof hen on a wet day, followed by a melancholy string of wish-they-had-never-been-hatched chickens; the other is to rush about in a demented fashion, as though one had invented the science of modern camp organization and had forgotten most of the details.

There are certain golden rules to be observed by the C.O.C. who wishes to make a success of his job.

Cultivate an indifference to human suffering; if Heaven intended hut-orderlies to be happy you have received no instructions on the point.

Develop your imagination; if the officer of the day remarks on the paleness of a joint of meat hazard the probable explanation that the beast it was cut from was fed on Sicilian clover, which fattens quickly, but gives a pale appearance; there may be no such thing as Sicilian clover, but one-half of the world believes what the other half invents. At any rate you will get credit for unusual intelligence.

Be kind to those who live in cook-houses.

It has been said that 'great men are lovable for their mistakes'; do not imagine for a moment that this applies, even in a minor degree, to Company Orderly Corporals. If you make the mistake of forgetting to draw the Company's butter till the Company's tea is over, no one will love you or pretend to love you.

A gifted woman writer has observed 'it is an extravagance to do anything that someone else can do better'. Be extravagant.

Of all the labours that fall to the lot of C.O.C. the most formidable is the distribution of the post-bag. There are about seven men in every hut who are expecting important letters that never seem to reach them, and there are always individuals who glower at you and tell you that they invariably get a letter from home on Tuesday; by Thursday they are firmly convinced that you have set all their relations against them. There was one young man in Hut 3 whose reproachful looks got on my nerves to such an extent that at last I wrote him a letter from his Aunt Agatha, a letter full of womanly counsel and patient reproof, such as any aunt might have been proud to write. Possibly he hasn't got an Aunt Agatha; anyhow the reproachful look has been replaced by a puzzled frown.

The Square Egg

A Badger's-Eye View of the War

Assuredly a badger is the animal that one most resembles in this trench warfare, that drab-coated creature of the twilight and darkness, digging, burrowing, listening; keeping itself as clean as possible under unfavourable circumstances, fighting tooth and nail on occasion for possession of a few yards of honeycombed earth.

What the badger thinks about life we shall never know, which is a pity, but cannot be helped; it is difficult enough to know what one thinks about, oneself, in the trenches. Parliament, taxes, social gatherings, economies, and expenditure, and all the thousand and one horrors of civilization seem immeasurably remote, and the war itself seems almost as distant and unreal. A couple of hundred yards away, separated from you by a stretch of dismal untidy-looking ground and some strips of rusty wire-entanglement lies a vigilant, bullet-spitting enemy; lurking and watching in those opposing trenches are foemen who might stir the imagination of the most sluggish brain, descendants of the men who went to battle under Moltke, Blücher, Frederick the Great, and the Great Elector, Wallenstein, Maurice of Saxony, Barbarossa, Albert the Bear, Henry the Lion, Witekind the Saxon. They are matched against you there, man for man and gun for gun, in what is perhaps the most stupendous struggle that modern history has known, and yet one thinks remarkably little about them. It would not be advisable to forget for the fraction of a second that they are there, but one's mind does not dwell on their existence; one speculates little as to whether they are drinking warm soup and eating sausage, or going cold and hungry, whether they are well supplied with copies of the *Meggendorfer Blätter* and other light literature or bored with unutterable weariness.

Much more to be thought about than the enemy over yonder or the war all over Europe is the mud of the moment, the mud that at times engulfs you as cheese engulfs a cheesemite. In Zoological Gardens one has gazed at an elk or bison loitering at its pleasure more than knee-deep in a quagmire of greasy mud, and one has wondered what it would feel like to be soused and plastered, hour-long, in such a muck-bath. One knows now. In narrow-dug support-trenches, when thaw and heavy rain have come suddenly atop of a frost, when everything is pitch dark around you, and you can only stumble about and feel your way against streaming mud walls, when you have to go down on hands and knees in several inches of soup-like mud to creep into a dug-out, when you stand deep in mud, lean against mud, grasp mud-slimed objects with mud-caked fingers, wink mud away from your eyes, and shake it out of your ears, bite muddy biscuits with muddy teeth, then at least you are in a position to understand thoroughly what it feels like to wallow – on the other hand the bison's idea of pleasure becomes more and more incomprehensible.

When one is not thinking about mud one is probably thinking about *estaminets*. An *estaminet* is a haven that one finds in agreeable plenty in most of the surrounding townships and villages, flourishing still amid roofless and deserted houses, patched up where necessary in rough-and-ready fashion, and finding a new and profitable tide of customers from among the soldiers who have replaced the bulk of the civil population. An *estaminet* is a sort of compound between a wine-shop and a coffee-house, having a tiny bar in one corner, a few long tables and benches, a prominent cooking stove, generally a small grocery store tucked away in the back premises, and always two or three children running and bumping about at inconvenient angles to one's feet. It seems to be a fixed rule that *estaminet* children should be big enough to run about and small enough to get between one's legs. There must, by the way, be one considerable advantage in being a child in a war-zone village; no one can attempt to teach it tidiness. The wearisome maxim, 'A place for everything and everything in its proper place' can never be insisted on when a considerable part of the roof is lying in the backyard, when a bedstead from a neighbour's demolished bed-room is half-buried in the beetroot pile, and the chickens are roosting in a derelict meat safe because a shell has removed the top and sides and front of the chicken-house.

Perhaps there is nothing in the foregoing description to suggest that a village wine-shop, frequently a shell-nibbled building in a shell-gnawed street, is a paradise to dream about, but when one has lived in a dripping wilderness of unrelieved mud and sodden sandbags for any length of time one's mind dwells on the plain-furnished parlour with its hot coffee and *vin ordinaire* as something warm and snug and comforting in a wet and slushy world. To the soldier on his trench-to-billets migration the wine-shop is what the tavern resthouse is to the caravan nomad of the East. One comes and goes in a crowd of chance-foregathered men, noticed or unnoticed as one wishes, amid the khaki-clad, beputteed throng of one's own kind one can be as unobtrusive as a green caterpillar on a green cabbage leaf; one can sit undisturbed, alone or with one's own friends, or if one wishes to be talkative and talked to one can readily find a place in a circle where men of divers variety of cap badges are exchanging experiences, real or improvised.

Besides the changing throng of mud-stained khaki there is a drifting leaven of local civilians, uniformed interpreters, and men in varying types of foreign military garb, from privates in the Regular Army to Heaven-knows-what in some intermediate corps that only an expert in such matters could put a name to, and, of course, here and there are representatives of that great army of adventurer purse-sappers, that carries on its operations uninterruptedly in time of peace or war alike, over the greater part of the earth's surface. You meet them in England and France, in Russia and Constantinople; probably they are to be met with also in Iceland, though on that point I have no direct evidence.

In the *estaminet* of the Fortunate Rabbit I found myself sitting next to an individual of indefinite age and nondescript uniform, who was obviously determined to make the borrowing of a match serve as a formal introduction and a banker's reference. He had the air of jaded jauntiness, the equipment of temporary amiability, the aspect of a foraging crow, taught by experience to be wary and prompted by necessity to be bold; he had the contemplative downward droop of nose and moustache and the furtive sidelong range of eye – he had all those things that are the ordinary outfit of the purse-sapper the world over.

'I am a victim of the war,' he exclaimed after a little preliminary conversation.

'One cannot make an omelette without breaking eggs,' I answered, with the appropriate callousness of a man who had seen some dozens of square miles of devastated country-side and roofless homes.

'Eggs!' he vociferated, 'but it is precisely of eggs that I am about to speak. Have you ever considered what is the great drawback in the excellent and most useful egg – the ordinary, everyday egg of commerce and cookery?'

'Its tendency to age rapidly is sometimes against it,' I hazarded; 'unlike the United States of North America, which grow more respectable and self-respecting the longer they last, an egg gains nothing by persistence; it resembles your Louis the Fifteenth, who declined in popular favour with every year he lived – unless the historians have entirely misrepresented his record.'

'No,' replied the Tavern Acquaintance seriously, 'it is not a question of age. It is the shape, the roundness. Consider how easily it rolls. On a table, a shelf, a shop counter, perhaps, one little push, and it may roll to the floor and be destroyed. What catastrophe for the poor, the frugal!'

I gave a sympathetic shudder at the idea; eggs here cost 6 sous apiece.

'Monsieur,' he continued, 'it is a subject I had often pondered and turned over in my mind, this economical malformation of the household egg. In our little village of Verchey-les-Torteaux, in the Department of the Tarn, my aunt has a small dairy and poultry farm, from which we drew a modest income. We were not poor, but there was always the necessity to labour, to contrive, to be sparing. One day I chanced to notice that one of my aunt's hens, a hen of the mop-headed Houdan breed, had laid an egg that was not altogether so round-shaped as the eggs of other hens; it could not be called square, but it had well-defined angles. I found out that this particular bird always laid eggs of this particular shape. The discovery gave a new stimulus to my ideas. If one collected all the hens that one could find with a tendency to lay a slightly angular egg and bred chickens only from those hens, and went on selecting and selecting, always choosing those that laid the squarest egg, at last, with patience and enterprise, one would produce a breed of fowls that laid only square eggs.'

'In the course of several hundred years one might arrive at such a result,' I said; 'it would more probably take several thousands.'

'With your cold Northern conservative slow-moving hens that might be the case,' said the Acquaintance impatiently and rather angrily; 'with our vivacious Southern poultry it is different. Listen. I searched, I experimented, I explored the poultry-yards of our neighbours, I ransacked the markets of the surrounding towns, wherever I found a hen laying an angular egg I bought her; I collected in time a vast concourse of fowls all sharing the same tendency; from their progeny I selected only those pullets whose eggs showed the most marked deviation from the normal roundness. I continued, I persevered. Monsieur, I produced a breed of hens that laid an egg which could not roll, however much you might push or jostle it. My experiment was more than a success; it was one of the romances of modern industry.'

Of that I had not the least doubt, but I did not say so.

'My eggs became known,' continued the *soi-disant* poultry-farmer; 'at first they were sought after as a novelty, something curious, bizarre. Then merchants and housewives began to see that they were a utility, an improvement, an advantage over the ordinary kind. I was able to command a sale for my wares at a price considerably above market rates. I began to make money. I had a monopoly. I refused to sell any of my "square-layers", and the eggs that went to market were carefully sterilized, so that no chickens should be hatched from them. I was in the way to become rich, comfortably rich. Then this war broke out, which has brought misery to so many. I was obliged to leave my hens and my customers and go to the Front. My aunt carried on the business as usual, sold the square eggs, the eggs that I had devised and created and perfected, and received the profits; can you imagine it, she refuses to send me one centime of the takings! She says that she looks after the hens, and pays for their corn, and sends the eggs to market, and that the money is hers. Legally, of course, it is mine; if I could afford to bring a process in the Courts I could recover all the money that the eggs have brought in since the war commenced, many thousands of francs. To bring a process would only need a small sum; I have a lawyer friend who would arrange matters cheaply for me. Unfortunately I have not sufficient funds in hand; I need still about eighty francs. In war time, alas, it is difficult to borrow.'

I had always imagined that it was a habit that was especially indulged in during war time, and said so.

'On a big scale, yes, but I am talking of a very small matter. It is easier to arrange a loan of millions than of a trifle of eighty or ninety francs.'

The would-be financier paused for a few tense moments. Then he recommenced in a more confidential strain.

'Some of you English soldiers, I have heard, are men with private means; is it not so? It is perhaps possible that among your comrades there might be someone willing to advance a small sum – you yourself, perhaps – it would be a secure and profitable investment, quickly repaid –'

'If I get a few days' leave I will go down to Verchey-les-Torteaux and inspect the square-egg hen-farm,' I said gravely, 'and question the local egg-merchants as to the position and prospects of the business.'

The Tavern Acquaintance gave an almost imperceptible shrug to his shoulders, shifted in his seat, and began moodily to roll a cigarette. His interest in me had suddenly died out, but for the sake of appearances he was bound to make a perfunctory show of winding up the conversation he had so laboriously started.

'Ah, you will go to Verchey-les-Torteaux and make inquiries about our farm. And if you find that what I have told you about the square eggs is true, Monsieur, what then?'

'I shall marry your aunt.'

For the Duration of the War

The Rev. Wilfrid Gaspilton, in one of those clerical migrations inconsequent-seeming to the lay mind, had removed from the moderately fashionable parish of St Luke's, Kensingate, to the immoderately rural parish of St Chuddocks, somewhere in Yondershire. There were doubtless substantial advantages connected with the move, but there were certainly some very obvious drawbacks. Neither the migratory clergyman nor his wife were able to adapt themselves naturally and comfortably to the conditions of country life. Beryl, Mrs Gaspilton, had always looked indulgently on the country as a place where people of irreproachable income and hospitable instincts cultivated tennis-lawns and rose-gardens and Jacobean pleasaunces, wherein selected gatherings of interested week-end guests might disport themselves. Mrs Gaspilton considered herself as distinctly an interesting personality, and from a limited standpoint she was doubtless right. She had indolent dark eyes and a comfortable chin, which belied the slightly plaintive inflection which she threw into her voice at suitable intervals. She was tolerably well satisfied with the smaller advantages of life, but she regretted that Fate had not seen its way to reserve for her some of the ampler successes for which she felt herself well qualified. She would have liked to be the centre of a literary, slightly political salon, where discerning satellites might have recognized the breadth of her outlook on human affairs and the undoubted smallness of her feet. As it was, Destiny had chosen for her that she should be the wife of a rector, and had now further decreed that a country rectory should be the background to her existence. She rapidly made up her mind that her surroundings did not call for exploration: Noah had predicted the Flood, but no one expected him to swim about in it. Digging in a wet garden or trudging through muddy lanes were exertions which she did not propose to undertake. As long as the garden produced asparagus and carnations at pleasingly frequent intervals Mrs Gaspilton was content to approve of its expense and otherwise ignore its existence. She would fold herself up, so to speak, in an elegant, indolent little world of her own, enjoying the minor recreations of being gently rude to the doctor's wife and continuing the leisurely production of her one literary effort, *The Forbidden Horsepond*, a translation of Baptiste Lepoy's *L'Abreuvoir interdit*. It was a labour which had already been so long drawn-out that it seemed probable that Baptiste Lepoy would drop out of vogue before her translation of his temporarily famous novel was finished. However, the languid prosecution of the work had invested Mrs Gaspilton with a certain literary dignity, even in Kensingate circles, and would place her on a pinnacle in St Chuddocks, where hardly anyone read French, and assuredly no one had heard of *L'Abreuvoir interdit*.

The Rector's wife might be content to turn her back complacently on the country; it was the Rector's tragedy that the country turned its back on him. With the best intention in the world and the immortal example of Gilbert White before him, the Rev. Wilfrid found himself as bored and ill at ease in his new surroundings as Charles II would have been at a modern Wesleyan Conference. The birds that hopped across his lawn hopped across it as though it were their lawn, and not his, and gave him plainly to understand that in their eyes he was infinitely less interesting than a garden worm or the rectory cat. The hedgeside and meadow flowers were equally uninspiring; the lesser celandine seemed particularly unworthy of the attention that English poets had bestowed on it, and the Rector knew that he would be utterly miserable if left alone for a quarter of an hour in its company. With the human inhabitants of his parish he was no better off; to know them was merely to know their ailments, and the ailments were almost invariably rheumatism. Some, of course, had other bodily infirmities, but they always had rheumatism as well. The Rector had not yet grasped the fact that in rural cottage life not to have rheumatism is as glaring an omission as not to have been presented at Court would be in more ambitious circles. And with all this dearth of local interest there was Beryl shutting herself off with her ridiculous labours on *The Forbidden Horse-pond.*

'I don't see why you should suppose that anyone wants to read Baptiste Lepoy in English,' the Reverend Wilfrid remarked to his wife one morning, finding her surrounded with her usual elegant litter of dictionaries, fountain pens, and scribbling paper; 'hardly anyone bothers to read him now in France'.

'My dear,' said Beryl, with an intonation of gentle weariness, 'haven't two or three leading London publishers told me they wondered no one had ever translated *L'Abreuvoir interdit*, and begged me –'

'Publishers always clamour for the books that no one has ever written, and turn a cold shoulder on them as soon as they're written. If St Paul were living now they would pester him to write an Epistle to the Esquimaux, but no London publisher would dream of reading his Epistle to the Ephesians.'

'Is there any asparagus anywhere in the garden?' asked Beryl; 'because I've told cook –'

'Not anywhere in the garden,' snapped the Rector, 'but there's no doubt plenty in the asparagus-bed, which is the usual place for it.'

And he walked away into the region of fruit trees and vegetable beds to exchange irritation for boredom. It was there, among the gooseberry bushes and beneath the medlar trees, that the temptation to the perpetration of a great literary fraud came to him.

Some weeks later the *Bi-Monthly Review* gave to the world, under the guarantee of the Rev. Wilfrid Gaspilton, some fragments of Persian verse, alleged to have been unearthed and translated by a nephew who was at present campaigning somewhere in the Tigris valley. The Rev. Wilfrid possessed a host of nephews; and it was, of course, quite possible that one or more of them might be in military employ in Mesopotamia, though no one could call to mind any particular nephew who could have been suspected of being a Persian scholar.

The verses were attributed to one Ghurab, a hunter, or, according to other accounts, warden of the royal fishponds, who lived, in some unspecified century, in the neighbourhood of Karmanshah. They breathed a spirit of comfortable, even-tempered satire and philosophy, disclosing a mockery that did not trouble to be bitter, a joy in life that was not passionate to the verge of being troublesome.

'A Mouse that prayed for Allah's aid
  Blasphemed when no such aid befell:
A Cat, who feasted on that mouse,
  Thought Allah managed vastly well.

'Pray not for aid to One who made
  A set of never-changing Laws,
But in your need remember well
  He gave you speed, or guile – or claws.

'Some laud a life of mild content:
  Content may fall, as well as Pride.
The Frog who hugged his lowly Ditch
  Was much disgruntled when it dried.

' "You are not on the Road to Hell,"
  You tell me with fanatic glee:
Vain boaster, what shall that avail
  If Hell is on the road to thee?

'A Poet praised the Evening Star,
  Another praised the Parrot's hue:
A Merchant praised his merchandise,
  And he, at least, praised what he knew.'

It was this verse which gave the critics and commentators some clue as to the probable date of the composition; the parrot, they reminded the public, was in high vogue as a type of elegance in the days of Hafiz of Shiraz; in the quatrains of Omar it makes no appearance.

The next verse, it was pointed out, would apply to the political conditions of the present day as strikingly as to the region and era for which it was written –

'A Sultan dreamed day-long of Peace,
The while his Rivals' armies grew:
They changed his Day-dreams into sleep
– The Peace, methinks, he never knew.'

Woman appeared little, and wine not at all in the verse of the hunter-poet, but there was at least one contribution to the love-philosophy of the East –

'O Moon-faced Charmer, with Star-drownèd Eyes,
And cheeks of soft delight, exhaling musk,
They tell me that thy charm will fade; ah well,
The Rose itself grows hue-less in the Dusk.'

Finally, there was a recognition of the Inevitable, a chill breath blowing across the poet's comfortable estimate of life –

'There is a sadness in each Dawn,
A sadness that you cannot rede:
The joyous Day brings in its train
The Feast, the Loved One, and the Steed.

'Ah, there shall come a Dawn at last
That brings no life-stir to your ken,
A long, cold Dawn without a Day,
And ye shall rede its sadness then.'

The verses of Ghurab came on the public at a moment when a comfortable, slightly quizzical philosophy was certain to be welcome, and their reception was enthusiastic. Elderly colonels, who had outlived the love of truth, wrote to the papers to say that they had been familiar with the works of Ghurab in Afghanistan, and Aden, and other suitable localities a quarter of a century ago. A Ghurab-of-Karmanshah Club sprang into existence, the members of which alluded to each other as Brother Ghurabians on the slightest provocation. And to the flood of inquiries, criticisms, and requests for information, which naturally poured in on the discoverer, or rather the discloser, of this long-hidden poet, the Rev. Wilfrid made one effectual reply: Military considerations forbade any disclosures which might throw unnecessary light on his nephew's movements.

After the war the Rector's position will be one of unthinkable embarrassment, but for the moment, at any rate, he has driven *The Forbidden Horsepond* out of the field.